Robert Crais is the author of seventeen novels, including the international bestsellers *The Forgotten Man*, *The Last Detective*, *Demolition Angel* and the Edgar-nominated *L.A. Requiem*. He has two additional Edgar nominations as well as Anthony and Macavity awards for his series of Elvis Cole and Joe Pike crime novels. Crais has also written for acclaimed television shows such as *L.A. Law* and *Hill Street Blues*. *Hostage* has been made into a major motion picture featuring Bruce Willis. He lives in Los Angeles. Visit his website at www.robertcrais.com.

By Robert Crais

The Monkey's Raincoat
Stalking the Angel
Lullaby Town
Free Fall
Voodoo River
Sunset Express
Indigo Slam
L.A. Requiem
Demolition Angel
Hostage
The Last Detective
The Forgotten Man
The Two Minute Rule
The Watchman
Chasing Darkness
The First Rule
The Sentry

lullaby town

AN ELVIS COLE NOVEL
· · · · · · · · · · · · · · · · · ·

ROBERT CRAIS

An Orion paperback

First published in Great Britain in 1992
by Piatkus Books
This paperback edition published in 1999
by Orion Books Ltd, an imprint of The Orion Publishing Group Ltd
Carmelite House, 50 Victoria Embankment,
London EC4Y 0DZ

An Hachette UK company

2

Reissued 2012

Grateful acknowledgement is made for permission to reprint
lyrics from 'Karn Evil 9, First Impression Part 2' by Emerson,
Lake & Palmer. Reprinted by permission of Leadchoice Ltd.

All the characters in this book are fictitious,
and any resemblance to actual persons, living
or dead, is purely coincidental.

A CIP catalogue record for this book
is available from the British Library.

ISBN 978-1-4091-3820-4

Printed and bound in Great Britain by
CPI Group (UK) Ltd, Croydon, CR0 4YY

The Orion Publishing Group's policy is to use papers that
are natural, renewable and recyclable products and
made from wood grown in sustainable forests. The logging
and manufacturing processes are expected to conform to
the environmental regulations of the country of origin.

www.orionbooks.co.uk

*Dedicated with love and respect to
my mother, Evelyn Carrie Crais,
who saved me from the monsters.*

There's a quaint little place they call Lullaby
    Town –
It's just back of those hills where the sunsets
    go down.
Its streets are of silver, its buildings of gold,
And its palaces dazzling things to behold.

There's a peddler who carries, strapped high
    on his back,
A bundle. Now, guess what he has in that
    pack.
No, he's not peddling jams nor delectable
    creams.
Would you know what he's selling? Just
    wonderful dreams!

– from *Lullaby Town**
by John Irving Diller

Welcome back, my friends, to the show that
    never ends.
We're so glad you could attend.
Come inside! Come inside!

– Emerson, Lake, & Palmer

* published in *The Best Loved Poems of the
American People* selected by Hazel Felleman,
Doubleday and Company, 1936, p. 399.

CHAPTER 1

Patricia Kyle said, 'Is this Elvis Cole, the world's greatest detective?'

'Yes, it is.' I was lying on the leather couch across from my desk, enjoying the view that I have of the Channel Islands. I used to have chairs, but a couch is much better to relieve one of the rigors of world-class detecting.

She said, 'Were you sleeping?'

I gave her miffed. 'I never sleep. I'm waiting for Cindy to come out onto the balcony next door.' The glass doors leading out to my little balcony were open to catch the breeze that was blowing up Santa Monica Boulevard into West Los Angeles. It was a nice breeze, cool and smelling of salt and sea birds. The open doors were also better to let me hear Cindy.

'Who's Cindy?'

I switched the phone from the left ear to the right. The left ear was still sore from having been hit hard two times by a Cajun with large forearms and no teeth. 'Cindy is a beauty supply distributor who took the office space next door.'

Pat Kyle said, 'Hmm. I'll bet I know what she distributes.'

'Your callousness and insensitivity are unbecoming. She is a very nice woman with a ready laugh.'

'Unh-hunh. I know what's ready.'

'The private-detecting life is a lonely one. After cleaning the guns and oiling the blackjack, what's a guy to do?'

'You could have lunch with me at Lucy's El Adobe Café across from Paramount.'

I said, 'Cindy who?'

Pat Kyle laughed. It was clear and without apology, the way a laugh should be. Pat Kyle is forty-four years old and five feet four, with curly auburn hair and good bones and an athlete's build. When we met six years ago, she looked like the Graf Zeppelin and was having trouble getting out of a bad marriage. I helped. Now she ran four fast miles every day, had her own casting agency, and was engaged to a dentist from Pasadena. Maybe one day I'd learn to like him. She said, 'I'm casting a film for Kapstone Pictures and a director named Peter Alan Nelsen. Do you know who he is?'

'He makes action pictures.'

'That's right. With great success. *Time* magazine called him the King of Adventure.'

'They called him a few other things, too.' Arrogant, demanding, brilliant. I had read the article.

'Yes. There is that.' You could hear something behind her. Voices, maybe. 'Peter has a problem and I mentioned your name. The Kapstone people want to talk with you.'

'Okay.' I swung up into a sitting position and put my feet on the floor. The detective, ready for action.

'When Peter was in film school, he broke up with his wife just after they had their only child. A boy. Peter hasn't seen or heard from his former wife or their son since, and he wants to find them. I told him that finding people is one of your best things. Are you interested?'

'It's what I do.'

'Kapstone has offices at Paramount. I'll leave a pass at the main gate for you to see Donnie Brewster. Donnie's the head of production.' Donnie. A twelve-year-old running a film company. 'Can you be here in about twenty minutes?'

'Let me check my calendar.'

She said, 'Ha. What calendar?'

'Callous. You dames are callous.'

She made the nice laugh again and hung up.

I pushed up off the couch and thought about Kapstone Pictures and Peter Alan Nelsen. The Big Time. I was wearing a white Mickey Mouse sweatshirt with a mustard spot high on the right shoulder. Mickey would be okay, but the mustard spot was definitely unacceptable. Did I have time to race home for the tux? I looked at the Pinocchio clock. Unh-unh. I took off the Mickey and put on a yellow-and-white Hawaiian beachcomber's shirt, a Dan Wesson .38 caliber revolver, and a light blue waiter's jacket. Dress for success. I began to hum. *There's no business like show business.* I turned on the answering machine and listened to the same message I'd been running for two months. *'Elvis Cole Detective Agency, we're cheap.'* Maybe it was time for a change. You work for a major film company, you need something a bit more show business. *Elvis Cole Detective Agency: There are no small cases, only small detectives – hire the biggest dick in the business!* I decided to leave well enough alone.

I walked the four flights down to the parking garage, got my car, and drove east along Santa Monica Boulevard through the belly of Hollywood. It was October, and the air was cool. I've got a 1966 Corvette convertible, but it wasn't so cool that I had to put up the top. It rarely was. Global warming. With the end of summer, the cars from Utah and Michigan and Delaware were gone, but the cars from Canada were arriving. Snowbirds, come down to beat the cold. At a red light on Santa Monica and La Brea I pulled up next to a maroon Buick sedan from Alberta with a very short man and a very short woman in the front seat and two very short children in the rear. The man was driving and looked confused. I gave them a big smile and a wave and said, 'Welcome to Los Angeles.' The woman rolled up her window and locked the door.

I stayed on Santa Monica to Gower, then turned right and followed Gower down past the Hollywood Cemetery to Paramount.

Paramount Studios is an Olympian structure on the corner of Melrose and Gower with a beige stucco siege wall running around its perimeter. The wall is very high, with a heaviness and permanence that has kept Paramount in business long after most of the other original Hollywood studios have gone. In a neighborhood marked by poverty and litter and street crime, it is free from graffiti. Maybe if you got too near the wall, thugs in chain mail poured boiling oil on you from the parapets.
. I rounded the corner at Melrose and tooled up to the guard at Paramount's front gate. 'Elvis Cole to see Donnie Brewster.'

The guard looked in a little file. 'You the singer?'

I shook my head. 'Elvis Presley died in 1978.'

The guard found a yellow slip, stuck it to my window with a piece of tape. 'Not the King. That other guy. With the glasses.'

'Elvis Costello. No. I'm not him, either.'

The guard shook his head sadly. 'Christ, I remember a time, you said "Elvis" there was only one.'

Probably just promoted from parapet duty.

Donnie Brewster was in a two-story earth-colored adobe building with a red tile roof and bird of paradise plants the size of dinosaurs. A receptionist led me to a secretary who showed me into a dark-paneled conference room. In the conference room were Patricia Kyle and a man in his late thirties with a sharply receding hairline and an eight-hundred-dollar sports coat that fit him like a wet tent. What hair he had left was pulled back tight into a short ponytail. Style.

Pat Kyle stood up and smiled and gave me a kiss. She'd

been working on her tan since I'd last seen her and it looked good. 'Elvis Cole, this is Donnie Brewster. Donnie, Elvis Cole.'

Donnie Brewster gave me a moist hand and looked nervous. 'Christ, where were you? I thought you'd never get here.'

'The pleasure is all mine.'

Donnie gave me everyone's-out-to-get-me eyes and glanced at Pat Kyle. 'She warned me you thought you were a riot. What you've gotta understand is that this isn't funny.' He held up three fingers. 'There's Spielberg, then Lucas, who doesn't direct anymore, then Peter Alan Nelsen. Peter's grosses total one point two *billion* worldwide over six pictures. He's the third most successful director in the history of film, and he knows it.'

'Hard to keep it a secret from him.'

Donnie rubbed his hand over his scalp and tugged at his ponytail. When he rubbed, he rubbed hard. Maybe that's why his hairline was receding. He said, 'Peter's gifted and brilliant. Gifted and brilliant people are sometimes difficult and have to be handled carefully.' I think he was saying it as much to himself as he was to me. He looked at Pat Kyle. 'Did you tell him what this is about?'

'Yes.' Pat repeated what she had told me.

Donnie nodded and looked back at me. 'That's about it. We need someone who can find the ex and the kid and not waste a lot of time doing it.'

'Okay.'

He sat in one of the swivel chairs, leaned back, and gave me the appraisal look. Getting down to the business of hiring a private eye. 'You charge by the hour or the day?'

'I get a flat fee. In advance.'

'How much?'

5

'Four thousand, plus expenses. The expenses I bill later.'

'That's absurd. We couldn't pay four thousand in advance.'

'How about six thousand?'

He tapped on the table and gave me his best business-affairs frown. 'You give it back if you don't find what you're looking for?'

'No.'

More tapping. Convincing himself. 'I had our lawyers call around. They spoke to a guy in the D.A.'s office and a policeman named Ito. They say you're pretty good at this sort of thing. How many cases like this have you handled?'

'Maybe three hundred.'

'Unh-hunh. And how many times out of that three hundred did you find the person you were looking for?'

'Maybe two ninety-eight.'

Donnie raised his eyebrows and looked impressed. Maybe he was feeling better about the four grand. 'Okay. We get you going on this, how long is it going to take to find them?'

'I don't know.'

'Well, can't you give me some sort of ballpark?'

I spread my hands. 'If she's living in Encino and telling her friends that she used to be married to Peter Alan Nelsen, maybe I find her tomorrow. If she's changed her name five times and working as a missionary in the Amazon, it takes longer.'

'Jesus Christ.'

I made a little shrug and smiled. Mr. Confident & Assured. 'It's rarely that bad. People usually don't change their names five times and move to the Amazon. People use credit cards, and credit histories list prior residences, and people own cars and driver's licenses and social security numbers, and any of these things are ideal for tracing someone.'

He didn't seem bolstered by my assuredness. He rubbed at his hair again and got up and paced. 'Peter is three weeks away from making a film, and he has to start this crap about finding his family. Christ, he hasn't seen the woman in over ten years. You'd think he could wait until the picture was finished.'

'Insensitive of him.'

Donnie crossed his arms and kept pacing. 'Hey, I know what that sounds like, but you've got to understand. We've got forty million dollars committed to Peter's film. I've already spent eighteen mil. I've got sets and soundstage rent. I've got stars with play-or-pay deals and a crew I'll have to carry. If Peter is distracted, we could run over budget into the tens of millions. We could end up with another *Heaven's Gate*. I could lose my ass.'

Maybe I'd be nervous, too. 'Okay. Then maybe it makes sense to wait until the picture is finished before we get started. The ex-wife will still be wherever she is. I'll still be around. Call me then.'

Donnie rolled his eyes and stopped the pacing and dropped into another chair. 'Did you see *Chainsaw*?'

'Yes.'

'*Chainsaw* was Peter's first picture. He made it for something like four hundred thousand. It grossed four hundred *million* and overnight Peter Alan Nelsen went from parking cars to being Hollywood's new wunderkind. Every picture he's made has grossed a fortune. Every studio in town wants Peter Alan Nelsen's next picture. The biggest actors in the business suck around him for a role and Oscar-winning screenwriters pimp their mothers for a shot at a development deal. You hear what I'm saying?'

'You're saying that Peter gets what Peter wants.'

'Abso-fucking-lutely. Peter being happy is the most

7

important thing there is. Peter wants to find these people, and we want Peter happy, so we're gonna hire somebody.'

I said, 'Make Peter happy.'

'Abso-fucking-lutely.' Donnie slapped his palms down on the table and stood. 'I like you. I like you fine. Peter knows about you, and wants to meet you, so all we have to do now is go over and see him. If Peter's happy, you're hired.'

'Making Peter happy is the most important thing.'

'Right.' Donnie Brewster lowered his voice, like maybe someone else might hear, and leaned toward me. Conspiratorial. 'Tell you the truth, I don't give a rat's ass if you find his ex or not. But if it makes Peter happy to have someone looking, then we'll have someone looking.'

Mr. Sincerity.

He made a little let's-go gesture and started for the door. 'We'll go over to meet him now. Whatever Peter says, just nod and say sure. Whatever he wants, say no problem. He asks how long, say a couple of weeks, max.'

'Make Peter happy.'

'Yeah. Peter being happy is all that matters.'

I looked at Pat Kyle, and then I looked back at Donnie Brewster and shook my head. 'You're asking me to lie to a client. I won't do that. You're also asking me to mislead him. I won't do that, either.'

Donnie stopped with his hand on the knob and looked horrified. 'Hey. Hey, I'm not asking you to do any of that. I love Peter Alan Nelsen like a brother.' He made a nervous glance out the door. Never know who might be listening. 'I'm just saying agree with the guy, that's all, and we'll work out reality later.'

'No.'

'No? What does that mean, no?' He ran back into the

room and spread his hands. 'You can't say no to Peter Alan Nelsen!'

'I'm not saying no to Peter Alan Nelsen. I'm saying no to you.'

Confused. 'Hey, you want Peter happy, don't you? Peter's not happy, you won't get hired. You know what a job like this could mean?'

'Ulcers?'

Donnie spread his hands even wider and gave incredulous, like how could I miss it? 'You work for Peter Alan Nelsen, you get on the A list. You get on the A list, you'll be working for the biggest names in the business. You might even get written up in *People* magazine.'

I said, 'Wow.'

Donnie raised his hands to the ceiling and looked at Pat Kyle. Her face was red and she was making a choking sound. He said, 'What kind of guy is this? What kind of guy did you bring me?'

She turned up her palms. 'Someone with principles?'

Donnie began rubbing at his head again and tugging at his ponytail. He rubbed so hard that I thought I saw hair fall, but that might've been my imagination. He said, 'This isn't going to work. Peter isn't going to go for this.'

Pat said, 'Peter and I spoke about Elvis at length. He sounded agreeable to me.'

Donnie gestured at me. 'But this guy's saying he won't play along. You know how Peter is. He can be a monster.' He made the nervous glance again, checking the door and the windows for ears. 'Hey, I love him like a brother.'

Pat said, 'He's expecting us in five minutes.'

Donnie said, 'Holy shit.' I think he was starting to hyperventilate.

I said, 'Donnie. Relax. Breathe into a bag.'

Donnie said, '*You* relax. I got forty million bucks

9

riding on Peter Alan Nelsen and you won't play along. This is Hollywood. Everybody plays along!'

I made a gun out of my hand and shot him.

Donnie slumped into his chair and looked depressed. 'Yeah, yeah, that's just what'll happen, too. In the back.'

Pat said, 'Donnie, Elvis is a professional and he gets results. He has done this before.'

'But not with Peter Alan Nelsen!'

'I told him what Peter is like, and I told Peter what Elvis is like. Peter knows what to expect.'

'Oh, Jesus. Oh, Jesus.'

I said, 'Donnie. Why don't we go see Peter and get it over with? I'm good. I might even find his kid. Think how happy he'll be then.'

Donnie squinted and thought about it. You could see gears moving and lights flashing behind his eyes. 'Yeah, yeah, that's right.'

'Tell him I'm brilliant and gifted. Everybody knows that brilliant and gifted people are difficult.'

Donnie's eyes got big and he slapped his hands on the table again as if he'd just found the Rosetta stone. 'Yeah, yeah. That's it! Brilliant and gifted are difficult.' He jumped up and charged toward the door. 'Let's go see him and get it over with.'

We went to see the monster.

CHAPTER 2

The monster had both floors of a two-story tropical-style plantation house hidden behind a stand of banana and rubber trees at the back of the studio. It had once been a bungalow like any other bungalow, but now it wasn't. Now, there was a veranda across the front and wide-slat Panamanian shutters and a lot of rough-hewn poles lashed together with coarse shipping rope to make you think you were on a tropical island someplace. Sort of like the Swiss Family Robinson's tree house. The roof was thatched with what looked like palm fronds, and running water trickled along a false stream, and a black skull-&-crossbones flag hung from a little pole. I said, 'Do we have to give him an E ticket before he lets us in?'

Donnie Brewster made the nervous frown. 'Stop with the humor, okay? I tell him you're brilliant and gifted, you make with the humor, he's gonna know that you're not.'

Some guys.

Inside, the floors were crude planking and the ceilings were done to match the roof, and Cairo fans hung down and slowly swirled the air. We went down a hall and into a room with two large couches and a little round glass table and posters of the six movies that Peter Alan Nelsen had made. The couches were covered in zebra skin and the posters were framed in what looked like rhino hide and a small, immaculate black man sat at a teak desk. Behind the man was a teak door. Behind the door, someone was yelling. Donnie Brewster rubbed at his scalp again and said, 'Holy Christ, now what?'

The black man nodded brightly when he saw us. Maybe he couldn't hear the yelling. 'Hello, Mr. Brewster. Ms. Kyle. Peter said to go right in when you got here.'

We went right in.

Peter Alan Nelsen's office was as long as a bowling alley and as wide as a check-kiter's smile and done up like the lobby of a Nairobi movie house. Posters from *The Wild Bunch* and *The Asphalt Jungle* and *The Magnificent Seven* hung along one wall and an old Webcor candy machine from the forties sat against the opposite wall between a Wurlitzer Model 800 Bubble-Lite jukebox and a video game called *Kill or Be Killed!* The Webcor featured M&M peanuts and Jujubes and Raisinets and PayDay candy bars. *Nothing beats a PayDay!* A blond woman with a neck like corded rosewood and shoulders like Alex Karras sat side-saddle on a sky-blue Harley-Davidson Electra-glide motorcycle parked at the far end of the office. She was wearing black spandex biking pants with a Day-Glo green stripe down the leg and a matching black halter sports top and pale gray Reebok workout shoes. Her thighs were massive and her calves thick and diamond-shaped and her belly looked like cut stonework. She glanced our way, then slid off the Harley and went to sit by a couple of guys who might've been reserve corners for the Dallas Cowboys. They were slouching on another one of the zebra couches, one of them wearing a Stunts Unlimited T-shirt and the other fatigue pants and eelskin cowboy boots. They glanced our way, too, and then they went back to watching Peter Alan Nelsen.

Peter Alan Nelsen was standing on top of a marble-slab desk, waving his arms and screaming so hard that his face was red. He was maybe six foot two, but skinny, with more butt than shoulders and the kind of soft, gawky frame that probably meant he had been a stiff-legged, awkward child. He had a rectangular Fred Mac-Murray face to go with the body, and he wore black leather pants with a silver concho belt and a blue denim work shirt with the cuffs rolled over his forearms. The forearms were thin. It was a style and a look that had faded away in the midseventies, but if you were the King of Adventure, I guess you could dress any way you wanted. The King yelled, 'Stop the tape! I don't want to see this crap! Jesus H. Christ, are you people out of your minds?!'

Peter Alan Nelsen was yelling at a neatly dressed woman and a man with a face like a rabbit's who were standing near a 30-inch Mitsubishi television. The man was scrabbling at a videotape machine, trying to eject a cassette, but his fingers weren't doing a good job and the woman had to help him.

Donnie ran forward, rubbing at his hair. 'Peter, Peter, what's going on? Hey, there's a problem here, that's what I'm for!'

The woman at the big Mitsubishi said, 'We showed him a tape of work by the new production designer. He liked it fine until I told him that the designer had worked in television.'

Peter made a loud, moaning sound, then jumped off the desk, raced forward, grabbed the tape from the rabbit-faced man, and threw it out the window. When Peter rushed toward them, the man jerked back but the woman didn't. Peter yelled, 'His quality is all wrong! Don't you people understand texture? Don't you understand image density? Tee-vee is *small*. Movies are *large*. I make *movies*, not *television*!'

Donnie spread his hands, like how could they do this. 'Jesus, Peter, I'm sorry. I can't believe they'd waste your time with a TV guy. What can I do to make it right?' I think he was trying to show me how to make Peter happy.

Peter screamed, 'You can kiss my ass on Hollywood Boulevard, you wanna make it right!' Peter didn't look any happier to me, but Donnie was the expert.

The neatly dressed woman said, 'You're out of your fucking mind.' Then she turned and stalked out, dragging the rabbit-faced man with her. When they passed, I hummed a little bit of 'There's No Business Like Show Business.' Pat Kyle gave me an elbow.

Donnie gave the big smile, telling everybody that he and his old pal Peter were in solid on this one. 'No, hey, Pete-man, I mean it.' Pete-man. 'You want a new production designer, you got one. I mean, we're making *film* here, am I right?'

Peter Alan Nelsen screamed, 'Shit!' as loud as he could, stalked back to the Harley-Davidson, and kicked it over. Hard. There were gouges in the floor where it had fallen before. The blond woman waited until Peter was through, then went over and righted it, her cut muscles straining against the weight. Peter paid no attention. He stood in the center of the floor, breathing hard, hands down at his sides like there was a terrible anger bubbling within him that he didn't know if he could control, but he would give it a game try. Drama. I said, 'I'm Elvis Cole. Is there a problem you want to discuss with me, or should I leave now during the intermission?'

Donnie Brewster said, 'Oh, shit,' and made more of the how-to-keep-Peter-happy hand moves. 'Hey, what a kidder, huh, Pete-man? This guy is the private cop we were talking about. He's –'

Peter said, 'I heard him,' and came toward me. He put out his hand and we shook. He squeezed harder than he had to and stood closer than you stand to someone you don't know. 'I'm sorry you had to see this,' he said. 'These guys give me the weight of making a major motion picture, then do everything they can to screw me up. It gets a little crazy.'

'Sure.'

He jerked his head toward the woman. 'That's Dani.' He gestured toward the two guys. 'That's Nick and that's T.J. They work for me.' Nick was the guy in the Stunts Unlimited T-shirt. T.J. had the eelskin boots. Each of them outweighed him by maybe sixty pounds.

Peter said, 'You see my movies?'

'I saw *Chainsaw* and *Hard Point*.'

'What did you think?'

'Pretty good. *Chainsaw* reminded me of *The Searchers*.'

He smiled a little bit at that and nodded. 'I was a twenty-six-year-old film-school flunk-out when I made *Chainsaw*. I didn't know my ass from a hole in the ground and I ripped off *The Searchers* every way I could.'

Donnie looked up from where he had gone to a phone. 'We were talking about *Chainsaw* before we came over. A dynamite film. Just dynamite. Tremendous gross.'

Peter went to the candy machine, slammed it with the heel of his hand, pulled a lever, and got a bag of M&M peanuts without putting in money. He tore open the bag with his teeth, dropped the paper on the floor, and poured half the bag of candy into his mouth. He didn't offer to share. Dani drifted over and picked up the paper.

Peter went to the big marble desk and sat on it, cross-legged. 'You look about my age. How old are you?'

'Thirty-eight.'

'I'm thirty-nine. We talked to some cop who said you were in the Nam. That true?' He leaned forward and said *the Nam* like they do on television, full of excitement and appeal and unreality. The way Bart Simpson would say it.

'Unh-hunh.'

He slurped up more of the M&Ms. 'The cop said you racked ass over there and got a fistful of medals.'

'What do cops know?'

'I tried to join up, but they wouldn't take me. I got this bone thing in my hips.' He was looking at a poster of John Wayne in *Blood Alley*. It showed the Duke firing a machine gun at some Commies. More shoulders than hips. 'The Nickster was in the Nam, too.' The Nickster.

The Nickster nodded. 'Airmobile.'

Peter said, 'Man, I wanted airmobile bad. Ride the skies. Ace a few Cong. I wasn't so old, I'd'a signed up for Saudi.'

The Nickster said, 'You woulda been a natural, buddy. I'd'a rather had you than half the turds in my unit.'

T.J. said, 'Fuckin' A.'

Peter nodded, regretting the lost opportunity to ride the friendly skies of Vietnam and Saudi Arabia.

Donnie put down the phone and turned back to us, making the big smile and the there's-no-problem-here hand gestures. 'Hey, Pete-man, you wanted that TV putz off the picture, he's yesterday. Gone. A memory. So tell me what you wanna do about a production designer? We've gotta make a decision and start building the rest of the sets.'

Peter said, 'Forget about it, Donnie. I'm into something now.'

Donnie's face pinched and he looked nervous. 'But, hey, Peter. We got a movie to make, man. We gotta get with it. These things won't wait.'

Peter didn't look at him. 'Donnie?'

'Yeah, Pete-man?'

Peter spit a chewed M&M at him. It hit Donnie's right pants leg, hung there a second, then fell. It left a green smear. 'Hit the road.'

Pat Kyle made a hissing sound. Donnie's face went white and his body stiffened as if the M&M had been a turd pie, and for just a moment, his face was clenched and hard and angry. Then, a little bit at a time, the anger was stored away as if little men inside of Donnie were disassembling it block by block. When enough of the blocks were gone, the little men built a smile. It wasn't a very good smile, but the little men were probably tired from all the overtime they put in. Donnie said, 'Sure, Pete-man. Whatever you say. I'll call later. Hey, I'm really sorry you got stuck with those TV clips.' His voice was tight. Trainee in the voice-box crew, no doubt.

Donnie Brewster turned and walked out without looking at me or at Pat Kyle or at Nick or T.J. or Dani. Peter poured the rest of the M&Ms into his mouth, crumpled the wrapper, then laid a hook shot toward a square wastebasket and missed. Dani picked it up.

The Nickster made a whiny voice. 'Sure, Pete-man, whatever you say.'

Peter and T.J. and the Nickster laughed. Dani didn't.

I looked at Pat Kyle. Her eyes were hard and her jaw was tight and she was staring at the floor. *What, and give up show business?* I looked back at Peter Alan Nelsen. Nick and T.J. were rolling around on the zebra couch, laughing and goosing each other and slapping hands. I said, 'Peter. I didn't come here for Pee-Wee's playhouse.'

The laughter stopped.

'I have come because my friend Pat Kyle asked me to come, and I have answered questions about myself because that's the way most people beat around the bush before they get down to business, but now we are at the end of the road. Unless you knock off the bullshit and get to the point, I will walk out of here and you can get someone else to do the job.'

Peter Alan Nelsen blinked at me through surprised, little-boy eyes. T.J. got up from the couch and put his hands on his hips and grinned at me. The Nickster said, 'Oh, man, Peter, this guy wants a piece.'

Dani uncrossed the big arms and came forward until her right hip was pressed against the desk, very close to Peter. Her left quadricep flexed like a beating heart. Peter stared at me for a long time, sort of smiling, but mostly looking like a little boy who'd been caught eating worms and knew it was wrong. He looked ashamed. Peter said, 'Nick, T.J., you guys go grab a beer or something, okay?'

Nick and T.J. glanced at Peter, then walked out, the Nickster making a big deal out of coming very close to me. When they were gone, Peter slid off the desk, dug out his wallet, took out a small color snapshot, and handed it to me. It was creased cleanly once, and yellowed the way old photos are yellowed when they have lain untouched between papers in a box for many years. It was Peter. Much younger and even thinner, with long frizzy hair and a dark maroon T-shirt that said USC FILM. He was sitting on an ugly cloth couch in a plain student's apartment and he was holding a tiny baby. Neither Peter nor the baby looked happy. He said, 'I've got an ex-wife and a son. The last time I saw my son, he was maybe a year old. His name is Toby. We named him Toby after *Toby Tyler, or, Ten Weeks with the Circus.* He's gotta be about twelve now, but I don't know if he's dead or if he's alive or if he's a crip in a ward somewhere. I don't know if he likes pizza. I don't know if he likes Teenage Mutant Ninja Turtles. You see?'

I nodded. 'Your ex-wife never came to you for child support?'

'No.'

'Or alimony?'

He spread his hands. 'For all I know she's on the moon.'

I said, 'Peter, you ever think maybe the woman doesn't want to be found?'

18

He stared at me.

'It's been ten years and you don't exactly lead a low-profile life. If she wanted to find you, she could've. I've done jobs like this before, and what happens is that everyone ends up wishing well enough had been left alone. The kids end up confused and scared and the parents end up fighting the old fights. You see?'

Peter took a deep breath and shook his head and looked around the office. With T.J. and the Nickster and Donnie Brewster gone, the office felt empty and he looked alone. He said, 'I'm worth, what? Maybe two hundred million, something like that? If I've got a kid, part of that's his, right?' Trying to convince me. 'What if he needs a car? What if he can't afford college?'

I said, 'You want to be a father.'

He took back the snapshot of the very much younger Peter Alan Nelsen and his baby son. Toby. Toby Tyler and the circus.

'Unless the kid's dead, I'm a father whether I want to be or not. That oughta mean something, right?'

I said, 'Yes. It should.'

'So Karen's mad. So I schmucked out back then and I blew it. Does that mean that I have to pay for it the rest of my life?'

'No.'

He shook his head and went over behind the marble desk and sat down the way a very old man would sit and he looked at the little picture again. He said, 'You know what's weird? It's like there's a piece of me out there that I don't know and have never seen. It's like I can feel him, like there's this other self, you see?'

I nodded. 'The boy may not feel that way. Your ex-wife almost certainly won't.'

He got up and walked over to the pinball machine and then to the video game and then to the Wurlitzer. He would stand, then move, then stand again, as if he didn't quite know what to do with himself or where he should be or how to say what he wanted to say.

I said, 'Just say it.'

He turned and his face seemed faraway and lost and hurt. 'I just want to say hello to my kid.'

I nodded. 'I don't blame you,' I said. 'I'll help you find him.'

The world's third most successful director took a deep breath, then said, 'Good. Good.' He came across the room and shook my hand. 'Good.'

CHAPTER 3

The black secretary stuck his head in the door and told Peter that someone named Langston needed to see him on the stage right away.

We trooped down out of his office and back into the real world of aliens and oil barons and people who looked suspiciously like studio executives. Patricia Kyle and Peter Alan Nelsen and I walked together, with Dani sort of drifting behind. Somewhere between Peter's office and the soundstage, Nick and T.J. reappeared, Nick giving me tough whenever I looked at him. Had me shaking, that guy. Make you turn in your license, a guy like that. I looked at Peter Alan Nelsen, instead. 'What was your ex-wife's name?'

'Karen Nelsen.'

'Not her married name. What was her maiden name?'

'Karen Shipley. That cop we talked to, Ito, he said you're big with the martial arts. He said you took out some killer from Japan.'

I said, 'What's your son's name?'

'Toby Samuel Nelsen. I got the Sam from Sam Fuller. Great director. You ever been shot?'

'I caught some frag once.'

'What did it feel like?'

'Peter, let's stick to the information about your ex-wife, okay?'

'Yeah, sure. What do you want to know?'

We walked along the little studio back streets and people stopped what they were doing and looked at him.

21

They saw celebrities every day, so they wouldn't look at Mel Gibson or Harrison Ford or Jane Fonda, but they looked at Peter Alan Nelsen, and Peter seemed to enjoy it. He stood tall and when he spoke he made broad, exaggerated gestures as if what was happening had been scripted and he was acting the scene and the lookers were his audience. Maybe the lookers thought so, too. Maybe, since Peter was the King of Adventure, they figured that a Stearman biplane would suddenly appear and begin a strafing run. Maybe they thought a Lamborghini Contach driven by Daryl Hannah would suddenly screech around the corner, chased by psychopaths in souped-up Fords, and Peter would have to save the day and it would really be something to see. If Daryl Hannah was driving the Contach, Peter would have to move pretty fast. I was planning to get there first.

I said, 'Okay. Do you have any idea where Karen might be living?'

'No.'

'You think she's still here in Los Angeles?'

'I don't know.'

'Did she ever talk about someplace in particular, like, "I'd really like to live in Palmdale one day," or, "Los Angeles is the greatest city in the world. I'll never leave it," something like that?'

'I never thought about living anyplace else.'

'Not you. Her.'

'I don't know.'

'Did she have any friends?'

He pressed his lips together and made a shrug. 'Yeah. I guess so.' Thinking harder. Then, 'I dunno. I was sort of into my own thing.' Embarrassed that he didn't have an answer.

I looked at Pat Kyle.

Pat said, 'Where was she born, Peter?'

'Someplace in Arizona or New Mexico. Phoenix,

maybe.' He frowned. 'We never talked about stuff like that.'

'Okay.'

'Why don't you ask me something I know?'

'Okay. What do you know?'

He thought for a while. 'About Karen?'

'Yeah.'

'I don't know.'

I said, 'How did you meet? Did she belong to any clubs or organizations? Did she have brothers or sisters or aunts or uncles or cousins or grandparents?' I figured if I listed enough stuff I would get lucky somewhere.

He said, 'I've got an older sister. She's married to a fat guy lives in Cleveland.' Everything was *I*.

'Great. But that's about you. What about Karen?'

'Oh.' Oh. Then, 'I think she was an only child. I think her people were dead.'

'But you don't know.'

'They were dead.' We walked along a little more, thinking about it. He said, 'Maybe she was from Colorado.'

We went through a pair of twenty-six-foot doors and into a battleship-gray soundstage that was being rebuilt to resemble the interior of a Mayan ziggurat. The doors were open to let in the air and the light. Above and around us dozens of men and women in shorts and T-shirts clung like spiders to scaffolding as they attached vacu-formed plastic panels to a wooden frame. The panels had been cast to look like great stone blocks. There were the sounds of hammers and saws and screwguns and the smell of plastic cement and paint, and somewhere a woman laughed. It was warming as the day wore on, and some of the men had their shirts off.

A heavy man with a Vandyke beard and a roll of architectural plans noticed Peter and started toward us.

23

Peter frowned and said, 'Nick, T.J., gimme some space here, huh?'

Nick gestured toward the beard and T.J. went over and intercepted him. Blocking backs.

We turned left past a couple of guys building something that looked like a sacrificial altar and squeezed between two backdrop flats and over a tangle of electrical cables into a little clearing that had been set up as a sort of office with a desk and a phone and a coffee machine. There was another Webcor candy machine next to the desk. Peter slammed it with his elbow and a PayDay candy bar dropped out. Dani said, 'Peter has a candy machine like this on all of his sets. It's part of his contract.' She said it like a press release.

Peter said, 'Go find Langston, willya, Dani? Tell'm we're hiding back here and ready to rock.'

Dani squeezed back between the flats and disappeared into the darkness. Nick hung back behind the flats, still not liking me.

Peter said, 'Man, I can't take a shit, the pogues aren't after me about something. That's why we gotta hide.' He tore the wrapper off the candy, stuffed most of the bar into his mouth, and dropped the wrapper onto the floor. I wondered how often he brushed.

I said, 'Tell me how you met.'

'I was at USC when I met her. I was casting a film and put up flyers for actors and Karen called for a reading. It was a ripoff of those biker flicks in the sixties. Eighteen minutes, synced sound, black and white. You wanna see it?'

'Is Karen in it?'

'No. I didn't give her the part.'

'Then I don't need to see it.'

'I made an audition tape for her. I couldn't find it, but I got the outtake tape. It was a long time ago, so it's Beta format, but I brought it into the office. We can probably dig out a machine if you wanna see. I did a pretty good job with her.' More of the *I*'s. *I* met. *I* married. *I* lived. Maybe Karen Shipley wasn't real. Maybe, like Pinocchio, she was a wooden puppet he had brought to life.

'What's an audition tape?'

Pat said, 'It's a way for an actor to introduce herself to casting agents. The actor tells you about herself and maybe reads a scene. Peter would've shot a lot more tape than Karen would need, then edited it down to three or four minutes. The outtake tape will be the takes they didn't use in the final product.'

Peter nodded and said something, but his mouth was full of candy again, and I didn't understand what he said.

I said, 'I'll want to look at it. Do you have a still picture?'

He swallowed the wad of chocolate and peanuts and shook his head.

Pat Kyle opened her briefcase and handed me a black-and-white 8 × 10 head shot of a pretty young woman with dark hair and eyes that would be either green or hazel. 'I phoned a friend at SAG and he came up with this.' The woman in the photograph was made up as a waitress with a fluffy apron and cap and a bright the-lemon-pie-is-very-nice-today! smile. She didn't look convincing. KAREN SHIPLEY was spelled out in block letters along a white border at the bottom of the picture.

I said, 'Pretty. Your friend at SAG say if Karen had an agent?'

Pat opened her briefcase again and took out an envelope large enough for the 8 × 10. 'A guy named Oscar Curtiss, with two esses. He's got an office over here, just off Las Palmas. His address is in the envelope.'

Peter came around next to me and looked at the 8 × 10. 'Jesus, I remember this.' He gestured at Karen's face. 'Nothing unique about the quality. See the nose, it's a little too ordinary. See the mouth, maybe it needs to be

25

fuller.' Peter the director. 'She had these made before we met. I said Christ, what do you want to look like a dopey waitress for? She said she thought it was cute. I said what a fucking waste.' He stared at the picture a little more, then looked at Pat Kyle. 'Can you get me one of these?'

Pat said, 'Sure.'

Peter looked back at the picture, and maybe there was something soft in his face, something less antic and less onstage. 'She got pregnant right away and then there was the kid and I just wasn't into the family scene. I was scrambling from job to job, trying to get a toehold, and she's talking about Huggies. I busted out of film school. It was crazy. So I said, look, this isn't my thing, I don't wanna be married anymore, and she didn't fight it. I don't think I've seen her or the boy since the day we signed the papers. A little while after that *Chainsaw* came along and things happened fast.' He spread the big hands, looking for a way to say it. 'I got larger.'

I said, 'Did Karen work, or was she just a wannabe?'

Pat said, 'Quite a bit of extra work and a couple of walkons. The sort of thing you get when all they need is a pretty face in the background.'

'Where do they send the residuals?'

'She's got four hundred sixty-eight dollars and seventy-two cents waiting for her for some work she did on *Adam* 12. Neither SAG nor the Extras Guild knows where to send it.'

Peter brightened and went back to the candy machine. He slammed it with his elbow and pulled out an Almond Joy. Another wrapper on the floor. 'I remember that gig. I went to the set with her and tried to talk the producer into giving me an episode to direct. The guy gives me the bum's rush. That TV prick. A lousy episodic producer and he's telling me I can't hack an *Adam* 12, he's saying that what they do is "highly stylized." Man, I ain't thought about that prick in years.' It was as if relating something of his to something of hers, he could remember it.

Dani came back between the flats with a fat guy in an argyle sweater. Peter said, 'That's Langston. He's my cameraman. I gotta talk to him about a shot move we're designing through the pyramid set. Is there anything else you wanna know about me?'

'Karen. We were talking about Karen.'

He looked annoyed. 'That's what I meant. Look, I gotta go. If you want anything, it's yours. Use my name. This town, it's like saying open sesame.'

'Ali Baba.'

He smiled. 'Yeah. Just like Ali Baba.'

He walked over to Langston.

Pat said, 'Well?'

I shook my head. 'He knows about him, but he doesn't know about her. How long were they married?'

'Fourteen months.'

I shook my head some more. You do that a lot in this business.

Pat and I went past the electrical cables and between the flats and toward the big doors. We were most of the way there when Peter Alan Nelsen yelled, 'Hey, Cole.'

I turned around. Peter was up on one of the framing catwalks, grinning at me. Dani was with him and the fat guy Langston, and a couple of other people who probably had to do with the construction rather than the design. He said, 'I'm glad you're on this for me. I like your style.' He tossed down a Mars bar. Maybe there was another candy machine up on the ceiling. 'Me and you,' he said, 'I think we're two of a kind. You're my kind of guy.'

I thought about ripping off the candy wrapper and dropping it on the ground, but decided that that would be small. I bit through the paper instead.

Peter smiled wider and said, 'Man, you are wild.'

27

Pat Kyle shook her head.

We walked out through the big doors and into the light. The paper tasted terrible. If Daryl Hannah was watching, I hope she was impressed.

CHAPTER 4

Pat Kyle and I walked back to the Kapstone offices where someone had set up a Sony Betamax VCR along with several yellow legal pads and sharpened pencils for the taking of notes. There was a check for four thousand dollars in an envelope taped to a Beta cassette on top of the VCR, along with a fresh pot of coffee on a side table with a tray of bagels and cream cheese and lox and sliced tomatoes and red onions. Pat said, 'Would you like company?'

'Sure.'

Pat turned on the machine and inserted the cassette and we watched as nineteen-year-old Karen Shipley Nelsen walked into an empty room and stood next to a stool. She wasn't made up like the waitress now. Now she was wearing faded jeans and an airy white top and red boots and she looked tanned and outdoorsy. The brown hair was cut in a sort of fluffy shag and the eyes were hazel. No makeup.

She looked at someone behind the camera and said, 'What do you want me to do?' The sound coming out of the television was hollow and sort of tinny. Even with that her voice was light and girlish. She giggled.

Peter Nelsen's voice came from where she looked. 'Give us the left and the right and the back. Try not to giggle.'

She showed her left profile, and then her back, and then her right. She said it as she did it, and when she moved she sort of squiggled and swayed and bounced,

29

the way fifteen-year-old girls do when they're acting grown-up and people are watching. 'This is my left side, and this is my back, and this is my right.' And then she giggled. 'Hee hee hee.'

Pat Kyle said, 'Oh, God.'

'She's not impressing you with her talents?'

Pat smiled sympathetically. 'I get tapes like this every week. Young women and young men come into my office and read for me, and they want you to like them so badly that you can feel them ache, but they aren't any better than this and they never will be any better than this.'

'Then you suspect she has not pursued acting as a vocation?'

She made an I-hope-not shrug.

The shot changed abruptly into a tight close-up. Closer, Karen's eyes showed an absence of line or character. She was talking about herself and trying to look serious. '... think my strengths lie in comedy, but I can also do drama. I think I'd make a really good ingenue.'

Peter's voice cut in sharply. 'You sound like an idiot in a malt shop, "really good ingenue." If you're an ingenue, just say it. Say "I'm a perfect ingenue."'

Karen looked unhappy and said, 'Oh, Peter, do I havta?' When she addressed Peter, she looked off camera. When she was acting, she looked directly out of the screen.

Peter's voice said, 'Why am I wasting my fucking time?'

Karen looked unhappy some more, then made a little smile and stared back into the lens and made herself serious and said it. Then she giggled.

It went on like that, cutting from bit to bit. Most of the bits were just fragments, five seconds of this, eight seconds of that, and many of them were repetitious. Peter would ask her a question or tell her to do something and she would answer or do it. There was something hopeful and naïve to her manner, maybe because she was nineteen. She tried hard even when she looked unhappy.

My stomach grumbled and I kept looking at the lox and bagels. I had to keep reminding myself that lunch at Lucy's was only moments away.

At one point, Peter walked into the picture and handed her a couple of script pages. He was wearing an orange Marine Corps T-shirt with a couple of stains on the back. *They wouldn't take me because of this hip thing.* He was young and skinny and built exactly as he was now, all wide butt and coat-hanger shoulders and intense eyes. His hair stuck out in a tremendous natural that, within the small confines of the TV monitor, seemed to be a full three feet across. Karen cleared her throat and read the speech from *Rocky* that Talia Shire says to Sylvester Stallone to give him the courage to go on. She didn't read it well. She giggled when she finished and asked Peter if that was okay. He said no.

The tape lasted twenty-two minutes. Karen Shipley never once mentioned her family or her friends or her hometown. She giggled sixty-three times. I counted. Giggling is not one of my favorite things.

When the tape ended, Pat Kyle turned off the monitor and we went to lunch. Kapstone Pictures paid.

One hour and ten minutes later, full of pork burrito and Dos Equis beer, Pat Kyle resumed work and so did I.

Las Palmas above Santa Monica Boulevard is a community of flat, faceless costume-rental shops and film-editing outfits and little single-story houses with signs that said things like flotation therapy. Women in flowered tops pushed baby carriages and men who looked like they wanted day work stood outside little markets and kids on skateboards practiced jumping curbs.

I stopped in a 7-Eleven on Fountain just past La Brea,

bought two dollars' worth of quarters, and ran outside to beat two fat guys to the pay phone on the side of the building. One of the fat guys was in a hurry and the other wasn't. The one who was in the hurry made a face like he had bowel trouble and said *Ah, shit,* when I got to the phone first. The one who wasn't leaned against the grill of a white window-repair truck and sipped at a Miller High Life. Did Mike Hammer use a 7-Eleven as an office?

I fed in a quarter and called a woman I know who works for the phone company and asked her if they had a listed or unlisted number for either Karen Shipley or Karen Nelsen anywhere within the state of California. She said she would have to get back to me, but it probably wouldn't be before tomorrow. I asked if she needed my number. She laughed and told me she's had my number for years. It's something I've been told before.

When I hung up, the fat guy in the hurry started forward. When I fed in another quarter, he raised his hands, rolled his eyes, and went back to the truck. Guess it wasn't a good day. His friend had a little more of the Miller and belched. When he belched, he covered his mouth with two fingers and said excuse me. Polite.

I called another woman I know who works the credit-verification department at Bank of America and asked if she would run a credit check on both Karen Shipley and Karen Nelsen, those names being either primary account names or maiden names listed to another unknown name. She said she would if I took her to a Lakers game. I told her to think of something else because I was going to take her to a Lakers game anyway. She made a little swooning sound, told me she'd get back to me tomorrow, and hung up. Some charmer, huh?

The fat guy was leaning past his truck like Carl Lewis set to come out of the starter's blocks, glaring at me. I showed him another quarter and fed it into the phone.

His face went white, he slapped the fender of the truck, and then stormed the long way around the truck and into the 7-Eleven. His friend sipped a little more Miller and shook his head. 'He's asking for a thrombo.'

I said, 'Get him into yoga. That'll help him relax.'

The friend shook his head, looking sort of sleepy and tired, and made a little shrug like they'd been through it a thousand times. 'You can't talk to him.'

I dialed the North Hollywood P.D. and got a gruff male voice that said, 'Detectives.'

'Elvis Cole for Lou Poitras.'

'Wait one.'

The phone got put down on something hard. There were voices in the background and the heavy laughter of men, and then the voice came back. 'I'm putting you on hold. He's gonna take it in his office.'

I got put on hold, then Lou Poitras came on. The laughter and the male sounds were still there, but now they were muted and farther away. Poitras said, 'I got my ass chewed good for trying to fix your last ticket. Don't ask me again.'

'Lou. One might think that our entire relationship is me asking favors of you.'

'So what do you want?'

'A small favor.'

'Shit.'

The fat guy in the hurry came out of the 7-Eleven with a Miller High Life of his own. He leaned against the truck next to his fat friend and looked tired. They drank. If you can't beat'm, join'm.

I said, 'I need to know if you have anything on a woman named Karen Shipley or Karen Nelsen. And I need you to go back ten years on the search.'

Lou Poitras said, 'Anything else?'

I said that should do it.

'You at the office?'

I told him where I was.

You could see him shake his head. 'Some big-time private op, working in a parking lot.'

'Beats sucking off the taxpayers.'

He said he'd get back to me tomorrow and hung up.

Everybody was going to get back to me tomorrow. Maybe there was something going on today that I didn't know about. Maybe that's why the fat guy was in such a hurry. Maybe he knew who to call to find out where the action was, and upon making the call, he and his buddy were going to whatever it was that I didn't know about. Maybe I could go with them.

I hung up the phone, looked at the fat guy in the hurry, and said, 'It's all yours.'

He sipped more Miller and didn't move, giving me who cares? His friend looked at him, then me, and shrugged. Go figure. Some guys are never happy.

CHAPTER 5

The Oscar Curtiss Talent Agency was two blocks below Sunset Boulevard in a small sky-blue clapboard house with a tiny lawn and a porch and a narrow sidewalk leading up to the porch. What looked like a Friedrich air conditioner stuck out of a window on the north side of the house and hummed loudly, water falling in a steady dribble from its underside. A couple of wine bottles were lying on the lawn. *Midnight Rambler*. The bottles were capless and empty.

I parked and went up the walk and through one of those frosty pebbled-glass office doors that no one has used since 1956. There was a large gold star on the door with *Oscar Curtiss Talent Agency* written in an arc above it and what were supposed to be little spotlights lighting up the sky.

Inside, there were three young women sitting on a hard L-shaped couch and a black woman in her sixties sitting at a scarred pecan desk that faced the room. Another frosted-glass door was behind her. This one said *Mr. Curtiss*. The three young women were spread around on the couches in a way that said they didn't know each other. Two of them were reading *Variety*. The other one was chewing gum. There were a couple hundred framed black-and-white head shots on the walls, but I didn't recognize any of them. The carpet was beige and worn and the hard couch was a kind of green and the walls were a sort of mustard and nothing went together, as if

35

the office had been built over the years without regard to style or esthetic. The Friedrich made it very cold.

The black woman looked up and smiled nicely. 'May I help you?'

'My name is Elvis Cole. I'd like to see Mr. Curtiss.' I gave her the card that said *Elvis Cole, Confidential Investigations*. The old cards had a picture of a guy listening at a keyhole. The new cards don't. Without the picture is probably better.

She took the card and nodded pleasantly, still smiling. 'Unh-hunh. And do you have an appointment?'

'No, ma'am. I was hoping Mr. Curtiss could squeeze me in.' I leaned forward and lowered my voice. Confidential. 'It involves a former client of his.'

More smiling and nodding. 'Unh-hunh. Well, why don't you just wait right there while I go see.' She got up, rapped once on the glass door, then let herself through.

I looked around at the three young women and gave them a smile. The two who had been reading were still reading, the one who had been chewing gum was still chewing gum. One of the readers wore a nice pastel pants suit and had a matching briefcase at her feet. She sat so that one foot was touching the case. The other was in blue jeans and knee boots and a purple sweater. The jeans and the sweater were too small, but she had the body for it. I made them early twenties, twenty-five tops. The gum-chewer had her legs crossed and her arms along the back of the couch and was looking at me with pale, steady eyes. She was wearing baggy culottes and pink Reebok tennis shoes and a blousy top that was tied off beneath her breasts so that her belly was bare. It was too cool outside for the top, but that's show biz. Her hair was pale and washed-out, and so was the spray of freckles across her nose. Younger than the other two. Seventeen, maybe. She blew a large pink bubble the size of a goiter, popped it, then used a lot of tongue to lick it off her lips. Maybe sixteen. Run away and come to the big town to be a star. I said, 'Pretty hot outside, huh?'

She blew another bubble, uncrossed her legs, then spread them.

I said, 'Pretty hot inside, too.'

She spread the legs a little wider, then popped the bubble and licked it off. Maybe I was a producer.

The glass door opened and the black woman came out with a short, thin guy pushing sixty. Oscar Curtiss. He had dark circles around his eyes and too many teeth and he was wearing a coarse-weave light sports coat and huaraches and baggy pants like they do in Italian fashion magazines. It looked silly. He gave me the teeth, stuck out his hand, and said, 'Hey, Cole, goodtaseeya.' Then he looked past me at the two readers and the gum-popper, mostly the gum-popper. 'You ladies excuse us for a few minutes, okay? Sydney, I'll see you next.'

The gum-popper nodded and blew another bubble. Sydney. Her knees were bouncing open-closed, open-closed.

Oscar gave her some of the teeth, too, then motioned me into his office. He didn't bother to look at me while he was doing the motioning.

The office was larger than the waiting room, with a lot of plants and one of those heavy, dark wood secretary desks they made back in the forties. It needed to be oiled. There was a leather couch against the wall and another Friedrich in the window behind his desk and more photographs on the walls, but I didn't recognize any of the people in these, either. Maybe Sydney would be there soon and I could recognize her.

He shut the door and followed me in, holding my card. 'Elvis Cole, huh? I like it. It's got catch. It's got pump and pizzazz. You got a nice look, too. You know who you look like?'

'Buddy Ebsen.'

'Nah. Michael Keaton. A little taller, maybe. A little better built. But sensitive and sharp. A guy you don't mess around with.'

'I always thought I looked like Moe Howard.'

'Take my word for it. You got the look and the name. Some of the kids come in here, Christ, they got names flat as piss on a plate. Pat Green. Steve Brown. I say that's no good. I say, you know what you need?'

'Pizzazz.'

'Fuckin' A. Look at Steve Guttenberg. Take away the Guttenberg, whattaya got? Nuthin!' He sat behind the desk and shot a glance at the door. 'Listen, I don't have a lot of time.'

'A long time ago you represented an actress named Karen Shipley. I'm trying to find her.' I took out the 8 × 10 and showed it to him.

He nodded. 'Yeah. Sure. I remember Karen. Great kid. Terrific body.'

'Do you still represent her?'

He handed back the head shot. 'Nah. I haven't heard from Karen in, what is it, ten years, something like that?' He put another glance on the door, anxious to get to other things. 'She musta went to another agency.'

I nodded. 'Did you continue to represent her after her divorce from Peter Alan Nelsen?'

Oscar Curtiss stopped looking at the door and sat forward in the chair and blinked at me. 'That's who she was married to?'

'Yeah.'

'Karen Shipley was married to Peter Alan Nelsen?'

'Yeah.'

'*The* Peter Alan Nelsen?'

'Peter Alan Nelsen wasn't Peter Alan Nelsen when they were married.'

Oscar slumped back in his chair and said, 'Jesus H.'

'He was in film school when they married. After he

38

busted out of USC, he divorced her. Now he wants to find her again.'

'Sonofabitch. I remember when she got divorced. She came here with the kid and sat down right over there and said she was divorced and needed to work. I said, sit-ups, Christ, a body like yours you wanna get it back, do sit-ups. Peter Alan Nelsen. Jesus Christ.' He wasn't looking at me anymore. He was staring somewhere in midspace, seeing the old scenes, worrying them through to recall if he'd done anything that could piss off Peter Alan Nelsen. All the worrying made his eyebrows dance around on his face.

I said, 'Do you know how we can contact her?'

'It's been years. Christ, I saw her a couple more times after that, then zippo. *Nada*. I never heard from her again.' The mouth started moving with the eyebrows.

'Okay. Where was she living?'

'It was somewhere over there.' He made a gesture that could mean anywhere in the northern hemisphere.

'That's a little broad, Oscar.'

'Christ, I never visited. She came here.'

'Maybe you've got records.'

He stopped all the moving around and looked at me with the kind of look they give you that tells you that the lights are going off behind their eyes. Getting The Big Idea. He said, 'Maybe I should deal direct with Peter on this. We might be getting a little personal here, you know, and he might appreciate keeping it in the family, as it were.'

I pointed at the phone. 'Sure. He's at the Paramount office now. Give'm a call and tell him that even though he's trying to find his ex-wife and his kid, you're foot-dragging because you want to suck after some kind of deal. He'll like you just fine for that.'

He said, 'Hey, I'm doing a favor here, right? I'm trying to help here, right?'

'Quit being small-time and tell me what you know, Oscar. You're coming across like a chiseler.'

'I look like I'm rolling in it here? I wanna help. I wanna do what I can. But, hey, Peter Alan Nelsen gives you the nod, my friend, you're made in this town.' Peter Alan Nelsen, spitting a green M&M on Donnie Brewster.

'Sure, Oscar.'

He worked it through some more, trying to get a fix on what was real and what wasn't and what he could get if he played it right and how much it could cost if he played it wrong. He said, 'Listen, Elvis, I help you out here, you tell Peter, okay?'

'I'll tell him.'

'You promise?' Like we were in fourth grade.

'I promise, Oscar.'

'Hey, I wanna help. I wanna do anything I can for Peter Alan Nelsen.' Nothing like sincerity.

'Where did Karen live?'

'I'm thinking.'

'Look in your files.'

'Christ, I'm supposed to keep files on people forever?'

'Returned checks. Tax information.'

'Nah.'

'Correspondence. Maybe an old rolodex.'

'Christ, I keep all that stuff I'd be buried in paper. We're talking a lifetime ago.'

'Okay. Maybe there's something else.'

'I'm thinking.'

'You know any of her friends?'

'No.'

'How about family?'

'Unh-unh.'

'Boyfriend?'

He shook his head.

'Did she say if she was thinking about moving away or taking a trip?'

40

His brow knotted and his face clenched and he hit the side of his head a couple of times with the heel of his hand. Worried that he wouldn't be able to come through and trying to shake something loose.

I said, 'Man, you two were really tight.'

He waved his hands. 'Hey, we never had no big heart-to-hearts. One day she just wasn't around anymore. I thought she dropped me. You know, went to another agency. I didn't hear anything from her and I tried calling the place she lived, but she was never around, so after a while I figured that's it.'

I stood up and walked to the door. 'Okay, Oscar. You tried. Thanks, anyway.'

He jumped up and came around the desk and grabbed my arm. He grabbed hard, like if he didn't something rare would get away. He grabbed the way you grab when the rare thing has visited once before, long ago, and you blew it, and now you're getting a second chance. 'Hey, you know what? I got some old stuff in storage. I'll dig through it. Maybe there'll be something, hunh? Maybe I'll find something that'll help out.' I don't think he meant help me.

'Sure. My phone is on the card.'

'You tell Peter I'm trying, okay? Tell'm I'm bending over backwards. Tell'm I really liked Karen, and I thought the kid was terrific.'

'Sure.'

I opened the door and we went out. The black woman was talking on the phone. The two young women who had been reading were still reading and the Sydney was still blowing bubbles. Oscar gave with the big teeth and made a big deal out of walking me to the outer door. 'Hey, you can tell Peter I'll get on the search tonight.' Putting on the act. 'And tell'm I'd appreciate it if he gives me a call. There's a couple of things I'd like to talk with him about.'

I said I would.

He made the big teeth some more, then left me at the door and sat on the couch next to Sydney with his hand on her thigh. The other two young women were watching him. He said that I worked for Peter Alan Nelsen and that he and Peter were thrashing out a deal together and that things were gonna start hopping around there soon. When he said it, he gave Sydney's thigh a little squeeze.

She watched him with the large pale eyes, blew another pink bubble, then popped it with her tongue. The eyes never once blinked and never once left him.

I walked out. So long, Norma Jean.

CHAPTER 6

The sun was dropping fast, the way it does in the fall, and the air lost its midday warmth and took on an autumn chill as I wound my way up Laurel Canyon to the little A-frame I keep off Woodrow Wilson Drive above Hollywood.

The cat that lives with me was sitting by his food bowl in the kitchen. He's thick and black, with fine shredded ears and broken teeth and the scars that come from a full, adventuresome, male-type-cat life. Sometimes he has fits.

I said, 'Is dinner ready?'

The cat came over and shoulder-bumped against my leg.

I said, 'Okay. How about meat loaf?'

He shoulder-bumped me again, then went back to his bowl. Meat loaf is one of his favorite things. Right up there with Kitnips.

I took a meat loaf out of the freezer, put it in the microwave to thaw, turned on the oven to preheat, then opened a can of Falstaff. It was twenty minutes after five. Business hours were until six. I drank some of the Falstaff, then phoned the Screen Actors Guild and spoke to a woman named Mrs. Lopaka about Karen Shipley. Mrs. Lopaka confirmed everything Pat Kyle had told me and added nothing new. I thanked her, hung up, then dialed the Screen Extras Guild and then AFTRA. Ditto. I called the machine at my office, hoping that there might be a message from the phone company or from B of A.

Nada. Somebody named Jose wanted someone named Esteban to call him back right away. Jose sounded pissed. I called my partner, Joe Pike.

Pike said, 'Gun shop.' Pike owns a gun shop in Culver City.

'We're on the job again. Backtrack to a woman and child.'

'You need me?'

'Well, I'm here at the house and I'm not yet pinned down by snipers across the canyon, so I guess not yet.'

Pike didn't answer.

'You know the director, Peter Alan Nelsen? He's our client.'

Pike didn't answer some more. Trying to talk with Pike is like carrying on a fill-in-the-blank conversation.

I said, 'Try to make conversation, Joe. It's easy. All you have to do is say something.'

Pike said, 'You need me, you know where I am.' Then he hung up. So much for conversation.

The microwave dinged. I took out the meat loaf, transferred it to a metal pan, opened a can of new potatoes, drained them, put them in the pan around the meat loaf and sprinkled them with garlic and paprika, then put bacon over the meat loaf and put the pan in the oven on high. I like the skin on my meat loaf to be crispy.

The cat said, 'Naow?'

'No. Not now. About forty-five minutes.'

He didn't look happy about it.

I finished the Falstaff, got another, drank most of it on the way up to the shower and the rest of it on the way back down. When the meat loaf was ready, I put out two plates and sliced off the ends for me and a center cut for the cat. He watched me put the end cuts and the potatoes in my plate and the center slice in his. He purred loudly as I did it. I sprinkled Tabasco on mine and

44

A-1 on his, then took the beer and both plates out to my deck. There's a Zalcona glass table out there with a couple of matching chairs and sometimes we eat at the table, but sometimes we take down the center section of the rail and sit at the edge of the deck and look out over the canyon. With the rail, you are separated from the view. Without the rail, you are part of it. We eat there often.

When we were finished, I said, 'Well? How was it?'

The cat stretched and broke wind. He's getting older.

I took the dishes inside, washed them, put them away, then stretched out on the couch with a finger of Knockando to read the latest Dean Koontz when the doorbell rang. It was Peter Alan Nelsen and his best friend Dani. Peter was dressed the same way he'd been dressed earlier, but Dani had shifted to buff-cut blue jeans and a designer sweatshirt with little pearl beads worked into the fabric. The sweatshirt was a pale lavender and looked good on her.

Peter walked in without being asked and said, 'Whadaya say, Private Eye? You ready to rock?' He was squinting a lot and swaying from side to side and he smelled like his clothes had been doused with bourbon.

He staggered into the center of the floor and looked around and said, 'Hey, this is neat. You live here alone?'

'Yeah.' The cat started to growl, a hoarse sound in his chest.

Peter saw my drink. 'What's that, scotch?'

I got a short glass and poured a little of the Knockando. I held the bottle toward Dani, but she shook her head. Designated human.

Peter went to the glass doors and looked out at the canyon. 'Hey, I like this view. This is okay. I got a place up on Mulholland with a view. You gotta come up sometime. We'll have a party or something.'

'Sure.'

Peter saw the cat sitting sphinxlike on the arm of the couch. 'Hey, a cat.'

I said, 'Be careful. He's mean and he bites.'

'Bullshit. I know about cats.' Peter swayed over to the couch and put out his hand. The cat grabbed him, bit hard twice, then ran under the couch, growling. Peter jumped back and shook his hand, then bent over and peered under the couch. I could see the blood from across the room. 'That sonofabitch is mean.'

Dani stood quietly to the side, maybe looking a little sad.

I said, 'Peter, it's late. I'm tired and I was getting ready for bed. What do you want?'

Peter straightened up and looked at me like I had to be kidding. 'Whadaya mean, sleep? It's early. Tell him, Dani, tell him it's early.'

Dani glanced at her watch. 'It's ten after ten, Peter. That's late for some people.'

Peter said, 'Bullshit. Ten after ten ain't nothing to guys like us.' He looked at me. 'I figured we could go out and knock back a few, maybe shoot a little pool, something like that.' He sat down on the couch and threw an arm over the back, forgetting about the cat. The cat growled, and Peter jumped up and moved to the chair across the room.

I said, 'Another time.'

Peter frowned, not liking that. 'Hey, you don't want to party?'

'Not tonight.'

'Why not?'

'Because I'm tired and I want to go to sleep, but most of all because you're so drunk you sound like you're speaking Martian.'

Dani made a soft, faraway sound, but when I looked at her, she wasn't looking at either me or Peter. Peter scowled and leaned forward in the chair. 'You got some smart mouth on you.'

'The rest of me ain't stupid, either.'

He poured himself more of the Knockando and got up and went over to the glass doors. 'I want to know what you've got on Karen.'

'You mean, how close have I come to finding her in the six hours since I started looking?'

'Yeah.'

'She is no longer a member of SAG or SEG or AFTRA, which probably means she no longer acts or works in front of the camera. I spoke with people I know at the Bank of America and the phone company and the police, all of whom are checking their computers for information about her past or present, but I probably won't hear from any of them until tomorrow. I talked with the man who was her theatrical agent, Oscar Curtiss, who is trying to be helpful but probably won't be. It goes like that sometimes. He wanted me to tell you that because he would like to do business with you.'

Peter made a little flipping gesture with his drink. 'Fuck'm.'

I shrugged.

Peter said, 'That's it?'

'Yep.'

'I thought it would go faster.'

'Most people do.'

Peter poured himself another three fingers of the Knockando, took it to the glass doors, and drank it. He stared out at the canyon for a while, then put the glass and the bottle on the floor and turned back to me. It took an effort to get himself turned around, like a tall ship in a wind with a lot of sail. He said, 'I'm calling you out.' Marshal Dillon.

I said, 'Yeah?'

He nodded. 'You're goddamned right. I didn't like the

47

way you spoke to me at the studio today, and I don't like the way you're speaking to me now. I'm Peter Alan Nelsen and I don't take shit.'

I looked at Dani. She said, 'Why don't we just leave, Peter? He doesn't want to party. We can go somewhere and party without him.'

Peter said, 'Hey, Dani, you wanna leave, leave, but I'm calling this sonofabitch out.' Peter sort of swayed forward, squinting the way you do when you're seeing three or four of something that there's only one of.

He said, 'C'mon, goddamnit, I'm serious,' and put up his fists. When his fists went up the cat howled loud and mournful and flashed out from under the couch. He grabbed Peter's ankle and bit and screamed and clawed with his hind legs. Peter yelled, 'Sonofabitch,' jumped sideways, stumbled into the chair, and fell over backward. The cat sprinted back under the couch.

I said, 'Some cat, huh?'

Dani helped Peter up, then righted the chair. Peter said, 'Lemme alone,' and pulled away from her. When he did he fell to his knees. He said, 'I'm all right. I'm all right.' Then he passed out.

I said, 'Is he like this a lot?'

Dani said, 'Pretty much, yeah.'

'I'll help you get him outside.'

'No, thanks. You could get the door, if you want.'

'You sure?'

'I can bench two-thirty. I squat over four.'

Nope. She wouldn't need the help.

Dani lifted him into the chair, then squatted in front of him and pulled him onto her shoulders and stood up. She said, 'You see?'

I got the door.

She moved out past me and stopped on the porch and looked back at me. 'I know it doesn't show, but he really likes you. You're all he talked about this afternoon.'

'Great.'

She frowned, maybe looking a little angry. Defensive for him. I liked that. 'It's not easy being him. Here's a guy with all he has going, and he can't just go hang out, you see?'

'Sure.'

'Everybody in his life is there because they want to screw him. Any time there's a woman, he's thinking it's because she wants to rip him off. Any time a guy says he's Peter's friend, it's because he wants to be in business with Peter Alan Nelsen, the big deal, not with Peter Nelsen, the guy.' She said it as if we were just standing there, as if Peter Alan Nelsen wasn't an outsized yoke across her shoulders.

I said, 'He's got to be getting heavy.'

She smiled softly. 'I can hold him all night.'

I followed her out to a black-on-black Range Rover and opened the right front door. She eased him into the front seat and carefully placed his head on the headrest and buckled the seat belt around him. She tested it to make sure it was snug. I said, 'Everybody's out to screw him but you.'

She nodded, then shut the door and looked at me, and there was something soft within the hard muscle. She said, 'Are you going to quit? He pulls stuff like this and most people quit.'

I shook my head. 'I'm liking you too much to quit.'

She made the little soft smile again, then went around to the driver's side, got in, and made a U-turn onto the little road that winds down the blackness toward Laurel Canyon and Mulholland Drive.

I went back into the house and picked up the empty glasses and the Knockando bottle and cleaned up the spilled booze. The cat came out from under the couch and watched me for a while, and then he left. Off to do cat things, no doubt.

When the glasses were put away, I went out onto the deck again and looked down into the dark canyon below. It was open and free and, beneath me there, lights moved along the curving roads.

Maybe they were Dani and Peter, but maybe they weren't.

CHAPTER 7

The next morning I rose early and was out on the deck again while the sun was still low in the east. The canyon below was cold and green with a faint hint of haze, and high overhead a red hawk rode a growing thermal, looking for gophers.

I did slow stretches and then the Twelve Sun Salutes from the hatha yoga and then an easy tae kwon do *kata* and then a hard one, snapping the moves with power and speed and certainty of purpose. It feels clean to do it that way. Sometimes when I practice in the early evening, the two little boys who live in the cantilevered house down the street come over and watch and we talk about things that are important to small boys. I find that they are important to me, too. In the morning, I am always alone. Lately I've noticed that I work out less in the morning and more in the evening. Maybe Peter Alan Nelsen was feeling that way, too.

I showered and shaved and put out two eggs for poaching and made a batter for blueberry cottage cheese pancakes. While I waited for the griddle to heat, I called my answering machine. There were messages from my friends at the Bank of America and the phone company and from Lou Poitras. My friend at the B of A said that their credit check showed that no one named Karen Shipley or Karen Nelsen or listing either of those names as either a maiden or former name possessed a credit card of any kind anywhere within the United States. My friend at the phone company said pretty much the same.

Lou Poitras said that Karen Shipley had once gotten a ticket for parking in a red zone but had paid it promptly. Her address at that time was the apartment she had shared with Peter Alan Nelsen. He said that if I found her, I probably wouldn't have to assume she was armed and dangerous, but that I might want to bring along backup just in case. That Lou. He's a riot, isn't he?

I made four pancakes and the poached eggs, then crushed the poached eggs on top of the pancakes, poured a large glass of nonfat milk, and brought the food and the milk to the table. The cat had left during the night. Sometimes he eats breakfast with me, but sometimes he doesn't. When he doesn't, I don't know what he eats. Maybe small dogs.

Karen Nelsen had no phone in either name, but I had sort of expected that. After ten years, the odds were large that she had remarried. The credit cards were another matter. If she had a credit card under Nelsen or Shipley, or with Nelsen or Shipley listed as a former name, she should've turned up. That was odd, but there were explanations. Maybe she had joined a cult and no longer had a name. Maybe she had given over all earthly traits and artifacts to a higher being named Klaatu, and in return Klaatu had blessed her with eternal bliss and escape from snoopy private cops. Or maybe she simply didn't like credit cards. Hmmm.

I had run through all of my leads and I had come up with nothing and it made me feel small. I needed another line. Maybe I should ask Klaatu.

The phone rang and Oscar Curtiss said, 'I think I got a line on Karen Shipley for you.'

I said, 'Thanks, Klaatu.'

'Hunh?'

'I sneezed. What do you have?'

'I dug out that stuff and I found an old address. It's

3484 Beechwood Canyon Place, Apartment 2. It's where she lived after the divorce.'

'Okay. Thanks.'

'I really broke my ass to find this stuff. Christ, I had it in storage in Glendale and I was two hours in traffic. You gonna tell Peter? You gonna tell Peter that I came through?' *Peter making a little flipping gesture with his drink. Fuck'm.*

'Sure, Oscar. I'll tell him.'

Oscar said, 'Oh, man.' Excited at the possibilities.

I said, 'Hey, Oscar? Thanks. I appreciate it.'

Oscar Curtiss laughed. 'Yeah, your thanks and appreciation won't buy dick. Just tell Peter, okay? This town, you're on Peter's team, you're *made.*'

'You bet, Oscar. Made.' *Fuck'm.*

I hung up.

At nine-forty that morning, I looped down Mulholland to the Cahuenga Pass, then followed the pass down to Franklin Avenue and across the northern part of Hollywood to Beechwood Canyon. Beechwood Canyon starts high, just beneath the Hollywood sign, and winds its way down to Franklin at the bottom of the Hollywood Hills. There is a school at the bottom and a gas station and a lot of large apartment houses that used to be small apartment houses and don't look as nice large as they did small. Urban redevelopment. Between the big places sat small stucco bungalows that were neat and pretty and still managed to look like garages. The higher up the mountain you went, the more you saw of the bungalows and the less you saw of the developers.

3484 was four narrow green stucco apartments stepping up the side of the hill in a line from the street, each one higher than the one in front. Cement steps went up along the left side, the steps cracked and uneven where a couple of ancient yucca trees had lifted them. The front apartment had a little porch with wooden wind chimes and lots of little cactuses in old clay pots that were painted the way maybe Indians would paint them, only the paint was chipped and faded just like the apartments. Four big century plants nested at the street, overgrown with the silver weeds you always see around them. All of it looked clean and all of it looked tended to, but only partway, as if whoever did it couldn't quite get the high spots and couldn't quite get in the corners and couldn't quite get all the grime or the weeds or the litter out. There was no driveway and no garage. Curb parking only.

I drove past, turned around, and parked the Corvette on the steep grade across the street, then went up onto the little porch. The door opened before I could knock and a woman in her seventies looked out past three security chains. She was wearing a paisley housecoat. She said, 'Can I help you?' high and hard, like maybe if she didn't like my answer the sort of help she'd give me was the LAPD's Metro Squad.

I showed her the license. 'About ten years ago a woman named Karen Shipley Nelsen lived here with a baby. I'm trying to find her. Do you have a few minutes to talk?'

She stared at the license, then at me. 'How do I know that's you?'

I took out my driver's license so she could see the picture. Outside on the street a very tall white man and a short, slender Hispanic man walked past. The white guy was bald and wore a tie-dyed dashiki like people used to wear in 1969. The Hispanic guy combed his hair straight back and traced his hand along the lines of the Corvette as they went past. The woman squinted from the picture to the guys on the street, then to me, and said, 'That your car?'

I said it was.

She nodded once, knowing. 'You'd better watch after it. That little sonofabitch will steal it.'

I said I would keep an eye out.

She craned around to watch the two guys on the street until she couldn't see them anymore, then she closed the door and unlatched the chains and opened it wider. 'My name is Miriam Dichester. You can come in, but I think we'll leave this door open.'

'Sure.'

The living room was small and musty, with gray lace drapes and an ancient RCA black-and-white console television and a deep purple wingback couch with crocheted doilies on the arms. A long time ago the doilies had been white. The drapes had probably been white, too. Very old movie magazines sat in neat stacks on either side of the couch, and on the console television were framed photographs of Clark Gable and Walter Brennan and Ward Bond. The picture of Ward Bond was autographed. Ashtrays sprouted from the furniture like mushrooms and an open carton of Kent 100s sat on the coffee table. The air was sour with cigarettes and perspiration and Noxema skin cream.

Miriam Dichester took a single cigarette and a little blue Cricket lighter from her housecoat and fired up. I sat on the couch. She sat on a Morris chair. I hadn't seen a Morris chair in years. She said, 'I watch the street out here and I know. These days, you better watch. That's why I have my place down here by the front. I can keep an eye on anything that comes up that walk.' She waved the cigarette at the little broken walk that went up alongside the building. 'Anything I don't like goes up there, I know about it. I got a little something to take care of it, too.'

I showed her the 8 × 10. 'This is Karen Shipley. Her son's name was Toby.'

'I know who you're talking about.'

I put the picture away. 'Do you know how I can get in touch with her?'

'No, I do not.' She sucked more of the Kent, looking down the flat planes of her face at me. 'I take care of my people. I guess I take care of them even when they don't live with me anymore.'

I said, 'She's not looking at trouble here, Miriam. The ex-husband hasn't seen her or the boy since they were divorced, and he's feeling pretty bad about it. He wants a shot at knowing his son.'

She breathed in the rest of the Kent, then crushed it out. Three puffs, and she had drawn through 100 millimeters down to the filter. She said, 'I don't like this. A woman gets dumped, then the sonofabitch who dumps her wants to come back to stir the pot again. And I'll bet you a high hand to heaven I know what he wants to stir it with, too.'

I gave her a little shrug. 'They're adults, Miriam, they can work that out. The boy isn't. He's about twelve now and he's never met his father.'

She pursed the wrinkled mouth. She was wearing only the upper teeth. The lowers were in a glass by the telephone. She finally took out another Kent and lit up. Succumbing to the inevitable. 'She lived with me for almost a year. She lived in number two, that's the one right behind.'

'Okay.'

'She wanted to be an actress. A lot of them come out here wanting that.' She looked at the picture of Ward Bond and drew heavy on the Kent.

'Only it wasn't happening.'

'She tried, though. She'd ask me to mind the baby so she could go out on readings, and I would, and for a while she worked at one of these carhop places, and I minded the baby then, too. She was good about it. She didn't abuse.' Miriam leaned past me and peered out the open door. The flash of a bird. A passing car.

'How long did that last?'

'Two months. Maybe three.' She leaned back as if whatever had caught her eye was gone. 'I heard her crying one day and I went to see. She said she couldn't keep on like she was going. She said she had the baby. She said there had to be a way to make a life for herself. She was very serious about it. She talked about going to school.'

I thought of the Karen Shipley I had seen on the tape. *Giggle. Do I havta, Peter? Giggle.* 'Did she enroll?'

Miriam Dichester shook her head and finished off another Kent. 'She didn't have the money. And what was she going to do with the baby?'

'Did she have friends? Boyfriends, maybe.' As soon as the one Kent was dead, she fired up another.

'No. She was alone. Just her and the baby. Not even any family to go to. After a while she didn't even leave the apartment. She just sat there, a young girl like that. Then she moved out.'

'She tell you where she was going?'

'She didn't say nothing when she moved out. She just up and left, owing me three months' back rent.'

She leaned forward again to look out the door. This time when she looked, I looked with her. It was catching. I said, 'You seem to like her.'

'I do.'

'Even though she stiffed you on the rent.'

She waved the cigarette at me. 'She paid it back. Couple of years later I got a letter. There was a U.S. postal money order in it for every nickel and the interest, too. How many people you know would do that?'

'A couple.'

'Then all right. There was a little note in there

apologizing and saying she hoped I wouldn't think bad of her for what she did but it couldn't be helped.'

'You like her a lot.'

Another nod. More of the Kent.

'You keep the letter?'

She said, 'Oh, Lord, I got so much stuff scattered around.'

'Maybe you could take a look.'

She squinted out past the drapes to the street. 'I go digging around in the back, I can't see the front.'

'I'll watch the front for you.'

'That little sonofabitch is looking to steal something, mark my words. They're coming back.'

'I'll watch. I'm good at watching.' I tapped my cheek under my right eye. Watchful.

She nodded and bustled over to a little secretary that was against the wall near where the living room L'd into the dining room. Three small drawers were fit across the top of the secretary, and she opened them one by one, looking through pens and pencils and note cards and small envelopes and photographs and a crushed flower and newspaper clippings that looked, from across the room, like obituary columns, and things that might've been forty years old. Precious things. She rustled around in it for a while, talking to me but really talking to herself, saying how she'd have to clean the place up, saying that she started to last week but then someone named Edna called and that had been that, no one ever calls until you're about to do something. She went through the drawers and she came up with a small white envelope that had been torn along the top edge. It had been in the little drawer for so long that the ragged tears were crushed flat and smooth and the paper was dingy. She took out a single sheet of folded yellow notepaper and read it and then showed it to me. It was exactly as Miriam Dichester had said it was, Karen apologizing for leaving while still owing money, saying she hoped Miriam hadn't experienced a hardship because of it, saying a check had been enclosed to pay Miriam back in full, including 6½% interest, and that she appreciated the kindness and friendship that Miriam had shown her and her son while they had lived with her. There was no return address and no hotel letterhead and no mention of where Karen was or where she was going. The envelope was postmarked *Chelam, CT*.

Miriam said, 'Does it help?'

I nodded. 'It's more than I had before.'

She said, 'You find them, you do right by them, hear?'

'That's my intention.'

'Well, you know what they say about that, don't you?'

'No. What do they say?'

'The road to hell is paved with good intentions.'

When we were in the door the tall white man and the shorter Hispanic man were walking down the street in the other direction. She said, 'You see. I told you they'd be back.'

'Maybe they live down the hill. Maybe they're just out for a walk.'

'My dying ass.' She was a pleasant old gal. 'Mark my words, that little sonofabitch is out to steal something.'

I thanked her and gave her one of my cards in case she remembered anything else, and then I went out to the Corvette. A hundred yards down the street, the white guy and the Hispanic guy were using a two-foot steel shim to pop the door on a white 1991 Toyota Supra.

I yelled and ran after them, but by the time I got there they were gone.

59

CHAPTER 8

Two hours and ten minutes later I was on a United Airlines L-1011 as it punched its way up through the haze layer and climbed out over the Pacific. The air was slick and clear and, below us, the red of the mountains and the desert and the gray of the ocean looked clean and warm. It was your basic outstanding Southern California afternoon. The people around me were relaxed and pleasant, and the flight attendant had a deep tan and when her smile was wide enough she dimpled. She was from Long Beach. Outstanding.

Five and one half hours later we landed at Kennedy airport beneath an overcast layer so thick and so dark that it looked like casket lining. Unseasonal cold snap, the papers had said. Arctic air down through Canada, they'd said. First snow of the season. I had brought a brown leather Navy G-2 jacket and a couple of sweaters and a pair of black leather gloves. It wasn't enough, even for standing around in the terminal.

While I waited for my suitcase at the baggage carousel, three different guys asked if they could borrow cab fare and another wanted to know if I'd found Jesus. An airport security cop arrested a pickpocket. The air smelled like burning rubber. A woman with a baby told me she didn't have enough money to feed her child. I gave her fifty cents and felt like I'd been taken. Maybe I looked like a tourist. I frowned and looked sullen and tried to make like a native. That seemed to work. I got a couple of road maps and a metallic-blue Taurus from

Hertz and drove over to the Kennedy Hilton and took a room for the night. Dining-room service was slow and the food was bad and the hostess in the bar had an attitude. A guy on the radio said that the cold air was going to keep pushing down from Canada and that maybe we'd get some more snow. The room cost two hundred a night and nobody had deep tans and dimples. This was my fourth time visiting New York in eleven years. Nothing much had changed. I ♡ NY.

The next morning I checked out of the Hilton and took the Van Wyck Expressway north to Connecticut. Through most of Queens and the Bronx everything looked dirty and gray and old, but farther along the building density diminished until, as I approached White Plains, stretches of empty land appeared, bordered by stands of trees, and, just north of White Plains, there were lakes. The empty land became fields and the woods grew deeper, and though some of the trees were dark and bare, most were still locked in their explosions of yellow and red and purple, and the sight and the smell of them made me think of squash and wild turkeys and neighborhoods where children yelled 'Trick or Treat!' Maybe the Northeast wasn't so bad after all.

Four miles east of Rockwood Lake, there was a Howard Johnson's Motor Lodge and a green exit sign that said *CHELAM next right*. I got off and followed a state road for a mile and a half through woods and farmland and there it was, a little place of clapboard and brick buildings around a town square, maybe two blocks on a side. There were plenty of trees and lawns, and the streets were narrow and without curbs and looked more like they were made for velocipedes than for automobiles. The overcast and the cold gave a barren quality to the town, but there was still enough green in the lawns and color in the leaves to let you know that, come spring, Chelam would look like one of those quaint little upstate hamlets that are always pictured on the post-cards your cousin Flo sends.

I let the Taurus roll down the main street past a Texaco station and a White Castle hamburger stand and the First Chelam National Bank and a barbershop with an honest-to-God barber's pole. A whitewashed gazebo sat on the town square across from a courthouse that was big and old, with a second-floor balcony ideal for mayoral speeches on the Fourth of July. Several big elms dotted the square, their dead leaves a fragile brown carpet over the lawn. Two young women in down jackets stood in the leaves, talking. An old man in a bright orange hunter's parka sat on the gazebo steps, smoking. Next to the courthouse there was a mobile home permanently mounted on cement footings. A big gold star was painted on the side of the mobile home along with the words CHELAM POLICE. Across the square there was a little building just about the size of a pay toilet that said *U.S. Post Office*. Eight years ago Karen Nelsen had gone in there and mailed the letter to Miriam Dichester. Maybe she had been on her way up to Maine, just passing through when she thought, oh, Christ, I've gotta get this money back to Miriam, and she had stopped and bought the money order and mailed it and continued on her way. But maybe not. Maybe she had stayed the night or had gotten something to eat and had said where she was going and someone would remember.

One block past the post office the town ended. I turned around and drove back to the Texaco station and pulled up to the full-service pumps. An old geez in a stained gray Texaco shirt and a cammie hunting cap was leaning back in a chair beneath a sign that said WE HAVE PROPANE. I turned off the engine and got out and said, 'How about some high-test?'

He tilted the chair forward and came over and put in the nozzle. A dirty blond Labrador retriever was lying between the chair and a Pepsi machine. The Lab had its chin down and its paws out to either side. He didn't move when the old man got up, but his eyes followed the old man to the car. Someone had put down a piece of cardboard for the dog to lie on.

I said, 'Pretty town.'

The old man nodded.

'Picturesque.'

He made a sucking sound through his nose, then hocked up something heavy and spit it toward the road. 'You want me to check the hood?'

'Hood's okay. If I wanted to stay a few days, where would I go?'

'Ho Jo's out on the highway.'

'Here in town.'

He squinted at the gas pump. Nine-forty and rising.

I said, 'There a little hotel? Maybe a boardinghouse? Something established?'

He made the sucking sound again, and this time he swallowed it.

I fed seventy-five cents into the Pepsi machine, pulled out a Barq's root beer, opened it, then sat down in the old man's chair. The dog still hadn't moved, but now it looked at me. So did the old man. Neither of them liked me in the chair. I said, 'Think I'll set for a spell and chew the fat.' Elvis Cole, the Bumpkin Detective.

The old man said, 'Guess you might try May Erdich's place.'

'She the only place in town?'

'Ayuh.' I guess that meant yes.

'Were there any other places, say, about ten years ago?'

'Shit.' I guess that meant no.

'How do I get to the Erdich place?'

The gas pump *dinged*. He put the nozzle back in the pump, then reset the counter. The dog's eyes moved from the old man to me, then back to the old man. Every time its eyes moved, its eyebrows shifted like it was watching a tennis match. It looked like Fred MacMurray.

I said, 'May Erdich.'

He told me, but only after I got out of his chair.

I drove back through the town and found May Erdich's place on a residential street two blocks behind the square. It was a big yellow two-story house with a gravel drive and a covered porch and a little sign out front that said *rooms to let*. Pockets of hard snow hid in the eaves and under the porch, safe from the sun. I parked in her drive and went up to the front door and knocked.

A woman in her late forties opened the door and looked out at me. She had fair skin and a pale green apron over blue jeans and a coarse yarn sweater, and her hair was held up with bobby pins so that wisps of it floated down into her eyes. It was warm in her house, and the warmth rolled out at me and felt good.

I said, 'Are you May Erdich?'

'That's right.'

'My name is Elvis Cole. I'm a private detective from Los Angeles. I'm trying to find someone who may or may not have stayed here about eight years ago.'

She smiled. The smile was where the lines came from. 'A private detective.'

'Pretty hokey, huh?'

The smile got wider and she nodded.

I showed her one of my cards and gave her a little Groucho Marx. 'Sam Grunion, private eye. Secrecy is our motto. We never tell.'

She laughed and slapped the towel against her thigh and said, 'No shit.' I was going to like May Erdich just fine.

She opened the door wider, let me come in, took the G-2, then had me sit on a big overstuffed couch in a room she called the parlor. 'Would you like a cup of hot tea? I just put some up fresh.'

'That'd be great. Thank you.'

She went out through a swinging door. The parlor was neat and clean, with a hardwood floor that showed neither dust nor scuff marks.

She came back with two glass cups of honey-colored tea on a beaten-pewter tray. There was a bowl of sugar with a little gold spoon in it and a few packets of Sweet'n Low and a saucer of sliced lemons and two glass spoons for stirring the tea and another saucer mounded with what looked like homemade blueberry cookies. The apron was gone and the wisps of hair were now neatly under the pins. I took one of the cookies. 'Delicious.'

'Would you like sugar or lemon?'

'I take it plain.'

She made a face. 'Ugh. It's so bitter that way.'

'Private detectives are pretty tough.' I had some of the tea. It was mellow and sweet with mint. Sugar would've ruined it.

She said, 'Is it exciting to be a detective in Los Angeles?'

'Sometimes. Most of the time it's doing things that people never think of when they think of private investigators.'

'Like what?'

'Like looking through phone bills and credit card receipts and being put on hold when you're talking to people at utility companies and the DMV and that kind of thing.'

She nodded, trying to imagine Tom Selleck on hold.

'But sometimes you get to help people and that feels pretty good.'

'Who are you trying to find?'

'A woman named Karen Nelsen. She might've been using the name Karen Shipley. Eight years ago, she would've had a toddler with her. A little boy, maybe three or four years old.'

She sipped more of the tea and thought about it, then shook her head, a little half shake. 'No. No, that doesn't ring a bell.'

I took out the 8 × 10 and showed it to her. The photo had been folded and there were creases that I tried to smooth.

May Erdich leaned forward and smiled the wide smile and said, 'Are you serious?' like maybe I was pulling her leg.

I said, 'What?'

'That's Karen Lloyd. She works at the bank.'

I looked at the picture as if it might've changed. 'She works at the bank?' We exciting L.A. detectives are quick on the uptake.

'She's got a twelve-year-old boy named Toby. I see her in the market. We used to be in PTA together.'

'This woman lives here, this woman and her son, Toby.' Swift, we are.

'That's right.'

I folded the picture and put it back in my pocket. Sonofagun. 'Karen Lloyd.'

May Erdich nodded. 'That's right. She works at the First Chelam. I think she's the manager or something.'

I finished the tea and stood up and May Erdich stood up with me. 'Why are you trying to find her? Did she do something bad?' Her eyes were bright and mischievous, thinking how great it would be if someone in town had done something bad.

I said, 'It involves family business, and you won't be doing her a favor if you tell people that a private cop has been asking about her. Do you understand that?'

May Erdich gave me some Groucho and squeezed my arm. 'Secrecy is our motto.'

'Right.'

She led me to the door. 'You must be a pretty good

detective, all the way from Los Angeles to find some-body here in Chelam.'

I put on the G-2 and went out into the cold. 'That's right. I am. In another life I could have been Batman.'

CHAPTER 9

The First Chelam National Bank was a small redbrick building across from the grocery store and next to a place called Zoot's Hardware. There was a single drive-through window for their customers' convenience on the west side of the bank and a small L-shaped parking lot wrapping around the east. Someone had planted a couple of young elms at the edge of the parking lot and their leaves were scattered over the cement. The drive-through window was closed.

I parked in the lot and went in. A teenage boy was filling out a deposit slip at a long table, and a heavy woman in stretch pants was talking to a teller at a blond-wood counter. An old guy in a gray security guard's uniform was reading Tom Clancy. He didn't look up. There were four windows built into the tellers' counter, but only one teller was on duty. Another woman sat at a desk behind the counter, and behind her were a couple of offices, but the offices looked empty. Neither the teller nor the woman at the desk appeared to be Karen Shipley.

I gave the woman at the desk a hopeful smile. She was in her late twenties and wore a bright green top under a tweed suit jacket and a little too much makeup. A name plate on her desk said JOYCE STEUBEN. I said, 'Excuse me. I'm here to see Karen Lloyd.'

Joyce Steuben said, 'Karen isn't in right now. She has a couple of property appraisals, but she should be back around three. Of course, she might come in before then. That's always possible.'

'Of course.'

I left the bank and walked across the street to a pay phone outside the grocery. In L.A., they put phone books three inches thick with the pay phones, but most of the books are stolen and the ones that aren't are defaced. The Chelam book represented something called *The Five-Town Area*. Chelam, Oak Lakes, Armonk, Brunly, and Tooley's Mill. It was complete and immaculate and was this year's edition, and altogether it was maybe a quarter-inch thick. Karen Lloyd was listed on page 38. Number Fourteen Rural Route Twelve, Chelam. There were six Lloyds. Three in Tooley's Mill and two in Brunly. Karen was the only Lloyd in Chelam. No Mr. Lloyd. I copied her address along with her phone number and put the book back in its case, still complete, still immaculate. Jim Rockford would've ripped out the page, but Jim Rockford was an asshole.

I sat on the bench outside Milt's Barber Stylings and wondered at my good fortune. If Karen Lloyd was in fact Karen Shipley, maybe I could get this thing wrapped up and be on an evening flight back to L.A. In L.A., I wouldn't have to sit outside Milt's Barber Stylings with two sweaters under the G-2 and still be cold. Of course, maybe Karen Lloyd wasn't Karen Shipley. Maybe they just looked alike and May Erdich was wrong. Stranger things have been known to happen. All I had to do was hang around and wait for Karen Lloyd and ferret out the truth.

Portrait of the Big City Detective sitting on a small-town bench, ferreting. In the cold. People passed on the sidewalk, and when they did they nodded and smiled and said hello. I said hello back to them. They didn't look as cold as me, but perhaps that was my imagination. You get used to the weather where you live. When I was in Ranger School in the Army, they sent us to northern Canada to learn to ski and to climb ice and to live in the snow with very few clothes. We got used to it. Then they sent us to Vietnam. That's the Army.

A little bit after two-thirty kids started drifting past with books, and at five minutes before three a dark-haired boy in a plaid Timberland jacket came pumping down the street on a beat-up red Schwinn mountain bike. Toby Nelsen. He was horse-faced and gangly, with a wide butt and narrow shoulders, just like his father. His rear end was up and his head was down and he whipped the bike across the sidewalk and skidded to a stop by the front door of the bank just as a dark green Chrysler LeBaron pulled into the parking lot. He was laughing. A woman who might've been Karen Shipley got out of the Chrysler. A dozen years older than the Karen Shipley in the videotape, wearing a tailored rust-colored top coat and heels and tortoiseshell sunglasses. Together. Her hair was short and set off her heart-shaped face nicely and she stood straight and confident. She didn't bounce or wiggle. Toby raised his hands over his head and yelled, 'I beatcha by a mile!' and she said something and the boy laughed again and they went into the bank. I crossed the street after them. Elvis Cole, Master Detective. We Always Get Our Mom.

When I got into the bank, Karen Shipley was seated in one of the back offices, talking on the phone, and the boy was at a little coffee table, writing in a spiral notebook. I went to the end of the tellers' counter again and waved at Joyce Steuben. 'I'm back.'

Joyce Steuben looked around at Karen Shipley, still on the phone. 'She's on a call now. Can I tell her who wants to see her?'

'Elvis Cole.'

'Would you like to have a seat?'

'Sure.'

I walked back to the little round table and sat down across from the boy. He was writing in the workbook with a yellow pencil and didn't look up. Fractions. He was big for twelve, but his face was smooth and unlined and young. He looked exactly like his father, and I wondered if he knew that. I said, 'You Toby Lloyd?'

He looked up and smiled. 'Yeah. Hi.' He looked healthy and happy and normal.

'You're Karen's son?'

'Yeah. You know my mom?'

'I'm here to see her. I saw you guys racing down the street. You were really flying.'

His smile flashed a yard wide. 'I really creamed her today. Usually she wins.'

Karen Shipley said, 'Mr. Cole? May I help you?' She was standing in the little passage at the end of the tellers' counter.

I got up and went over and shook her hand. The handshake was firm and dry and poised, and she looked at me with a clear confidence that she could meet my every banking need. No wedding ring. Up close, and with the sunglasses off, you saw that she was the woman in the video, yet not. It was the face, yet not the same face. As if she had stepped into the transmogrifier with Calvin and Hobbes and had been changed. Her voice was lower and there was a light network of lines around her eyes and she looked better now than she had then, the way most women do as they move into their thirties. I said, 'I hope so. I'm going to be moving to the area, and I'd like to discuss financing for the purchase of a home.'

She opened the gate and gave me a warm, professional smile. 'Why don't we go back to my office and talk about it.'

'Sure.'

Her office was neat and modern, with a polished executive's desk and well-tended green plants and comfortable chairs in which people with legitimate business could sit and look at her. A Toshiba *My Café* coffee machine sat on a lowboy filing cabinet between a couple of smoked-glass windows that looked out on the parking lot, and on the wall behind her desk there were framed photographs and certificates and diplomas. Official-looking men and women were standing with Karen in the photos, and in some of them the official-looking people were presenting Karen with what looked like plaques and citations. Some of the citations were on the wall. *Greater New England Banking and Trust Award. PTA Meritorious Service Award. Appreciation Award from the Five-Town Area Rotary.* A framed real estate license hung beneath a diploma from the State University of New York for a bachelor's degree in finance. *Gee, Peter, do I havta?* It had been awarded two years ago. I blinked at her and maybe smiled a little. It had been a long time since she'd made herself up like a waitress. She said, 'Would you like coffee?'

'No, thank you.'

She went around and sat behind the desk and folded her hands and smiled at me. 'All right. How can I help you?'

I got up and closed the door.

She said, 'You don't have to do that.'

I left the door closed and went back to my seat. 'It's better if it's closed,' I said. 'I'm afraid I've come to you under false pretenses.'

She made a small frown, wondering what I was talking about.

I said, 'I'm not moving to the area, and I don't want to finance a house. I'm a private investigator. From Los Angeles.'

Her left eye flickered and she didn't move for several seconds. Then she made an effort at the professional smile and sort of cocked her head to one side. Confused. 'I'm afraid I don't understand.'

I took out the 8 × 10 of nineteen-year-old Karen

Shipley made up like a waitress, unfolded it, and put it on her desk. I said, 'Karen Shipley.'

She leaned forward and looked at the 8 × 10 without touching it. 'I'm sorry. My name is Karen Lloyd. I don't know what you're talking about.'

'Your ex-husband, Peter Alan Nelsen, hired me to find you.'

She shook her head, smiled patiently, then used a pencil to push the picture back toward me and stood up. 'I don't know anyone named Peter Alan Nelsen and I've never been to Los Angeles.'

I said, 'Karen. Come on.'

'I'm sorry. But if you're not here to discuss business with the bank, I think you should leave.' She came around the desk and opened the door and stood there, right hand on the knob. Outside, Joyce Steuben glanced at us from her desk and a woman with blue hair took money from the teller.

I picked up the 8 × 10 and looked at it and looked at the woman with her hand on the knob. They were one and the same. I had not lost my mind. 'Ten years ago you and Peter Alan Nelsen were divorced. Your theatrical agent was a guy named Oscar Curtiss. You lived in an apartment house on Beechwood Drive owned by a woman named Miriam Dichester for almost a year, and then you skipped out on three months' back rent. Twenty-two months after that, you mailed a U.S. postal money order for four hundred fifty-two dollars and eighteen cents to Ms. Dichester. It was postmarked Chelam. This is you in the picture. Your maiden name was Shipley. Then you were Karen Nelsen. And now you're Karen Lloyd.'

She was gripping the door knob so hard that the tendons in the back of her right hand were standing out like bow strings, as if the force of the grip was not so much to hold on to the knob as it was to hold together something that had been carefully constructed over many years and was now in danger of being pulled apart. Her eye gave the flicker again. 'I'm sorry. I don't know what you're talking about.'

'Don't know.'

She made the professional smile, but it didn't quite work this time. 'I'm sorry.'

I held up the picture. 'This isn't you?'

The little smile again. 'No. We do look alike, though, so I can understand your confusion.'

I nodded. Outside, the woman with the blue hair put money in a plain white envelope and put the envelope in her blouse and walked away. Joyce Steuben talked on the phone. The guard read Tom Clancy. Nobody seemed ready to jump up and give me a hand, but then they rarely do. I said, 'Peter doesn't want anything from you. He doesn't want to impose on you or to interfere with either your life or the boy's. He just wants to meet his son. He seems sincere in this. You're not going to gain anything by acting this way.'

She didn't move.

I spread my hands. 'Karen, you're found.'

She made a little shrug and shook her head. 'I hope you find whoever you're looking for. I really do. Now if you don't mind, I have work to do.'

She didn't move and I didn't move. Outside, a black man in a New York Yankees baseball cap approached the teller and Joyce Steuben hung up the phone and began to write on a yellow legal pad. Somewhere in the back of the little building the heating system clicked on and warm air came through the vents. I said, 'If there's nothing to anything I've said, call the guard and have him throw me out.'

She squinted to make the left eye stop moving. The knuckles on the hand holding the knob turned white. Neither of us said anything for quite a while. Then the tip of her tongue appeared and wet her lips. She said, 'I'm sorry that you've wasted your time, but I know nothing about any of this.'

I took a deep breath and let it out and then I nodded. 'Karen Lloyd.'

'Yes. That's my name.'

'Never been to Los Angeles.'

'Never.'

'Don't know Peter Nelsen.'

'I can understand your confusion. I do look very much like the girl in the picture.'

I nodded again. The black man finished his transaction and left and the teller walked over to Joyce Steuben's desk and sat down. Toby Nelsen appeared in the teller's window, reached through, took a pencil, then disappeared again. Karen Shipley stood very still, legs together, elbows tight at her sides, right hand on the knob and left hanging down at her side. The left was red as if blood had pooled there. I folded the 8 × 10 and put it in my pocket and stood up. 'Sorry,' I said. 'You do look very much alike.'

'Yes.'

'I'll be seeing you.'

'Have a nice day.'

I walked past her and past Joyce Steuben and around the end of the tellers' counter and out past the guard to the front door. I stopped and looked back at her. She had not moved. Her face was tight and contained and her right hand was still gripping the knob of her door. She stared at me a little longer and then she stepped back into the office and shut the door. Toby was concentrating on the math workbook and did not look up.

I went out to the parking lot and stood by my car beneath a sky that had grown heavy and dense and the color of shale. There was a cold wind coming from the northwest and a formation of large black crows beating their wings a hundred feet overhead. Because of the wind, the crows were pointing in one direction but traveling in another. I wondered if they knew it, and, knowing it, understood it, or if they were simply oblivious, carried along by a force that was felt but not seen. The same thing happens to people, but most of the time they don't know it, or when they know it, they think it an action of their own devising. They are usually wrong.

CHAPTER 10

Just after four o'clock I drove back to the Howard Johnson's and took a room for the night. I brought in my things, pulled off my clothes, then went into the shower, letting the hot water cut at my scalp and my neck and my shoulders. I let it cut for a long time. When I got out, I drank a glass of water, got dressed, and went down to the bar.

The bartender was a red-haired woman in her early forties with white lip gloss and heavy silver earrings that looked like little Rorschach patterns. She was cutting limes with a very large knife with a wide, flat blade. She said, 'You're the guy from Los Angeles.' These small towns.

I nodded. 'Really packing'm in tonight.' I was the only one in the place.

'Wait'll you have one of my drinks. You'll see why.'

'Unh-hunh.' You come to these small towns, the people think they're a riot. 'The beer cold?'

'Yeah, but it's flat.' You see?

I asked her for a Falstaff, but all they had was Rolling Rock. She put down the knife and went to a refrigerator with a see-through door and took out a long-necked bottle. She said, 'I always wanted to go out to Los Angeles. What they say about the smog true?'

'Yep.'

'Bet it's nice, though.' She opened the bottle and put it and an icy glass on a little napkin in front of me. I had some.

'It is.' I took a little more. Second pull and the bottle was almost empty. Maybe Rolling Rock just sort of naturally went down easy after a hard day of dealing with women who hung on to their lies as if the lies were living things. I had most of the rest of it.

The bartender said, 'I was a kid, I wanted to go out there. I used to think about it all the time, palm trees and people roller-skating at the beach and cruising down the freeways in a convertible.' The knife went through another lime. *Thunk*. 'Sometimes things just sort of get away from you.' *Thunk*. She stopped cutting and looked at me. 'You want a piece of lime in your beer?'

'No, thanks.'

'I heard people in California put lime in their beer.'

'No.'

She looked disappointed.

I left a two dollar tip and went next door into the restaurant. Two guys in plaid flannel L.L. Bean shirts and bright orange hunter's caps sat at a formica counter, holding heavy white coffee mugs in coarse hands. A chalk board that said *Today's Special: Homemade meat loaf* sat on a little easel on the counter across from a row of booths. Farther back, there were tables and chairs for people with a greater sense of formality. I sat in a booth by the windows with a delightful view of the parking lot.

A short woman in a black waitress outfit brought a menu and a glass of ice water, and asked whether or not I'd care for a drink before dinner. The first Rolling Rock had been so good I told her that I'd have a second. Without lime. She wrote on a little pad and said, 'We have a special tonight. It's the meat loaf. It's very nice.' She was in her sixties.

I handed back the menu without looking at it. 'Then that's what I'll have.'

She gave me an approving smile and went away. I felt the warmth of her smile and was glad that someone approved of me. Karen Shipley probably didn't. *You have me confused with someone else.* Not much you could do with that. A stranger walks in off the street and tells you that everything you've worked for was about to change. Who you gonna call? Gumshoebusters?

The waitress came back with the beer. An older couple strolled in and took a table in the dining room. Formal. A single guy in a gray business suit came in carrying the *New York Times* and sat at the counter, well away from the two guys in the orange hunting caps. He opened his *Times* to the real estate section. I drank the Rolling Rock and marveled at how good Karen and the boy and the Rotary awards had looked together, and wondered if that would continue with Peter on the scene. With Peter around, maybe their lives would disintegrate and Karen would fall into prostitution and Toby would end up running with a dope-fiend vampire motorcycle gang and the Rotary would take back their awards. It happens all the time with Hollywood families.

The waitress brought the meat loaf on a heavy white plate like the kind they used in cafeterias in the forties. The slice of meat loaf was wide and thick and weighed almost a pound. There was a large portion of creamed potatoes and about a million green peas, and a thick brown gravy had been ladled over the meat loaf and the potatoes. Nurture food. It smelled wonderful. She said, 'Can I get you anything else?'

'Tabasco sauce and another Rolling Rock.'

She brought the Rock and the Tabasco. I applied both liberally. Tabasco is great for clearing the sinus and putting the ruination of lives into perspective. So is the Rolling Rock. The meat loaf was excellent.

What's wrong with this picture? Peter Alan Nelsen was a celebrity, and the profits from his pictures were subject to stories in *Newsweek* and *Time*. Karen would read those stories and know that her ex-husband, the father of her child, was worth millions. Many people, perhaps most, would go after a piece of that, yet she hadn't. Either for herself or for the boy. Interesting. Maybe Peter wasn't the boy's father. Maybe Peter had done such hateful things to Karen that this was her way of punishing him and he deserved it. Maybe Karen was a nut case.

At five minutes before seven a tall guy with a nose like a chayote squash came in and looked around. He was wearing a bright turquoise shirt with a squash-blossom string tie and black slacks and a black duster. The black slacks were a half inch too short and the pointy black shoes were cut a half inch too low, so you ended up seeing a lot of black socks with little red triangles. He looked at me and the guy with the *Times* and the couple in the back and then he left. Probably looking for the disco.

I worked on the meat loaf and the potatoes and the peas and a growing depression. There were questions, and the questions bothered me, but I hadn't been hired to answer questions or even to get Karen Shipley to admit that she was Karen Shipley. I had been hired to find her whereabouts and I had done that. The rest was up to Peter Alan Nelsen. So what if Karen Shipley didn't like it, and so what if I didn't like it. They don't pay me to like it.

I ordered two more of the Rolling Rock to bring back to my room. A couple more Rock and I'd probably like it just fine.

Out in the parking lot the guy in the string tie met a white Thunderbird and said something to the driver. They talked for a minute, then the guy in the string tie got in on the passenger's side and the Thunderbird crept away around the side of the motel.

The waitress brought the beer in a little brown paper bag and the check and a single peppermint. I signed for the check and went out through the lobby. My room was on the ground floor, off the parking lot on the west side of the motel, halfway down a two-story row of rooms and just past a little alcove with an ice machine and a Pepsi machine and a stair leading up to the second floor. The Taurus was parked outside my room and a green Polara station wagon was parked closer up on the street side of the lot. A Peterbilt eighteen-wheeler took up most of the far end of the parking lot, looking like a supertanker in dry dock. No white Thunderbird.

When I got to the stairwell, the guy in the string tie and another guy stepped out. Guess they put the Thunderbird on the other side.

The guy with the string tie said, 'Hey, Joey, you think this is the guy?'

Joey was shorter and wider than me with a round cannon-ball head and caviar zits and a thick fleshy body that made him look sort of like an overgrown Pillsbury dough boy. He was wearing a blue Navy pea coat open over two layers of flannel shirts. The shirttails hung out. He said, 'Yeah, this is him. Looks like a fuck from out of town who don't belong around here. Like he needs a little help to find his way home.' He was maybe twenty-six, but he looked younger. He also looked mean.

The guy with the string tie nodded and made a sort of snickering sound. The snickering sound was a nose whistle. 'Fuckin' A. Let's get him on his way.'

I said, 'Are you guys for real, or is this going to be on *America's Funniest Home Videos*?' They sounded like Leo Gorcey and Huntz Hall. Brooklyn or the Bronx or Queens, but I couldn't tell which. New Yorkers all sound alike.

The guy with the string tie took out a piece of pipe maybe ten inches long and Joey took a half-step forward. Joey said, 'We got a message for you, Mickey Mouse.

81

Pack your fuckin' mouse ears and go back to Disney-land.'

I blinked at them. 'Did Karen Lloyd put you guys on me?'

The string tie waved the pipe so I could see it better. 'You don't ask questions, fuck face. You just do what we say.' He was breathing hard and the nose whistle was loud. Even Joey looked.

I said, 'That's some nose whistle. Is it natural or did you have to stick something up in there?'

Joey said, 'This fuck thinks we're kidding.'

Johnny Style swung the pipe from somewhere out around the North Atlantic.

I stepped to the inside and hit him in the forehead with the two bottles of Rolling Rock. The broken glass cut through the bag and beer sprayed back along my arm and across the wall and the sidewalk. Johnny Style said, 'Unh,' and dropped the pipe and fell backward over a curb stone. Joey sort of waddled forward, throwing a lot of overhand rights and lefts without much in the way of control, trying to do it the way he'd done it in school-yards and on playgrounds for most of his life.

I sideslipped and hit him twice in the face and once in the neck and drove a straight kick from the tae kwon do into his solar plexus. He stopped swinging and made a sort of coughing sound and stepped back. Surprised.

I said, 'What's this got to do with Karen Lloyd?'

Joey made the coughing sound again, then something hard hit me behind my right ear and I went down. Third guy in the Thunderbird. I kicked up and punched, but I don't think I hit him. My eyes weren't working too well and it was hard to see through the starbursts. Joey leaned over and punched me some more in the ribs and again in the back of the head, saying, 'You fuck! You fuck!' He was slow, and he was stupid, but he was strong. He lifted my head by the hair and sort of shook my head and said,

'Get out of town and keep your mouth shut or we'll turn you into a fuckin' piece of hamburg. You got that? You got that, you fuck?' I tried a claw move at his eyes, but I missed. The guy with the string tie said, 'Jesus Christ, I gotta get to a hospital.'

Joey kicked me again, then there were footsteps and, a long time later, an engine fired to life and faded away into the buzz of the highway.

I lay with my face pressed down into the parking lot, and no one came and no one saw. It was cold. Cars moved past on the service road, but none pulled in. Out front there would be people coming and going for the bar, but not back here. After a while I pushed myself up and tested my balance and went to my room.

I took four aspirin and peeled off my clothes and looked at myself. You get kicked in the lower back and you worry about the kidneys, and you get kicked in the ribs and you worry they're broken. I leaned forward and back and from side to side and raised my arms over my head. The places where I was kicked throbbed with a sort of a dull ache and when I raised my arms the right side of my back below the shoulder blade hurt but not the way it would hurt if anything was broken. I urinated. There was no blood. Kidneys were okay, but I'd have to check again later in the night.

I closed the toilet lid and sat on the seat and felt myself living. I felt the blood move and the lungs work and the muscles pull against bone. I hurt, but it was better than being in the hospital, and it was better than being dead. I had been hurt bad before, and I knew what that felt like. This wasn't bad.

I took a very cold shower, and then I dressed and went out to the ice machine and brought back a tub of ice. I undressed again and took another four aspirin and put some of the ice in one of the snowy-white Howard Johnson towels. I stacked the pillows at the head of the bed and sat against the pillows with the ice on my head. An hour later I dressed and put on my jacket and walked back to the bar. It was nine-forty-five. The bartender was gone and the bar was closed and so was the restaurant. That's life in Chelam.

I went back to my room and put more ice in the towel and lay there for a very long time thinking about Karen Shipley.

CHAPTER 11

The next morning my back felt stiff and hard, and the place behind my ear ached with a doughy, immediate presence. I took more of the aspirin, soaked in a hot bath to loosen the back, and then did yoga, starting with the simplest stretches and working my way through the spine rock and the cobra and the spine twist. The back hurt quite a bit at first but warmed and felt better as I worked.

By twenty minutes after nine I was back in Chelam. I drove down Main Street past the bank to the town square, turned one block south, then turned again and parked in front of a place that had at one time been a showroom for John Deere tractors. Now, it was empty.

The threat of snow had passed without incident, and the day was bright and clear except for a scattering of cottonball cumulus clouds that moved through the sky to the south. It was warmer. I walked back to the grocery store one block north and stood by the pay phone and looked at the bank. Karen Shipley's green LeBaron was in the lot. I could go into the bank and confront her, but chances were good that she would continue to deny that she was Karen Shipley. Chances were equally good that she would deny knowing the three leg-busters who had come to the Ho Jo. I could go in with the sheriff, but that would bring in the press and Peter Alan Nelsen. The press would like it, but Peter Alan Nelsen probably wouldn't. Also, I didn't like the way it felt for Karen Shipley. There was something acutely desperate and unprotected about Karen Shipley denying that she was Karen Shipley even as she stared at her photograph, and I didn't want the sheriff and the town and the press to know what it was before I knew what it was. Also, going to the sheriff seemed like a wimpy thing to do. There were alternatives. I could lie in wait for Karen Shipley and, when she stepped out of the bank, pistol-whip her into admitting her true identity. If that didn't work, I could shadow her every move until, in an unguarded moment, she revealed her true self. Or maybe I could just ask around. Hmm. Asking around seemed easiest and a lot less trouble. After all, Karen Shipley had lived here for eight years. The people here knew her and knew of her, and if I talked to them, I might learn what they knew and see what they saw. If I knew enough and saw enough, maybe I'd know what in hell was going on and what to do about it. Elvis Cole, detective in search of intelligence.

Rittenhauser's Diner was down the block, two doors past the barbershop. I went in and sat at the counter. A pinch-faced short-order cook in a blue apron was standing with his arms crossed near the cash register. He was watching a tiny Magnavox color TV that was sitting on a gallon can of pork and beans next to the register. Oprah Winfrey. Something about fat men being better lovers. He picked a clean coffee mug from a wire rack and filled it and put the mug in front of me without my having to ask. He said, 'What'll it be?'

'Three eggs, scrambled. Rye toast. Maybe put some mushrooms and some cheese in the eggs.'

'Sharp cheddar?'

'How about Swiss?'

'You got it.'

He made the eggs and a little patty of hash browns and two large pieces of rye toast. When it was done, he put it all onto a heavy white plate, then he put the plate in front of me. I said, 'Nice looking plate of eggs.'

He said, 'Unh,' and went back to the Oprah.

I ate some of the eggs. 'Just moved out from California. Transfer. Met Karen Lloyd at the bank yesterday.'

'Unh.'

'Nice looking lady.'

He said it again.

'You know if she's married or seeing someone?'

'Nope.' An obese man in his sixties told Oprah that he could ejaculate twenty-six times a day. He attributed it to his bulk. The cook looked interested.

'Nope, you don't know, or nope, she's not seeing someone?'

'Ain't none of my business.' The obese man said that when he was thin, he was sexually dysfunctional.

'She been working at the bank long?'

The cook leaned closer to the television. Something about high-fat content leading to increased fluids production.

I said, 'Great day for a nuclear holocaust, huh?'

The cook nodded and cut himself a piece of cherry pie, still staring at the Oprah.

Maybe looking for intelligence in Chelam was going to be harder than I thought. I decided to shadow her every move.

Being a stranger in a small town is sort of like being a Martian in Mayberry. You tend to stand out. Aunt Bea sees you hanging around a parking lot, pretty soon Barney Fife is looking at your driver's license. Opie rides by on his bike, pretty soon you got Andy in your shorts. Everybody in town knows you're there, and then you get your thugs in string ties asking why you're still around. You see how this works?

I drove back to the Howard Johnson's, changed rooms,

then drove down to the Hertz office in upper Westchester and traded the blue Taurus for a white one. I couldn't do much about Aunt Bea and Opie, but I could make it tougher for Joey and his pal with the tie.

By nine-fifty I was back in Chelam. By nine-fifty-two the new white Taurus was parked in a little alley outside the John Deere showroom and I had picked the lock on a side door and let myself inside. From the showroom I could see the bank and the grocery store and a fair part of Main Street. Aunt Bea and Opie might wonder about the Taurus, but it was better than having them wonder about me.

Between ten-thirty and noon eight people pulled up to the First Chelam, went in, did business, and came out. None of them were fat guys with caviar skin or people who wore string ties, but I held hope.

At five minutes after twelve Karen Shipley came out and got into her LeBaron. She was wearing a tweed pants suit and brown flat-heeled shoes under a slim leather topcoat, and she carried a briefcase. She pulled out of the lot and turned south, and I hustled out to the Taurus and went after her. Twenty minutes later we turned into a shopping mall in upper Westchester where Karen went into a little café. A man in a gray suit took her hand and kissed her on the left cheek and they sat at a window table. I sat in my Taurus. Midway through the meal she opened the briefcase and took out some papers and gave them to the man. He put on tortoiseshell half-glasses, read the papers, then signed them. She put the papers back in her briefcase and they resumed their lunch. Business.

At ten minutes before two Karen was back in the First Chelam and I was back in the John Deere showroom. Opie and Aunt Bea were nowhere to be seen.

At three o'clock Karen Shipley came out again, climbed back into the LeBaron, and drove half a mile out of town to the Woodrow Wilson Smith Elementary School. Toby got into the car and they drove back across Chelam to a single-story medical building with a little sign that read *B. L. Franks, D.D.S. & Susan Witlow, D.D.S., a dental corporation.* They stayed for just under an hour.

After the dentist, we went back through Chelam along a two-lane county road between fields and woods and a scattershot of ponds and small lakes until we turned down a broad new black-topped road past a stone sign that said *Clearlake Shores.* Someone had come in with a bulldozer and carved out a housing development around a couple of lakes that were too round and too sculptured to be natural. Most of the lots were still unimproved, but some of them had houses under construction, and some of them held completed houses warm with life.

Karen Shipley pulled into a one-story brick colonial with a wide cement drive and white pilasters and virgin landscaping. Maybe a year old. Maybe less. Four white birch trees and a live oak had been planted in the front yard. The trunks on the birch were only a couple of inches thick, the oak was maybe a little thicker. They weren't much now, but if you gave them a little time they would grow tall and strong and you would be glad you stayed with them. There was a basketball backboard suspended over the drive at the lip of the garage. Toby and Karen went inside through the front door and lights came on. They didn't come out again. Home.

I cruised through the development and parked in some high weeds near the county road and watched the house until the sky was dark. Joey and the guy with the string tie didn't show up. Shadows didn't skulk across the landscape. The new house and its hopeful landscaping didn't look like a place where people hid in fear or sicced leg-breakers on unsuspecting private eyes, but then they never do. When my stomach made more noise than the radio, I drove back to the Howard Johnson's.

Each day was pretty much the same. Toby would head for school on his red Schwinn mountain bike, then Karen would leave for the bank. She would get to the bank before anyone else and unlock the door. Joyce Steuben would get there two or three minutes later, and the teller would roll up by nine, just before the bank opened. Bank customers would come and go, and sometimes during midmorning or in the early afternoon Karen would drive to a house or a building or a piece of unimproved land where she would meet two or three people and they would look and smile and point, and then Karen Shipley would go back to her office.

Every day between four and four-thirty Toby would pedal up to the bank and go in and stay until Karen left, sometimes as soon as Toby arrived, sometimes not until five. They would go home, Karen sometimes stopping to do a quick errand on the way, but most times not. Once, they drove fourteen miles to a McDonald's, and once they drove to the next town to see the new Steven Segal film. One day Toby didn't come to the bank. Karen left early and drove to the school where the Woodrow Wilson Smith Barking Bears took on the Round Hill Lions in a basketball game. I went in through the rear of the auditorium and watched from the stage. Toby played right forward and he was pretty good. Karen sat on the lowest bleacher and cheered hard, once screaming at an official and calling him a jerk. The Barking Bears lost 38 to 32. Karen took Toby out to a place called Monteback's for a malt. Portrait of the successful single-parent family in action.

At six-oh-five on the morning of the fourth day it fell apart.

I was driving down the county road toward Karen

Shipley's when Karen Shipley passed me going in the opposite direction, an hour before she usually left.

I turned around in a gravel drive and waited for a pickup with a beagle in the back to pass, then pulled out and followed her. She went past Chelam, then picked up the state highway and drove most of the way to Westchester. Traffic heading down toward the city was dense and made keeping her in sight easy. She stayed in the right lane and took an exit marked *Dutchy*. Less than a mile off the interstate she pulled into the parking lot of an abandoned Eagle service station and parked. There was no one else around. I stayed behind an old guy in a 1948 Chevy for another half mile, then pulled over, parked off the road, and walked back through a jumble of birch and elm trees until I was behind the Eagle station. She was still in the car.

The cold air and the winter woods smell made me think of when I was a boy, hunting in the autumn for squirrel and whitetail deer, and I felt the peace that comes from being alone and in a wild place. I wondered if Karen Shipley felt that peace, and if that was why she came.

At twenty-two minutes before seven a black Lincoln Town Car with smoked glass and a car phone antenna turned off the road and parked behind her. The door opened and a dark man with a thick neck and a wide back got out. He was in his early forties and taller than me, and he wore an expensive black Chesterfield topcoat and gray slacks and black Gucci loafers shined so cleanly that he probably kept them in his refrigerator. He took a green nylon bag out of the trunk of his Lincoln and walked over to Karen's LeBaron and gave Karen an off-white smile, but I don't think he was trying to be friendly. Karen got out without smiling back. She took the bag and tossed it into the passenger side of the LeBaron. They talked. Karen's mouth was tight and her eyes were edged on a frown and she stood with her bottom pressed against the LeBaron. The dark man reached out and touched her arm and I could see her stiffen from eighty yards away. He said something else and touched her again and this time she pushed his arm away and as fast as she touched him he slapped her. It was a single hard pop that turned her head. She didn't scramble away from him and she didn't scream for help. She stood there and glared and he raised his hand again, but then he lowered it and went back to the Lincoln and drove away with a lot of spinning tires and spraying gravel and roaring engine. I copied down his license number.

Karen Shipley watched him drive away and then she got back into her LeBaron and started the engine and put her face into her hands and cried. She slapped the LeBaron's steering wheel and screamed so loudly that I could hear her even with the windows up and the engine running.

She cried for another five minutes and then she dried her eyes and checked her makeup in the rearview mirror, and when it was perfect she drove away.

I ran back through the woods and pushed the Taurus over a hundred on the roads back to Chelam and picked up Karen Shipley again just as she turned into the bank's parking lot. I pulled up beside the grocery and watched. It was six-fifty-two. Still plenty of time before Joyce Steuben or the teller would arrive.

Karen got out of the LeBaron and carried the duffel bag into the bank. Ten minutes later she came out with the duffel now deflated and folded into a tight roll. She walked across the street to a public waste can in front of the hardware store and threw the duffel away.

Someone in a green and white Chevy Blazer drove by, beeped his horn, and waved. Neighborly. Karen Shipley did not wave back. She walked with her eyes forward and her face set all the way back into the bank. She looked tired and old. Older than the lemon-pie girl in the 8 × 10.

I sat in the Taurus in the empty grocery store lot and watched the town come to life. A rural town with small-town ways. The air was cool and smelled of maple and the coming of Halloween. I turned on the radio. A man and a woman were discussing all the fine recipes you could make with pumpkins and the other autumn squash. A little bit of butter. A little cinnamon. A little sugar. After a while I turned off the radio.

Fall used to be my favorite time of the year.

CHAPTER 12

I called the New York State Department of Motor Vehicles from a pay phone at a Shell station just off the interstate and said, 'This is foot patrol Officer Willis Sweetwell, badge number five-oh-seven-two-four. I need wants and warrants on New York plate sierra-romeo-golf-six-six-one. And gimme the registration on that, too.' They either go for it or they don't.

There was a little pause, then a guy with a deep voice said, 'Wait one.' Score for the Jack Webb.

The deep voice came back on and told me there were neither wants nor warrants on six-six-one, and that it was registered to the Lucerno Meat Company at 7511 Grand Avenue in lower Manhattan.

I said, 'You don't have an individual on that?'

'Nope. Looks like a company car.'

I said, 'Thanks for the help, buddy. Have a good day.' Cops like to say 'buddy.'

I took the Merritt Parkway down through White Plains, then went across the peninsula to the Henry Hudson Parkway and down along the western rim of Manhattan with the Hudson River off to my right. A green treesy park followed along the river with joggers and old people and kids who should've been in school hanging out and laughing and having a good time. I passed Grant's Tomb and the Soldiers and Sailors Monument and then the Hudson parkway became the West Side Highway and the green strip of park was gone and the road ran along the waterfront. Lee J. and Marlon,

94

slugging it out. You hear that the Hudson is ugly and barren, but I didn't see any dead fish or floating bodies, just a couple of nice sailboats and about a million Japanese container ships and a Cessna floatplane tied to a short pier.

At the Holland Tunnel I went east along Canal, crossing lower Manhattan between Little Italy and Chinatown. The buildings were old and made of red brick or yellow brick or stone, some painted and some not, each webbed with a tarnished latticework of fire escapes. People jammed the sidewalks, and yellow cabs roared over the streets without regard to traffic lanes or bicyclists or human life, and no one seemed to see anyone else, as if each person was inalienably alone and liked it that way, or at least was used to it.

Lucerno's Meat Packing Plant was in a two-story redbrick industrial building between a tire wholesaler and a textile outlet, four blocks from the Manhattan Bridge. There was a drive and a large crushed-gravel parking lot on the side where Econoline vans and six-by trucks turned around and backed up to a loading dock. Five cars were parked at the far end of the lot, out of the trucks' way. The second car from the end was the black Lincoln.

I pulled into the lot past the six-bys, whipped a snappy turn like I was trying to get out of the place, put it into reverse, backed up, and crunched the Lincoln nicely. I turned off the Taurus, got out, and made a big deal out of looking at what I had done. The Lincoln's left front headlight was popped and the chrome around it crumpled and the bumper compressed. A couple of black guys in dirty white aprons up on the loading dock were watching me. One of the black guys went into the warehouse and yelled something, and then a little guy in a white jumpsuit and a clipboard came out. I walked over and said, 'I was trying to turn around and I backed into that Lincoln. Do you know who owns it?'

The little guy came over to the edge of the dock and stood with his boot tips hanging over and looked at the cars. *Lucerno's Fine Meats* was embroidered on the back of his coveralls with red thread and FRANK was sewn over his left breast pocket. His face was sour and lined, like maybe he'd just checked his lunch pail and discovered that his wife had given him a roach sandwich. He said, 'Jesus Christ, where'd you learnta drive? Wait here a minute.' He went back into the warehouse. The two black guys finished loading a dolly of white boxes into a six-by. They took the boxes off the dolly two at a time and slid them into the six-by so hard that the boxes slammed into the truck with a heavy thud. Tenderizing the meat.

In a little while Frank came back and said, 'Forget it. You're off the hook.'

I looked at him. 'What do you mean, forget it?' Best-laid plans.

'Just what I said. You had a bad break, but we're not gonna bust your chops about it. Take off.' The old smash-their-car-and-offer-to-pay-for-it routine wasn't getting me very far.

I said, 'The headlight's smashed and the bumper's pretty dinged up and the frame around the light is busted. Maybe the owner should come take a look.'

'It's a company car. Forget it.'

'I don't want to forget it. I'm responsible. I oughta pay something to somebody.'

He gave me Desi looking at Lucy, the look saying, Jesus Christ, what did I marry? 'I'm giving you a pass, *capisce*? What, are you stupid?'

I said, 'You know, that's the trouble with America today. Everybody's looking for a pass. Nobody wants to own up. Well, not me. I own up. I take what's coming to me. I pay my way.' Maybe I could appeal to his national pride.

One of the black guys adjusted his crotch and laughed. He had two gold inlays on the right side of his mouth. Frank took a deep breath, let it out, and said, 'Look, I got work to do. You came in here, you busted the car, and you came looking for someone to do right by it. Great. But I'm standing here telling you that it's okay. I work here. We seen what happened and it's okay. I'm telling you that you ain't gotta pay a dime, you ain't gotta say you're sorry, you ain't gotta do dick. Okay?'

'But you don't own the car?'

He spread his hands and blinked. 'What?'

'And you don't own the company.'

'What?' His voice was getting higher.

'If you don't own the car and you don't own the company, then how do I know you've got the right to tell me it's okay?'

He shook his head and looked at the sky. 'I can't fuckin' believe this.'

'Tell me who drives the car,' I said. 'Maybe the guy who drives the car should tell me it's okay.'

'Jumpin' Jesus fuckin' Christ with a hard-on.'

'It seems only fair.'

One of the black guys said, 'Oo-ee.'

Frank threw down the clipboard and stalked back into the building. The two black guys flashed a lot of inlay work and gave each other the Spike Lee treatment. After a little while Frank came back with a large, bald man in his fifties with pop eyes and a melon head and a voice so soft that it might have come from a sick child. He told me that he was the manager and he gave me his card. It said *Michael Vinicotta. Lucerno Meats. Manager*. He said that if my insurance company wanted to speak with anyone, they could speak with him. He told me that he

very much appreciated my concern and my consideration in trying to make sure I had done right by the owner
of the car, but that restitution by me was neither sought
nor needed.

I said, 'Maybe we should leave the cars where they are
and call the police and get an accident report.'

He said, 'Get the fuck outta here or there's gonna be
more broken than a goddamned headlight.'

I went back to the Taurus and drove around the block
and parked in a garage on Broome Street. I walked back
to a pastry shop across from Lucerno's and bought a
double decaf espresso and sat in the window. Maybe I
should go back and pretend to be Ed McMahon and tell
them that the guy who drove the Lincoln had just won
the Publisher's Clearing House Sweepstakes for a million bucks. That sounded better than the old busted-
headlamp routine, but now they knew I wasn't Ed
McMahon. Probably should've tried that one first.

Most of the way through my third espresso the fat guy
with the caviar skin came out of Lucerno's. Joey. He was
wearing the white coveralls and insulated work boots
and the same blue Navy pea coat that he had worn at the
Howard Johnson's. Well, well. He wasn't the guy in the
Lincoln, but he was close enough.

I paid for the espressos and followed Joey two blocks
east to a place with a big sign that said SPINA'S CLAM BAR.
I watched through the front glass as he took a stool at the
end of the bar and said something to the bartender. The
bartender put a glass of draft beer in front of him, then
set up an iced tray and started opening clams. Four other
guys sat at the bar, but no one seemed to know anyone
else and no one seemed particularly talkative. Another
half-dozen people sat in little booths. It was the kind of
place you could go in your work clothes.

When the tray was filled with clams, the bartender put
it in front of Joey and then walked away to see about the

other guys. Joey was slurping a clam off its shell when I walked up behind him and said, 'Say, Joey.'

Joey turned and looked at me and I thumbed him in the throat.

His face went red and his eyes got big and he grabbed at his throat and started to cough. Most of a clam popped out and fell on the floor.

I said, 'You oughtta not eat so fast, you're going to choke.'

The bartender came down. 'Is he okay?'

I said sure. I said I knew how to do the Heimlich. A couple of the people at the other end of the bar looked over, but when they saw the bits of clam all over the place they turned away. The bartender went back to his other customers.

Joey sort of half fell and half slid off his stool and pushed a slow right hand at me. I pushed it past with an open hand then thumbed him in the right eye. He went white this time and stumbled backward and fell over his stool into the bar and down to the floor.

The bartender and the other four guys at the bar looked at me. I said, 'Think I did the Heimlich a little too hard.'

The nearest guy said, 'You want I should call an ambulance?'

'Maybe in a bit.'

Joey was scrambling around on the floor, holding his face with one hand and trying to get up. He screamed, 'You poked out my fuckin' eye! I'm gonna be blind!'

I pulled him up and led him farther back into the bar. The bartender and the other guys were making a big deal out of not seeing it. I said, 'Nah. I took it easy. Let me see.'

He let me see. I thumbed him in the other eye.

Joey made a sort of gasping sound and grabbed at the other eye and tried to turn away but he was against the wall and there was no place to go. The eyes were red and tearing but he would be fine.

He said, 'You sonofabitch, you're supposed to be gone. We got rid of you.'

'You did a lousy job.'

He lurched forward and threw another right hand and I pushed it past just like the first and drove a spin kick to the right side of his head. It slammed him sideways into the bar and he fell down again. The guys at the other end of the bar and a couple of people in the booths stood up. The bartender said, 'Hey, I'm gonna call the cops.'

I said, 'Call'm. This won't take long.'

I reached down and pulled Joey up again and sat him on the stool and dug out his wallet and looked at his driver's license. *Joseph L. Putata. Jackson Heights.* I put the wallet back in his pocket. 'Okay, Joey. What's a used rubber like you got to do with Karen Lloyd?'

One of his eyes was looking up and the other was sort of rolling around and he was blinking a lot. He shook his head, like he didn't know what I was talking about. 'I dunno. Who's Karen Lloyd?' His hands were down at his sides.

'The lady at the bank.' Maybe she hadn't sent them.

Joey's eyes started coming together and he looked scared. 'Oh, shit, I told him we run you off. I said you were outta here.'

'Who? The guy in the Lincoln?'

The bartender said, 'I just called the cops.'

Joey looked from me to the bartender, then back to me. Confused along with the scared.

I said, 'Why'd the guy in the Lincoln want me to forget about Karen Lloyd?'

'I dunno. He said you were bothering her. He said she was a friend.' He looked even more scared, like talking about the guy in the Lincoln brought it out in him. 'I told him you were gone.'

'Who is he?'

'Who?'

'The guy in the Lincoln.'

Joey looked at me like I'd just beamed down from the *Enterprise*. 'Jesus Christ, you don't know?'

'No.'

He looked at the other people at the bar and then he lowered his voice. He said, 'We're talking about Charlie DeLuca. Sal DeLuca's kid.'

'So?'

Joey shook his head and put on a face like he was about to wet his pants. 'Sal DeLuca is the godfather, you dumb fuck. The *capo de tutti capo*. He's the head of the whole damned mafia.'

CHAPTER 13

It was twenty minutes before five that afternoon when I turned down the neat, clean blacktop off the county road above Chelam and pulled into Karen Shipley's drive. The sun was most of the way down in the southwest, and would set in another hour. The LeBaron was parked in the garage.

Toby Lloyd was pounding a basketball on the drive, hopping sideways and swiveling his head as if he were being covered by David Robinson and Magic Johnson. I parked about thirty feet back to give him room to work the ball and got out. 'Hi. Remember me from the bank?'

'Sure.' He bounced the ball a couple of times, then turned and launched one toward the basket. It banged off the backboard and went through the net.

I said, 'Gotta be tough shooting in the cold. Gets your fingers stiff.'

He nodded and scooped up the rebound. 'You want to see my mom?'

'Yeah. She inside?'

'Sure. C'mon.' Elvis Cole, friend of the family, comes to call.

He led me through the garage and a laundry room and into their kitchen. The walls and the ceilings and the floors and the appliances were still new-house bright, without the ground-in dirt that comes as the years put their wear of life on a place. A thick spaghetti sauce was simmering on top of a Jenn-Air range, a fine spray of the sauce a red shadow on the enamel. Toby yelled, 'Hey, Mom, there's somebody here to see you!'

We went out of the kitchen and through the dining room and into the living room. Karen Shipley came out of a hallway from the back of the house in a pink sweatshirt and faded blue jeans and white socks with little pompoms at the heels. She said, 'What did you say, hon?' Then she saw me.

I said, 'Hi, Karen.'

There was a small part of a moment as she saw me when her eyes flickered and her breath might have caught, but then she forced a pretty good smile for the boy like everything was fine. 'You're still here.'

'Unh-hunh.'

More of the smile for the boy. 'Tobe. Mr. Cole and I have something to discuss. Would you leave us alone for a while?'

'Okay.' Like he was used to having to be out of the way when she talked business and that was just fine with him. He charged back through the kitchen and the laundry.

The living room was large and comfortable, with a vaulted beamed ceiling and peg-and-groove floors and Early American furniture across from a used brick fireplace with a mantel. Colonial. A white and orange cat was asleep on the couch.

Karen Shipley said, 'You're wasting your time, Mr. Cole. My name is not Karen Shipley.'

I said, 'You're owned by the mob.'

She went very still, and then her left foot moved as if her balance had abruptly and without warning shifted and she had to catch herself. Her mouth opened, then closed, and she wet her lips. She did not look away from me. Outside, Toby bounced the basketball. There was a faraway electric hum from something in the kitchen and something else behind me in the living room. Clocks. She said, 'That's,' and then she said, 'Silly.'

'Two hours after I saw you in the bank four days ago, three men came to the Howard Johnson's and told me to forget about you and get out of town. I didn't. This morning you met a man driving a black Lincoln Town Car at a secluded place off the road near Brunly. The man in the black Lincoln gave you a nylon duffel bag, then made advances on you which you refused. He struck you. The man left first and then you brought the duffel to the bank. The Lincoln Town Car is registered to the Lucerno Meat Company in lower Manhattan and was driven by a man I've identified as one Charlie DeLuca, son of Sal DeLuca, head of the DeLuca crime family. I went to the meat plant and observed one of the three men who had come to the Howard Johnson's. His name is Joseph Putata. That links Putata to Charlie DeLuca. I didn't see what was in the bag, but I'd bet it was money, and I'd bet you wash it for the DeLucas by running it through an account without reporting it to the IRS. I'd also bet that if I went to the cops with this, they'd be pleased as peaches to see me.'

Karen Shipley's eyes got red and wet, and she sat down next to the cat with her hands in her lap. She said, 'Oh, damn,' over and over.

I went into the kitchen, turned off the Jenn-Air so that the sauce wouldn't burn, then drew a glass of water and brought it out to her. She sipped it.

I said, 'The three guys gave you away. Where would you get three guys like that?'

'I'm sorry. I didn't think they would send anyone to do that. I didn't mean for them to threaten you.'

'It's okay. I've been threatened before.'

'I'm not a bad person. I don't like this.'

'I know. I saw the way it was with DeLuca.'

Karen Shipley wiped at her eyes, then got up and went

to the big triple-glazed window and looked out at her son. Bounce. 'What happens now?'

'I don't know. I'm trying to figure that out.'

She looked back at me, surprised. 'What do you mean? Haven't you told Peter?'

'No.'

'And you haven't told the police?'

'No.'

'But those men beat you up.'

I said, 'I knew something was wrong and I wanted to find out what it was. Cops deal with the law. The law isn't usually concerned with right and wrong. Ofttimes, there are very large differences.'

She shook her head as if I'd spoken Esperanto.

I said, 'All you do is launder their money?'

'Yes.'

'Ever done any other crimes for them? Drugs, murder, stolen goods?'

Surprised again. 'Of course not. What do you think I am?'

'An employee of the mafia.'

She looked away and crossed her arms. Embarrassed. Back at the boy. Bounce, bounce. 'When I met Charlie DeLuca all I knew about the mafia was Al Pacino. I was working as a waitress on Seventh Avenue in the Village and Charlie introduced me to his father and the old man said he could help me get a better job and I said sure. Nobody said anything about the mafia.'

'They never do.'

'I came out to Chelam and met with the woman who used to be the manager here and she hired me as a teller. I rented a little house. I started taking night classes at the college in Brunly. I didn't see Charlie again for months.'

'Then he needed a favor.'

She gave me the eyes.

I said, 'It would've been Charlie's father, Sal. He would've said that he was in a bind with a couple of business partners and he needed a place to put some money and could you open an account for him that no one would know about and maybe transfer the money out of the country without reporting it to the IRS.'

She shook her head and made the kind of smile you make when you feel stupid and used. 'Is it so obvious?'

I made a little shrug. 'You weren't thinking in terms of crime. You were helping a friend. It's the way they do it.'

'He had gotten me the job. He had been so nice.' She uncrossed the arms and walked back across the room to the hearth. Embarrassed again and angry because of it. The orange and white cat stretched, then sat up and stared at her. 'Toby was in nursery, I was in school, I was studying for the real estate exam, I had a life. It was months before I heard from Sal again, and when he called I was surprised. I didn't think there would be a second time. The third time it was Charlie, and then the calls were every few weeks, and then every week, and then there it was. The *New York Times* runs an article on organized crime and they feature the DeLuca family. That's how I found out. I'm laundering money for the mafia. I'm taking the cash profits they're making from prostitution and gambling and whatever else they do and I'm cleaning it for them. I called Charlie. I said I can't do this anymore and Charlie comes to the bank and he says that I will keep doing it for as long as they want because I'm a stick of furniture and then he locks the door to my office and takes out his penis, and I thought, oh God, he's going to rape me, he's going to use me to show me what I am, but he doesn't. He urinates on the carpet and he says, you see, this is what I can do, and then he left.'

She was trembling as she said it. The cat hopped down from the couch, walked over to her, and rubbed against her ankles. I don't think she felt it.

I said, 'If you want out, go to the cops. You're in with Charlie and Sal. That's worth something. You could cut a deal.'

She shook her head again and walked back to the window and looked at the boy. The cat followed her. He wasn't as big as the cat who lives with me, or as scarred, but he was okay. 'No. Going to the police means witness protection. We'd have to give up everything we have.'

'Looks like you're giving up a lot right now.'

Her eyes hardened and an edge came to her voice. 'All I had when I left Los Angeles was my son and a lot of bad memories. I wanted a job with a future. I wanted an education. I wanted to work and see the work pay dividends and be a worthwhile person. I am. I have a good home. I do a good job with my boy. He's not on drugs and he does all right in school. Witness protection means we change our name and our life and start over. I won't do that. I've already started over and I've built the thing I wanted to build and I don't want to lose it. I've come a long way from stupidville.'

'Far enough to make it worth being owned by the mob?'

The eyes went back to the boy and turned red again. 'I don't know what I can do, but I'll find a way out. It's been eight years, but I will find a way out. I promise you.' She wasn't saying it to me. She was saying it to the boy.

I looked around the house. I looked at the cat. I looked at the boy bouncing the ball. It was a good house, well put together and warm and filled with the things that a family home should be filled with. It couldn't have been easy. *Peter, do I havta?* I said, 'I know what you can do.'

She made a tired little laugh and looked back at me. 'What shit. You're here, and Peter's here, and any chance I might've had to get away from these people is gone. There isn't anything else I can do.'

'Sure there is. You can hire me to get you out of this mess.'

CHAPTER 14

We were sitting on the Early American furniture across from the fireplace, me on the couch, Karen on one of the wingback chairs, drinking white wine from glasses that were simple and without adornment. The cat had left the room. She said, 'They give me money, and I transfer it out of the country without reporting it to the Treasury Department. Any deposit over $10,000 we're supposed to file a form with the Treasury Department, but I don't. That's what it's all about, taking in the money and not reporting it. I put the money into an account, then transfer it to a bank in Barbados. In, then out. It doesn't seem like much, does it?'

I said, 'Who gives you the money?' I was looking for a way out for her. I didn't know what that would be, but maybe if I heard enough, something would present itself. It's the scattershot approach to the detective business.

'Either Charlie or a man named Harry. It's usually Harry, but sometimes it's Charlie.'

'Who's Harry?'

'Just this guy. He works for Charlie and he's usually the one who brings the money.'

Outside, the sun was dropping down and the sky was taking on a deep blue cast, but there was maybe a half hour of good light left. Toby was still working the ball. 'I'm surprised you see Charlie. The top guys like Charlie and Sal always stay away from stuff like this. They use guys like Harry. Something goes wrong, Harry takes the fall. That's what he's paid for.'

She sipped some of the wine, then set down the glass as if the wine had lost its taste. 'This is common to you, isn't it? You deal with things like this all the time.'

'Not exactly like this, but close enough. People look for ways to trap themselves and they usually find what they look for. I see people at their extremes.'

'Are you good at what you do?'

'Not bad.'

'I'm surprised you found me. I took great care to hide myself. I erased my maiden name from all my credit records. I took the name Lloyd from a billboard.'

'You left a trail a mile wide.'

She picked up the wine again and had some, as if she needed the wine to help her talk about these things. 'I want you to know that what I've built, I've built without their help and without their money. I didn't use Peter's help and I didn't use theirs.'

'All right.'

'Three days after I made the first transfer, a man came to the bank and gave me an envelope containing one thousand dollars. I called Sal and told him to take the money back, but he wouldn't. He told me that friends have to take care of one another, that kind of thing. He was sweet and charming, and it was a thousand dollars, so I let myself get talked into keeping it. That first time, after I got used to the idea, it was even sort of exciting. Do you see?'

I nodded.

'But after more calls, and more money, it wasn't. I knew it was wrong and I was scared, and finally they said, okay, if you don't want to get paid, we won't pay you. But they had already paid me a total of sixty-five hundred dollars, and I had spent it.' She got up and went back down the hall again and came back with a 5 × 7 manila envelope. She opened it and shook out a small stack of papers and handed them to me. 'Over the past three years I've put forty-two hundred dollars into various charities. I didn't want to keep any of the sixty-five hundred. That's all I can do.'

I looked. The receipts totaled forty-two hundred dollars. Twenty-three hundred dollars until a clean conscience. Extremes.

She said, 'Does this help at all?'

'If you got caught and went to trial, or if you went to the cops, maybe. Other than that, no.'

She nodded. 'Oh.'

'Has Charlie ever mentioned any other way he launders money?'

'No.'

'How about the woman who hired you, was she in their pocket?'

'I don't think so.'

'Do they own anyone else at the bank now?'

'No.'

'Does anyone else at the bank know what's going on?'

'No.'

'Is there a paper record that passes between you and the DeLucas?'

'No.'

Maybe the scattershot approach wasn't going to work so well. Sort of like trying to find intelligence. 'How about a record of the bank transfers?'

'Not for the first few times. The first few times, I was scared and I didn't want there to be a record so I erased it from the computers. Then I got scared to not have a record and I started keeping a file.'

'Okay. That's something. I'll need to see it.'

She nodded. 'All right. I can print out a transaction record at the bank.'

I said, 'Is there anything you can think of that maybe I'm missing?'

'I don't think so.'

The cat came down the hall and walked across the dining room and into the kitchen. Karen Shipley Nelsen leaned toward me and clenched her hands together. 'What about Peter?'

I spread my hands. 'I have what we in the trade call an ethical dilemma. I've taken Peter's money to find you, and now I have. I owe him that information.'

She stared at me, still clenching the hands.

'I've found people before and kept their secrets, but that won't work here. Peter wants to find his son and he has unlimited resources with which to do it. If I tell him that I couldn't find you, he will simply hire someone else and they will find you. You weren't that hard to find.'

Her jaw tightened. She wasn't liking it much, but she knew that she didn't have to like it.

I said, 'What does Toby know?'

'He doesn't know anything about the DeLuca family or how I'm involved with them. I don't want him to know.'

'What does he know about Peter?'

'He knows that his father's name is Peter Nelsen, and he knows that his father left us because he didn't want a family and he didn't want to be married. We don't talk about it. He doesn't know that his father is the guy who makes movies and has articles written about him.'

'You should think about telling him.'

She stood up and went to the window and looked out at her son. The ball was sitting motionless on the drive and Toby was sitting against one of the birches. She said, 'Tell me the truth. Do you see any way out of this?'

'Guys like the DeLucas, they won't do something out of the goodness of their hearts. If we want something, we'll have to give something.'

'Like what?'

'They might let you go if we could put one of their

people in your place. That way they don't lose anything. Would you walk away from the bank?'

'Yes. Yes, I'd walk away.' Her face was pale when she said it.

I nodded. 'Okay. That's a place to start. I'll ask around, find out about the DeLucas, see what's there that we can give them or what we can use as leverage. What you can do is get together all the information you have about the accounts and about what you know about Charlie and Sal. Don't leave anything out. Even if it seems small or silly or beside the point.'

'Okay.'

'I'll go to Charlie and give him a little push and see what happens. Charlie won't like it, but there isn't any other way. Is that all right with you?'

She nodded.

'Maybe I can get you away from the DeLucas before we bring Peter in. If they're away and you're not a part of them anymore, it might work.'

She nodded again.

'If it works, Peter doesn't have to know about the DeLucas and they don't have to know about Peter.'

She was looking hopeful. 'That's what I want.'

'But it may not work out that way. It may get messy and you have to be ready for that, too. Focus on DeLuca. DeLuca is who is important. Not Peter. Do you understand?'

'Of course.'

'We'll take it a step at a time.'

She nodded some more, then we stood up and went to the door. When we got there, she said, 'How much?'

I looked at her.

'How much do you want for this?'

'Fifty billion dollars.'

She stared at me and then she nodded and made a little smile. 'Thank you, Mr. Cole.'

'Don't mention it. We're a full-service agency.'

CHAPTER 15

I called Joe Pike at seven-thirty that night, L.A. time. 'It's me. I'm in New York on this thing, and it's heating up. Looks like the mafia is involved.'

'Rollie George.'

'You got his number?'

Pike gave me a phone number. 'Where are you staying?'

I told him.

'Wait ten, then call Rollie. Try to survive until I get there.'

He hung up. That Pike. Some partner, huh?

Fifteen minutes later I called the number and a deep male voice said, 'I've got an apartment on Barrow Street in the Village, just east of Seventh. You need a place to stay, it's yours.' Roland George.

'How ya doin, Rollie?'

'Can't complain. My friend Joe Pike says you want to know some things about your classic, all-American-style mafia.' He dragged out *mafia* into three long syllables. Street black.

'The DeLuca family.'

'Figured it might be the Gambinos, you being the guy who burned Rudy when he was out on the coast.' Nobody in the rest of the world refers to Los Angeles as 'the coast.' Only New Yorkers.

'A woman named Ellen Lang did him. I was just along for the ride.'

'They after you?'

'No. This is something else.'

'Whatever you want, it's yours, you know that.'

'Sure.'

'Whatever I've got, whatever I can get for you or for Joe, it's yours.'

'I'm coming in tomorrow morning. From Chelam, Connecticut.'

'Come in after the traffic, say about ten. Take you an hour. I'll meet you downstairs in front of the building at eleven-thirty.'

'All right.'

He gave me the address and we hung up.

The next morning I retraced the route I had driven before, this time turning off the West Side Highway on Twelfth and picking up Bleecker at Abingdon Square and following it down through the Village to Barrow.

Two black men and a very old Boston terrier were standing in front of a redbrick building at the east end of Barrow by Fourth Street. One of the men was younger and tall and muscular in a plain navy suit with a white button-collared shirt. The other was in his early sixties in a dark brown leather trench coat and had maybe looked like the younger guy a couple of lifetimes ago, before twenty-two years with the NYPD's Organized Crime Control Bureau and two 9mm high-velocity parabellums in the liver had taken it away from him. Roland George. The little black and white Boston terrier sat at his feet, rear legs stuck out at odd angles, its pushed-in, once-black face white with gray, staring at nothing through eyes heavy with cataracts. Its tongue was purple and didn't fit in its mouth. It drooled. Roland's dog, Maxie.

Eleven years ago, Roland George and his wife, Liana, had been driving up the Rahway Turnpike from a weekend at the Jersey shore when a dark brown Mercury had pulled up alongside them and two Puerto Rican hitters had cut loose with a couple of Sig automatics, payback from a Colombian dope dealer whom Roland had busted. Roland survived the bullets and the subsequent crash, but Liana did not. Maxie had been left in the care of a neighbor. They had had no children. Roland George took a forced medical retirement, drank heavily for a year, then sobered up to write thick, violent novels about New York cops tracking down psychopathic killers. The first two didn't sell, but the last three had ridden the *New York Times* bestseller list to a couple of penthouse apartments, a twenty-eight-room home on a lake in Vermont, and substantial contributions to political candidates favoring the death penalty. Fourteen weeks after Liana George died, the two Puerto Rican hitters held up a Taco Bell in Culver City, California, and were shot to death by a uniformed police officer named Joe Pike. That's how Joe and I knew Roland George. Roland still wore the wedding ring.

I pulled to the curb, got out, and Roland shook my hand. His grip was hard and firm, but bony. 'You hungry?'

'I could eat.'

'Let Thomas here put your car in the parking garage across the street. There's an Italian place we can walk to not far from here.'

'Sure.' I gave the younger man my keys, then leaned down and patted Maxie on his little square head. It was like petting a fire hydrant. 'How ya doing, old boy?'

Maxie broke wind.

Roland shook his head and looked concerned. 'He's not doing so well.'

'No?'

'He's gone deaf. He's got the arthritis, he's blind as a bat, and now he can't hear. I think he sees things.'

'Growing old is hell.'

'I bear witness to that.'

Thomas said, 'Shall I pick you up at the restaurant, Mr. George?'

'That's all right, Thomas, I think we'll walk back. Be good for old Max.'

'Very good, sir.'

Thomas climbed into the Taurus and pulled away. I said, 'I never heard anyone say "very good, sir" in real life before.'

'I keep trying to break him of it, but, you know, he's working his way through Columbia Law.'

Roland and I turned off Barrow onto Fourth. To get Maxie going, Roland had to lift him to his feet, then give little tugs on the leash to point him in the right direction. Maxie's tongue stuck out and a ribbon of drool trailed along the sidewalk and his back legs lurched along with a mind of their own. The arthritis.

As we walked, Roland's eyes flicked over faces and storefronts on both sides of the street, sometimes lingering, mostly not. Still a cop. He said, 'Sal DeLuca is your old-line dago. Came up as a hitter through the Luchesi mob back in the forties, and by the time that broke up, he had a big enough crew and enough power to form his own family. Sal the Rock, they call him. These dagos are big on the names.'

'What are they into?'

'Gambling and loan-sharking and the labor rackets here in lower Manhattan. We're in DeLuca family territory right now.'

I looked around for shadows lurking in doorways or people with tommy guns, but I didn't see any. 'How can you tell?'

'Over in OCCB they got a territory map hung on the wall with New York carved up so it looks like its own little United States, here to here the DeLucas, here to here the Gambozas, here to here the Carlinos, like that. A bunch of guys called *capos* each have their own crew of soldiers and run their own businesses, but the *capos* all answer to the *capo de tutti capo*, the boss of the bosses.'

'The godfather.'

'That's it. In the DeLuca family, that's Sal. Charlie's got his own crew, and his own business, but he's still got to answer to Sal. Most of the time, the *capo de tutti capo* retires, he passes it on to his kid. He's lined things up so that the kid has the biggest crew, the most money, like that. Sal bought Charlie a meat-packing plant.'

'I've been there.'

Rollie made his hand like a gun and touched his temple. 'He's a nut case. Absolutely out of control. They call him Charlie the Tuna. You see, with the names? They call him the tuna because he's put so many guys in the ocean.'

Great. Just what you want to hear.

We turned off Fourth onto Sixth and started south toward Little Italy. When we were waiting for a light to change, Maxie suddenly growled and ran sideways, back legs moving faster than his front legs, drool trailing from the corners of his wide shovel mouth like wet streamers, trying to bite something that wasn't there. A couple of guys in watch caps waiting next to us traded looks and moved out of range.

Roland looked sad and said, 'It's hardest when their minds go.'

Maxie snapped at the air until he wore himself out and then he broke wind again and sat down. One of the guys who had moved away frowned and shook his head. I said, 'Sounds like digestion problems, too.'

Roland made more of the sad nod. 'Yes.'

When the light changed, Roland helped Maxie up and got him pointed in the right direction and we crossed.

We turned off Sixth onto Spring and went into a little place called Umberto's. A bald guy in a vest hustled up to Rollie with a lot of smiling and a lot of *buon giorno* and brought us to a booth across from the bar. A couple of dozen people were already eating and more than half of them were speaking Italian. Dark eyes moved with Rollie and voices lowered. The maître d' snapped his fingers and a kid with spots on his face brought water. Maxie sat on the floor next to Rollie and panted. When the maître d' and the kid were gone, I said, 'They don't mind the dog?'

'Max and I been eating here for years. When I was with the cops, I kept book on half the guys in this place. We nod, we smile, it's like a game we play. This place is owned by the Gamboza family.'

'Here in DeLuca territory?'

Rollie sipped his water and nodded. 'Used to be there were only five core families, with everybody killing everybody else over territory and business, but now there's eight, nine families and these guys all like to make like they're Lee Iacocca, everybody polite, everybody doing business with everybody else as long as the other guy pays *rispetto*. You know *rispetto*?'

'You want to do business in another guy's territory, you don't just move in. You pay respect. You ask permission and you give him a piece of the action.'

'Yeah. Vito Ratoulli, the guy owns this place, he's a soldier for Carlino. He pays the DeLucas six percent of his gross to do business here. Vito makes the best calamari diablo around, he treats DeLuca with respect, old Sal even comes here to eat sometimes. Works both ways. Some of DeLuca's people have businesses in Carlino territory.'

The maître d' came back and put a large white plate between us. There was a little white bowl of olive oil and basil in the center of the plate and a dozen paper-thin slices of prosciutto fanned out around it and a row of small hot rolls around the edge of the plate. The rolls were warm and slick with olive oil and little pieces of garlic. Rollie folded up a slice of the prosciutto, swirled it in the olive oil, ate half of it along with one of the little rolls, then gave the rest to his dog. He said, 'You like spicy food?'

'Yes.'

Rollie told the maître d' that we wanted the calamari. The maître d' went away. I said, 'What part of Italy are your people from?'

Rollie made a booming laugh. 'You eat enough macaroni, you lose your taste for red beans and fatback.'

I said, 'Why'd the families make peace?'

Rollie spread his hands. 'Organized crime isn't just the dagos and the kikes anymore. The brothers up in Harlem used to be under the mafia's thumb, but now you got civil rights. The black man figures he can do his own crime and not have to pay the dago. You got your Crips and Bloods and they ain't just street punks anymore. You got your Jamaicans and your East Indians, and those cats come up here believing in voodoo and shit. They don't give a damn about no Sicily. You got your Cubanos and your Chinese Triads and all these little bastards from Southeast Asia. Shit.' Rollie frowned and thought about it. 'The families knew that if they didn't hang together, they'd be run out of business, but it ain't an easy peace. There's still plenty of bad blood. No one likes showing polite, and no one likes showing respect, and a lot of bodies were buried before the families decided how they were going to divide up the crime and the territory. Your DeLucas and your Gambozas hate each other all the way back to Sicily, but they hate the niggers and the chinks worse. You see?'

'Anybody do business with the other guys?'

'Shit.'

'I want Charlie DeLuca to turn loose somebody he owns.'

Rollie ate another piece of prosciutto. 'Charlie the Tuna isn't a guy you can talk with.'

'They never are.'

Rollie smiled. 'You got anything to give him?'

I shook my head.

Rollie made a little shrug. 'I'll ask around. Maybe I can help you out.'

'I figured I'd go talk to him, see how he feels about it. You know where I can find him?'

'Try the meat plant.'

'I did. He's sorta tough to see.'

'Probably ain't there most of the time, anyway. The wise-guys own these businesses, but they don't like to work. Try a place called the Figaro Social Club up on Mott Street, about eight, nine blocks from here.'

'Okay.'

Rollie frowned at the last piece of prosciutto, picked it up, then swirled it in the oil. 'This guy, he gets hot, he ain't so good at controlling himself. That's why he's always in trouble. That's why his daddy has to clean up after him.'

'I know.'

'He's a nut case, Elvis. Certifiable.' He spoke slowly. 'This ain't L.A.'

I said, 'Rollie, in L.A. we got Richard Ramirez and the Hillside Strangler.'

Roland stared at me for a minute, then nodded again and ate the prosciutto. 'Yeah. I guess you do.'

Maxie suddenly charged sideways, snapping and barking at something that only he could see. Roland George got the sad look again and gently reeled him in and mumbled soft things that the dog could not hear and petted him until he was calm. I thought I heard him say Liana.

After a while the little dog took a deep breath and sighed and sat at Roland's feet. He broke wind loudly.

Everyone in the restaurant must have heard, but no one looked. Showing polite, I guess. Paying respect, I guess. When the calamari came, it was excellent.

CHAPTER 16

The Figaro Social Club was on Mott Street, squeezed between a shoe repair shop and a place that sold fresh ground coffee, looking sharp with one of those padded doors upholstered in red naugahyde. The naugahyde was cracked and had maybe been wiped down in 1962 but not since, and the doorstep and the gutter were littered and oily and wet. A small CLOSED TO THE PUBLIC sign was hanging on the door. I thought it all looked sort of crummy, but maybe I was just suffering from West Coast Bias. On the West Coast, big-time mobsters spent a lot of money and lived in palaces and acted like they were related to the Doheny family. Maybe on the East Coast such behavior was considered gauche. On the East Coast, the well-established mobster probably went in for the rat-hole look.

I pushed through the red door and stood in the entry for a moment, letting my eyes adjust. Charlie DeLuca and a couple of guys built like bread trucks were sitting at a bare wooden table, shoveling in pasta with some sort of red sauce. Behind them, Joey Putata and a short, muscular guy were wrestling a full beer keg onto the bar. An old guy in a white barman's bib yelled at them to go easy with the goddamned thing. In the back of the place a tall bony man with a long face and a hatchet nose was shooting pool by himself. His shoulders were unnaturally wide, as if he should have been twins but wasn't, and he was X-ray thin, with pale skin pulled tight and lean over all the bones. His hair was black and shaggy and stuck out in spikes on top, and he wore black Ray Ban Wayfarer sunglasses and black roach-killer boots with little silver tips and tight black pants and a black silk shirt buttoned at the neck. All the black made the pale skin look as white as milk.

The bartender saw me first and flagged his hand. 'Hey, can't you read? We're closed to the public.'

'I know. I'm here because I want to see Mr. DeLuca.' You give them the mister when you're hoping for cooperation.

DeLuca and the two guys at his table looked over, and so did Joey Putata. When Joey Putata saw me, he stopped wrestling with the beer keg and said, 'Oh, shit.' He hadn't said anything about the clam bar.

'My name is Elvis Cole, Mr. DeLuca. I want to talk with you about Karen Lloyd.' I was laying it on thick with the mister.

DeLuca blinked at me, then looked at Joey Putata. 'I thought you got rid of this fuck.' Probably wasn't laying it on thick enough.

Joey said, 'Hey, Charlie, we gave him the word. I took Lenny and Phil with me. We gave him the word real good.'

Charlie turned back to me and went back to work on the pasta. I think he was eating tongue. 'You're the creep from Disneyland, right?'

'Nope. I'm the creep from Los Angeles.'

'What's the fucking difference? It's all talking rabbits out there anyway, ain't it?'

The two guys sitting with Charlie and the little bartender thought that was a good one. One of the guys sitting with Charlie had big arms and a lot of gut and a gray sharkskin jacket over a blue shirt. His collar tips were long and stuck out over the jacket. Twenty years out of style. He said, 'Hey, Charlie, you think this mook knows Minnie Mouse? You think he plays hide the salami with old Minnie?' Everybody laughed except the guy back at the pool table. He was staring at the pool table and holding the cue stick as if it were a guitar, gently bobbing his head in time with the music.

Charlie said, 'You got some nut coming here. Didn't Joey tell you to knock it off and go home?'

'Joey didn't do a good job.'

Joey said, 'Hey, fuck you.'

Charlie turned back to me with the same hard eyes he was giving Joey. 'Joey's a piece of shit. I got guys who can do better, Mickey Mouse.' He turned enough to look back toward the pool table. 'You think you can do better than this piece of shit, Ric?'

The guy with the pool cue nodded, still staring at the pool table. Ric. He looked almost seven feet tall.

Charlie said, 'You're bothering my friend Karen, Mickey Mouse. That's not good.'

'Not anymore, Charlie. Now I'm working for her because she's working for you and she wants to stop. You see?'

Charlie stopped with the knife and fork and said, 'Karen.'

'She'd like to retire.'

'Karen been talking to you?' He wasn't liking it.

'I found out some things and I asked her about them. She's hoping we can work something out.'

Charlie put down the knife and fork and made a little hand move to the guy with the twenty-year-old clothes. 'Tudi, see if he's wired.'

Tudi came around the table and patted me down. I stood with my hands raised and sort of out to the side while he did it. He took out the Dan Wesson, opened it, pushed out the bullets, closed it, put the bullets in my left pants pocket and the Dan Wesson back in my shoulder rig. He took out my wallet and tossed it to Charlie DeLuca. Tudi started at the tops of my shoulders

126

and went down each arm and my back and my front and my crotch and each leg. He took off the G-2 and went over the seams and the fabric, and then he took off my belt and checked that, too. While he did it, Ric knocked pool balls around and Charlie DeLuca looked through my wallet. Tudi said, 'He's clean.'

DeLuca closed my wallet and tossed it back to me. 'I never met a private dick before. Private dicks around here know they fuck with Charlie DeLuca, they end up with the fish. You know what they call me?'

'Charlie the Tuna.'

'You know why they call me that?'

'They can't think of anything better.'

Joey said, 'You see? The guy's a wiseass. I couldn't help the wiseass wouldn't listen.' Whining.

Charlie said, 'Shut up, you piece of shit.'

Joey shut up.

I said, 'Karen wants to move on. Maybe we can work something out so that you get what you want and she gets what she wants.'

Charlie nodded, two guys sitting around a bar, shooting the breeze. 'What's your cut? You fuckin' her?'

'No cut. I'm just trying to help a friend.'

'Yeah. You know the old saying, if it ain't broke, don't fix it?'

I said, 'There are ways we can work this. You can find another bank to launder your money.'

He smiled and spread his hands and looked at Tudi. 'Tudi, you know what this guy is talking about, launder our money?'

Tudi said, 'Shit.'

I said, 'Okay. How about you move someone else into Karen's place. She'll stay on until they're in place, and then she'll leave. That way you don't lose a thing and everything stays just as it is.'

Charlie made the smile again and did more with the

hands. 'I don't get this guy. I say one thing, he says another. Maybe he don't speak English out there in Disneyland. Whatta they talk there, mousetalk?'

Tudi went, 'Eep, eep.' Everybody thought that was a riot.

I said, 'Karen wants out, Charlie. She's leaving.'

Charlie pushed his plate of pasta carefully to the side and leaned forward. 'Try to get this through your head, mook. What she wants does not matter. Do you know what matters?'

'What you want.'

'Right. And you know what I want right now?'

'To fit into size-34 pants.'

Joey said, 'You see, Charlie? You see? A wiseass.'

Charlie DeLuca's eyes went dark and he looked at me the way you look at a parking ticket you've found under your wiper blade. He said, 'I want you to watch this.' He turned and made the little hand move to Joey Putata. 'Come here, piece of shit.'

Joey glanced at the short, muscular guy and then at the bartender, and then he walked out to stand in front of Charlie DeLuca's table. The principal's office. 'What?'

'You told me you got rid of him. I sent you on the job to get rid of him, and here he is. I don't like fuckups, piece of shit.'

Charlie wasn't looking at Joey; he was looking at me. Joey was staring at Charlie, sweating now, scared and wondering what was going to happen, and everyone else was staring at Joey. Except for Ric. Ric made a nice, smooth shot and the *clack* of the balls was the only sound in the bar.

Charlie said, 'Smack yourself, piece of shit.'

Joey said, 'C'mon, Charlie, please. I took Lenny and Phil. We gave him the word.'

Charlie still didn't look at him; he stared at me. 'Do it, piece of shit. Hit yourself in the face.'

Joey sort of slowly raised his right hand and looked at it, then slapped himself in the face. It wasn't very hard.

'Close your hand.'

Joey started to cry. 'Hey, c'mon, Charlie.'

'Piece of shit.'

Joey closed his hand and sort of punched at his jaw.

'Harder.'

Joey hit himself harder, but it still wasn't very hard.

Charlie said, 'Ric, this piece of shit needs some help.'

Ric put down the pool cue and moved up by the bar, head still bobbing to music only he could hear. When he moved, he sort of glided, as if the tight pale skin were laid over steel cables and servo motors instead of muscle. He took off the Wayfarers and put them away in the black shirt and then he took out a stainless-steel Smith & Wesson 10mm automatic. You don't see many 10-mils. Style.

Joey said, 'Hey, Charlie, hey, I'll do it, look at this.' This time his lip split.

Charlie nodded. 'That's better, piece of shit. Now a couple more.'

Joey hit himself twice more. The second time opened the split and blood ran down Joey's chin and dripped onto his shirt. Ric put away the 10mm. Charlie DeLuca got up from the little table and came around and looked at me. 'You see the way it is.'

I said, 'Sure.'

'I want you gone. Ric, you and Tudi walk this fuck outta here and show him that I get what I want.'

I said, 'Does this mean I can't stay for lunch?'

Ric peeled himself away from the bar and the guy with the big arms took out a short-barreled Ruger .38 revolver. He showed it to me, then put it in his coat pocket just like they do in the movies. Ric didn't bother with the 10mm. I guess he just brought it out on special occasions.

Charlie DeLuca was turning away as if he were going around the table to finish his tongue when he hit Joey Putata a wide, looping right hand that caught Joey blind and knocked him over a couple of chairs and down to the floor. Joey covered up and DeLuca kicked him in the kidneys and the back and the legs, yelling, 'Piece of shit, rotten piece of shit.' He grabbed a fork from somebody's plate and stabbed Joey in the fleshy part of the shoulder. Joey Putata screamed and Charlie went back to kicking him. Tudi and the bartender and the other guys watched, but took a step back as if they didn't like what they were seeing and they were frightened that they might be pulled into it. Except for Ric. Ric glided up behind Charlie and put his hands on Charlie's shoulders and mumbled until Charlie stopped kicking and cursing and was finally standing there, breathing hard and finished with it. Ric the cooler, talking down the nut case. Charlie went back to the table, sat, but stared at the plate as if he didn't recognize what was in front of him.

The little bartender said, 'Jesus.'

Ric straightened his jacket, then came back over to me and pushed me through the red naugahyde door out into the light. It took Tudi a couple of steps to catch up. I said, 'He gets sort of carried away, doesn't he?'

Ric said, 'Shut up and let's go.'

We went up along the street, then turned into a little alley. The alley was black and wet and gritty, with dumpsters and steel garbage drums sprouting like mushrooms along the base of the buildings. A couple of six-wheeler vegetable trucks were parked to the side, enveloped by restaurant steam venting from greasy pipes. Surly white kids and Puerto Rican kids in dirty aprons hung around outside of the kitchen doors, smoking and scratching at tattoos that someone had cut into them with Bic pens and sewing needles. Rotten cabbage was the big smell. I said, 'Gee, fellas, I think I can find my way from here.'

Tudi said, 'We get finished with you, mook, you ain't even gonna be able to find the hospital.'

Ric didn't say anything.

Tudi took the little .38 out of his coat pocket and pointed it at me and that's when Joe Pike stepped out from behind one of the vegetable trucks, twisted the gun out of Tudi's hand, cocked it, and pressed it against Tudi's right temple. It had taken him maybe a tenth of a second.

Pike said, 'Do you want to die?'

CHAPTER 17

It happened quickly and without apparent effort, as if Pike had somehow assembled himself from the air and the trucks and the earth.

Tudi blinked and looked confused, response lagging behind event, and then his eyes bulged and he sucked in a single sharp breath. 'Jesus Christ.' His right hand stayed up and out, as if he were still holding the gun.

I said, 'You're five minutes too soon. I was just about to let these guys have it.'

Pike's mouth twitched. He never smiles, but sometimes he'll give the twitch.

Pike is maybe six-one and lean, all taut cords and veins. He was in straight-legged blue jeans and Nike running shoes and an olive-green Marine Corps parka over a gray sweatshirt and G.I. pilot's glasses so dark that they were without depth or dimension. He cocked his head to look at Ric. He had to look up.

Ric lifted his hands to the sides, letting Pike see that they were empty. He moved with great care, but he didn't look scared. Outside in the light, his skin was so pale I wondered if he used makeup, his eyes black dots set far back in dark hollows, angry weasels staring out of ice caves.

Pike said, 'Your call.'

Ric smiled. His teeth were small and yellow and angled backward like a snake's. If he bit you, you'd have a helluva time getting away from him. He reached out and pushed Tudi's gun hand down. 'He's got your gun, stupid. All you're holding is air.'

Tudi looked at his hand, maybe wondering where his gun had gone. 'The guy japped me.'

Pike stepped back and lowered the gun.

I gave Tudi the tsk-tsk. 'First Joey the Potato, now you. Charlie's gonna love it.'

Tudi's face was red and angry. He looked at his empty hand again like maybe he had made a mistake the first time, like maybe if he looked again, it wouldn't be empty and he could shoot Pike and me and he wouldn't have to tell Charlie that he'd been japped by a guy who came out of nowhere. Only when he looked, the hand was still empty. He looked back at Pike, then grunted and charged, head down. Pike's right knee snapped up hard, and Tudi popped over as if he'd been jerked backward by a leash. He hit the ground flat on his back with a loud slapping sound and that was the end of it.

'Dumb,' I said. 'This man has the market cornered on dumb.'

Ric smiled some more. 'He thinks he's good. All these guys, they think they're good.'

Pike was back to looking at Ric. 'How about you?'

Ric reached down with the emaciated white scarecrow arm and picked up Tudi and lifted him over his shoulder like a bag of dirty laundry. Tudi had to go two-thirty-five, at least. It was a long way to lift two-thirty-five. 'We'll talk again,' he said.

Pike nodded, then opened Tudi's gun, shook out the bullets, and dropped the gun into a steel garbage drum. We walked away, me leading and Pike walking backward, keeping an eye on Ric until we got to the street, then we moved against the traffic down toward Broome, trying to blend in with the natives.

I said, 'How'd you find me?'

'Went by Rollie's when I got in and dropped off my

stuff. He said you'd be here. He said you were going to go one-on-one with the mafia.' He shook his head, unimpressed. 'The mafia.'

'What they lack in skill, they make up for in numbers. Except for Ric. Ric is maybe pretty good.'

Pike shrugged, still giving it unimpressed. You want to impress Pike, you've got to use the neutron bomb.

We picked up a cab at the corner of Mott and Broome. The cabbie was an older guy with a bald, misshapen head and a lot of ear hair. He said, 'Where to?'

I told him an intersection near Rollie's. 'You know where that is?'

He flipped down the flag on the meter. 'Hey, I'm driving the Big Apple thirty-five years.'

We went west on Broome.

The cabbie said, 'You guys here on business?'

'Yeah.'

'You from California?'

I said, 'We're from Queens.'

The cabbie laughed. 'Yeah, right. I got you made for somewhere out west, L.A. or maybe San Diego.' So much for blending with the natives.

We picked up Pike's things and the Taurus from the parking garage across from Roland George's building, and worked our way out of the city and then north through the countryside to Connecticut and Chelam. While we drove I told Pike about Peter Alan Nelsen and Karen Lloyd and their son, and Karen's involvement with the DeLuca family. Pike sat in the passenger seat and never once moved or spoke or acknowledged what I was saying. As if he weren't even in the car. Maybe he wasn't. You hang around Pike enough, you begin to believe in out-of-body experience.

Twenty minutes after four we pulled off the highway into the Ho Jo, and I used the phone in my room to call Karen Lloyd at the bank. She said, 'Charlie called.' Her voice was low, as if Joyce Steuben might be outside the door, listening.

'I thought he might.'

'He was livid. He told me I shouldn't have brought you in.'

I said, 'It's not anything we didn't expect, but we had to try. Did you print out a record of the transactions for me?'

'Yes. I have them here.'

'Okay. I need to see them.'

'Don't come to the bank.' There was a pause, as if she had to think through the variables and find the best one. 'Come to the house, say at seven-thirty. We'll be finished with dinner then and Toby will be doing his homework. Is that all right?'

'Fine.'

There was another pause and then she said, 'Thank you for trying.'

'Don't mention it.'

I put down the phone and looked at Pike. 'We'll go out to her place at seven-thirty.'

Pike nodded, then went out to the lobby and checked in, taking one of the rooms adjoining mine. I stood in the door and watched him bring in an olive-green Marine Corps duffel bag and a long metal gun case that looked like something for a Vox guitar. Anyone saw it, they'd think Pike played bass for Lou Reed. After he was settled he came back into my room and we looked at each other. It was four-forty-five. He said, 'Anything around here to do until seven?'

'Nope.'

'Any good places to eat?'

I shook my head.

Pike looked out of my window down onto the parking lot and crossed his arms. 'Well,' he said. 'We didn't have it this good in Southeast Asia.'

Nothing like support from your friends.

At five o'clock we went down to the bar and drank beer, then enjoyed an early dinner in the restaurant. I had a very nice chicken-fried steak. Pike had lentil soup and a large mixed vegetable salad and four slices of whole-wheat toast and a thick wedge of Jarlsberg cheese. Vegetarian.

The female bartender who was thinking about moving to California came in from the bar and kidded around with us until two older couples in heavy coats and loud shirts walked in and then she had to go back to the bar. The two older couples didn't eat. They just drank.

After a while we bought four beers to go and took them back to my room and watched the local New York news. The weather forecast said that the skies would continue to clear for the next few days, but that then another front would move down from Canada bringing cold and snow. The sports report was fine, but the hard news stories were mostly about subways and city strikes and local personalities and things indigenous to New York. They seemed alien and sort of empty.

Midway through the newscast, a male anchor with a lantern jaw and a rough-hewn face and squinty eyes reported a federal study that concluded that the L.A. basin had the dirtiest air in the country. He grinned when he said it. The black female co-anchor grinned, too, and reported a corollary story that Angelenos drive more than urbanites in any other major American city. The jut-jawed anchor grinned even harder and said that maybe Los Angeles wouldn't have such a bad smog problem if they put in a subway to the beach. That got a big laugh from everybody. Especially the weatherman.

Joe Pike said, 'Assholes.'

I turned off the television.

It was ten minutes before six.

We sat and stared, neither of us saying much, and then

136

Joe Pike went into his room. After a while I heard his water running. I took off my clothes and did a little yoga, stretching to warm myself, then working through the cobra, and the locust, and the wheel pose, but I couldn't concentrate. I tried doing push-ups and sit-ups instead, but with no better luck. I kept losing count. After a while I got off the floor and called the local news station in New York and told a young woman that I wanted to speak to the jut-jawed anchor. When the young woman asked me why, I said that I wanted to call him a prick. She wouldn't put me through.

Pike stayed in his room and I stayed in mine, and at twenty minutes after seven we went down to the Taurus and drove to Karen Lloyd's.

Tough guys like me never miss home.

CHAPTER 18

The air was crisp and cold and the sky was a velvety black as we parked in Karen Lloyd's drive and walked up to the door. I rang the bell and Karen Lloyd answered. When she saw Joe Pike, she said, 'Oh.'

I said, 'Karen Lloyd, this is Joe Pike. Joe, this is Karen Lloyd. Joe is my partner. He owns the agency with me.' Dark, and he still wore the glasses.

Pike said that he was pleased to meet her. Karen looked uneasy but she said hello. Another person invading her life.

The three of us went into the dining room. There was a 9 × 12 manila envelope on the table and a glass of white wine next to it. Most of the wine was gone. I said, 'Where's Toby?'

'In his room, doing homework. I told him that people were coming and that I had work to do. He has his radio on. He won't be able to hear us.'

'All right.'

Karen picked up the 9 × 12, handed it to me, then picked up the wineglass. 'This is what I had in the computer.'

'Okay.'

Pike and I took off our jackets. When Pike took off his jacket, Karen leaned forward and made a little sound like *ssss*.

Pike had two bright red arrows tattooed on the outside of each deltoid when he was in Vietnam. They pointed forward, and looked like the kind of red arrows you see on jet intakes or rocket nozzles or other dangerous things. With the jacket off and Pike in a sweatshirt with no sleeves, you could see the tattoos as clearly as if neon tubes had been laid beneath his skin. Karen looked away, not wanting him to catch her staring. People do that.

The orange and white cat came in from the hall, walked over to Pike, and rubbed against his ankles. Pike bent down and held his fingers out. The cat began to buzz. Karen said, 'Do you like cats, Mr. Pike?'

Pike nodded.

She said, 'His name is Tigger.'

Pike nodded once, then stood and walked into the kitchen. Karen said, 'Excuse me, the bathroom isn't that way.'

Pike went through the door without looking back.

I said, 'He isn't looking for the bath. He's looking for how someone might get into your home, or get out, and for where they might hide while they are within it.'

She blinked at me.

'It's one of his more colorful habits.'

The back door opened and Pike went outside. Karen went to the window and tried to look out at him, but she couldn't see out of the light and into the darkness. No one ever can. 'What a strange man.'

'Perhaps, but he is someone that you want on your side. He will never lie to you, and he will give you every piece of himself.'

She looked doubtful. 'Has he been your partner for a long time?'

'Yes. Since I bought the agency. We bought it together.'

She looked out of the window again. Worried. 'What if he scares Toby? What if one of the neighbors sees him and calls the police? Then we'll have to explain.'

'No one will see him and no one will hear him. You ever see a ninja movie? That's Pike.'

She squinted out the window some more, then came back to the table and picked up her glass. 'How can he see at night while he's wearing those sunglasses?'

I gave her a little shrug. There are some things even the great and wonderful Oz does not know.

In a little while Pike came back and we went through the records. Karen got more wine.

There were two hundred fourteen entries made into eight different First Chelam account numbers, all of which were immediately transferred into two accounts in Barbados. The records were spread over six pages of computer printout, showing single-spaced rows of numbers without meaning, dates to the far left, account numbers to their right, amounts to the right of that, destination accounts on the far right, with dates going back four years and eleven months. I would read the sheets, then pass them to Pike, and he would read them. Karen watched us and drank the wine. It was sort of like reading a phone book with phone numbers but without names.

I said, 'Let's start with the most recent deposit and you can walk us through every transaction.'

'God, they're all the same.'

'You told me that most of the deposits come through Harry, but some of them come through Charlie.'

'That's right.'

'Then they're not all the same. There are Harry deposits and there are Charlie deposits.'

She nodded and said, 'All right. What are you looking for?'

'I don't know. All we can do is dig into what we have and see if something presents itself.'

'Oh.'

'Most of the time, in what we do, there are no clear or ready avenues. Detectives look for clues, and clues tell you what's going on and what to do about it. Do you see?'

'Of course.' She didn't look convinced. I think she was trying to relate it to banking.

'I'll need a pad and a pencil.'

She got up and went down the little hall and came back with a yellow legal pad and a Paper Mate Sharpwriter pencil. She also got more wine. She seemed tired, but I didn't think it was just the booze. Her hip brushed the jamb when she came back through the door. I said, 'Let's start with the transaction I saw in Brunly. Tell us how it was arranged and who arranged it, and how you were told to do what you did and as much as you know about where the money came from and where the money went. Don't leave anything out. Things that you take for granted we don't know anything about. We'll do that one, and then we'll walk through every transaction for as far back as you can remember.'

She nodded gamely, and we began.

We went through as much of each transaction as she could remember, starting with the latest and working backward. She remembered more than she thought she would because a lot of what had happened was repetitious. Most of the answers were the same. Charlie's secretary at the meat plant would set the meetings just as she would for Charlie and any other business associate. At the meetings, Charlie would tell Karen which of the eight First Chelam accounts the money should go into and into which of the two Barbados accounts it should be transferred. There were no receipts given and no statements mailed and nothing to prove that someone named Charlie DeLuca was either putting cash into the First Chelam Bank or moving money from one account to another. Karen assumed that someone in Barbados checked to make sure that the right amount of money was being fed into the accounts, but she wasn't sure.

Somewhere in the middle of it, Toby came into the hall and looked at us with big eyes. 'Mom?'

I said, 'Hi, Tobe.' Mr. Bright and Cheery.

Karen put down her wine and gave him the Barbara Billingsley smile and went over to him. 'Hey, pal, you get the homework done?' She'd had three or four glasses of wine by then, but she was doing okay.

'Unh-hunh.'

'You know Mr. Cole? And this is Mr. Pike, his associate.'

Toby smiled uneasily, knowing that something wasn't right, that his mom didn't get sauced and have late-night meetings with guys sporting tattoos and sunglasses to talk over wrap-around financing and short-term mortgage envelopes. He looked nervous. 'You okay?'

She ran a hand through his hair and looked sad. 'Sport, it's been a helluva day. Why don't you get ready for bed?'

He glanced at Pike and me, then he gave his mom a kiss and went back down the hall. Karen watched him go and then she turned and trudged back to the table and Barbara Billingsley was gone. Karen Lloyd's face was older.

I said, 'You want to knock off until tomorrow?'

She shook her head. 'No. Let's get this done.'

Two hours and eleven minutes later we had filled the legal pad with two columns. HARRY had been written above one column and CHARLIE had been written above the other, with deposit dates on the left of the columns and amounts in the middle and destinations accounts on the right. There were seven different account numbers under the HARRY column, but only one account number under the CHARLIE column. All of the HARRY accounts were transferred to the same Barbados destination. The CHARLIE account went to the other Barbados location. There were one hundred eighty-one entries under the

HARRY account and thirty-three entries under the CHARLIE, with all of the HARRY deposits coming every Thursday, as regular as the sunset. The HARRY deposits were from $107,000 to $628,000, and they were spread more or less equally among the seven accounts. The CHARLIE deposits were different. They started about twenty-eight months ago, and sometimes they would be made twice in one week and other times there would be eight or nine weeks between them. Irregular. The first couple of years the deposits were relatively small, with nothing over $9,800. A little less than five months ago the deposits went from four figures to five, with a high of $68,000. All of the deposits since then had been large, but still much smaller than any of the HARRY deposits.

We stared at our numbers and our chart, and Pike said, 'You see it?'

Karen said, 'What?'

I turned the yellow pad around so it would be easier for her. 'Harry brings money, and Charlie brings money, but only Charlie tells you where to put the money.'

She nodded. 'Yes.'

'Look at it. Every time Harry brings money, it goes into one of seven accounts, but it never goes in the eighth. Every time Charlie brings money, it goes in the eighth and never into any of the other seven.'

She frowned and brought the pad closer. The frown made her look more strained, but now there was maybe a little hope. 'I've never thought about it, but I guess that's right. Do you think this means something?'

I made a little shrug. 'I don't know. I'm looking at things in a certain way and they're adding up, but maybe they add up in other ways, too. Maybe the Harry accounts are DeLuca family accounts, and the Charlie account is a personal account. Maybe the money Charlie gives you is the piece that Sal cuts for him, and maybe it's bigger than the piece Sal cuts for the other *capos*, so

Charlie and Sal don't want anyone else to know to keep peace in the family.'

Pike grunted. 'Or maybe not. Maybe it means something that we can use.'

Karen looked from me to Pike and then back to me. The hope you could see in her faded. She said, 'It seems iffy.'

'It is iffy. If you want certainty, go to the cops. There's witness protection.'

Her face set, then she got up and went to the hearth. The cat followed her with his eyes. 'We've been through that.'

'It's still an option.'

'No. It is not. It is not an option for me.' Her frown deepened and she stared at the mantel. The pictures of her and Toby were there. She chewed her upper lip, then looked back at me. 'Charlie's secretary called back this evening. She said I'm supposed to meet Charlie tomorrow. I told her no. I said that I'm not going to do it.' That's why the drinking.

Pike said, 'Bad move.'

Her nostrils tightened and she looked at him. 'What do you know?'

I said, 'He's right. Charlie's already pissed, and we shouldn't make it worse. Pike and I will be there, and we won't let him hurt you.'

She pulled herself erect and stepped away from the hearth and gave me the sort of eyes she must've given herself ten years ago when she'd decided to change her life. Hard, focused, don't-get-in-my-way eyes. 'No. It's not about being scared. It's about not wanting it in my life anymore. I've got Peter coming back. I've got you in my home. I'm not going to pick up his money. I'm not going to take any more deposits from Harry. I've made up my mind. Do you understand?'

I said, 'Yes, ma'am.'

Pike nodded once, and his mouth twitched.

Karen Lloyd said, 'Will you need me for anything else tonight?'

'Nope,' I said. 'I think that about covers it.'

She went to the front door and opened it. The cat slipped out and was gone. She said, 'I appreciate what you've done, and I don't mean to be abrupt, but it's late and I'm tired. If you need to speak with me tomorrow, you can call me at the bank.'

'Sure.'

'Good night.'

She closed the door before we were off the porch.

Pike said, 'Tough lady.'

'Unh-hunh.'

'Maybe too tough. Like she's got something to prove.'

I nodded.

Outside, the night air was crisp and chill and sparkling in its clarity, smelling strongly of oak and elm. Orion hung sideways in the southern sky, and a three-quarter moon hung in the east. We walked out onto the lawn and stood by the Taurus and watched Karen Lloyd's house. One by one, the lights went out and the house grew dark. With every light that died, the night grew closer.

I said, 'A long time ago, she made the choice to be the way she is. She earned the job and the house and the position within the community. She rose above the bad thing in her life and has tried to get it out of her life and is trying again. I think she made gutsy choices. Be a shame if she had to regret them.'

Pike moved in the dark, and the orange and white cat came from beneath the car and rubbed against him. Pike bent and picked up the cat and held him close. 'You're right when you say that Charlie's already pissed. She doesn't show when he expects her, he might drive around to find out why. He might try to make sure it doesn't happen again.'

'Think you could stay close to her, keep him from doing that?'

Pike's mouth twitched in the moonlight. 'Unh-hunh.'

I nodded, and Pike put down Karen Lloyd's cat and we got into the Taurus. The final light went out in Karen Lloyd's house, and all was darkness.

CHAPTER 19

Roland George called at 7:32 the next morning and said, 'NYPD owns a guy named Walter Lee Balcom. Busted him seven weeks ago on two counts of murder and one count kidnapping and about two dozen ancillary counts. Most of them smut and sex crimes.'

'Do the DeLucas run porno?'

'No. That's the DeTillio family. But Walter's not mob. He's just been around for a long time and knows people who know people who know people. He's been singing up a storm to try to cut a deal, and Charlie DeLuca's name has come up a few times.'

'Can I talk with him?'

'Ten o'clock at the Hall of Justice, downstairs, room B28. I'll meet you there.'

'Right.'

Rollie hung up.

At a quarter before ten I pulled into the parking garage next door to the Criminal Courts Building on Centre, just north of Foley Square in Chinatown, then walked across and down to subbasement B. A fat cop sitting behind a narrow table asked my business. I told him I was looking for Roland George in room B28. The fat cop looked through a little box, took out a pass with my name on it, and jerked a thumb to the right. 'That way.'

Subbasement B of the Criminal Courts Building looked like a breeding ground for cops with green cement walls and tile floors that were maybe a thousand years old and the faraway smells of disinfectant and urine.

Cops of both sexes moved through the halls, uncomfortable in spotless, starched uniforms, called in by prosecutors to rehearse before appearing in court. Defense attorneys on their way into or out of interview rooms glared at the cops with angry eyes that were looking to cut a deal for clients everyone knew were guilty. The lawyers looked like chronic gamblers. The cops looked like drunks.

When I got to B28, Rollie George and a fireplug-shaped guy with a blond crew cut were standing outside the door. Rollie said, 'Elvis, this is Sid Volpe. Sid's with the Justice Department, and he's the guy who's letting us see Balcom.'

We shook. Volpe's hand was dry and hard. He said, 'I got you sandwiched in between the IRS and the feds. You can have him for twenty minutes starting now, so let's not waste time.'

We went in.

Walter Lee Balcom was a pale man in his late forties with fine, straw-colored hair that was thinning on top. He was sitting at a narrow wooden table, chain-smoking Lark cigarettes and wearing gray prison fatigues. A boxy Nagra reel-to-reel tape recorder sat to his side on the table, along with a couple of gray legal pads. There were four metal chairs scattered around the table, but there weren't any pencils or pens or other sharp things.

Walter Lee Balcom gave me a nice smile as we walked in. 'Hello, Mr. Volpe, hello, Mr. George, is this the gentleman you told me about?' His voice was soft and papery.

Volpe said, 'This is him, Walter.' Volpe sat in one of the chairs and turned on the Nagra. 'Don't let Walter's manner fool you, Cole. Walter recruited a sixteen-year-old male prostitute named Juan Roca to help him kidnap a nineteen-year-old nurse's aide named Shirley Goldstein. They took her over to a tank farm outside Newark where Roca raped her and tortured her to death with a butane torch while Walter here got it all on videotape. Then Walter walks out in front of the camera in a Groucho Marx nose and shoots Roca four times in the chest and back with a .45 automatic butt-packed with hollowpoints.'

Walter Lee Balcom sat impassively while Volpe said it, using the stub of one Lark to light another. The air smelled of pipe tobacco from the Larks.

Volpe said, 'There's no business like show business, right, Walter?'

Walter said, 'That wasn't me in the videotape, Mr. Volpe. That was someone made up to look like me.' A voice like whispers.

Volpe said, 'Shit,' then grinned at Rollie. 'This asshole is so fucking perverted even the goddamned DeTillio family wouldn't touch half the smut he handled.'

Walter shrugged, as if this were all part of a meaningless conversation he was having with strangers at a bus stop.

I said, 'Do you know many organized-crime figures, Walter?'

Another shrug. A deep puff. 'A few. I've been in the industry for quite a long while. It has always been profitable.'

'Do you know Charlie DeLuca?'

'Not personally. I know who he is, of course.'

Rollie said, 'We're told that DeLuca's name has come up a few times in the songs you been singing.'

Shrug. A whisper. 'You hear things.'

Rollie crossed his arms and sat back in the chair. 'Your kind of business, they've got to be dirty things.'

Walter made the nice smile again. 'One man's garbage, Roland.'

Sid Volpe leaned across the table and hit Walter Lee Balcom in the face with the back of his left hand. Walter went backward out of the chair and landed on the floor. The broken Lark landed on the table next to the pack, its coal still red and smoking. Walter Lee slowly got up, righted his chair, and sat again. There was a trickle of blood from his right nostril.

Volpe said, 'It's *Mister* George, Walter.'

Walter made an embarrassed smile. 'Yes, of course. My apologies.' Walter took a fresh Lark out of the pack and lit it with what was left of the coal. Volpe took a white handkerchief out of his pants and tossed it onto the table next to Walter. 'Get your nose.'

Walter dabbed at his nose.

Roland watched without moving, then said, 'Thanks, Sid. I think we can take it from here.'

Volpe said, 'Whatever you want,' then got up and left.

When he was gone, Rollie turned off the Nagra. 'You want some ice for that, Walter?'

'No. Thank you.'

Rollie said, 'When I was starting out, we used to call these rooms the garden rooms. Can you guess why?'

Walter shook his head the slightest bit, made the gentle smile.

'We called'm the garden rooms because this is where we took out the hoses. You see?'

'Ah.' The smile.

'I didn't like it then, and I don't like it now, but I don't like you, either. I just can't abide beating on a man when he can't fight back. Even a piece of trash like you.'

'Ah.'

'Just so we understand each other.'

Walter nodded and took more of the Lark. Rollie crossed his arms and settled back.

I said, 'I'm looking for a handle on Charlie DeLuca, Walter. Do you have any ideas?'

'As I said, I don't know him.'

'But you hear things.'

'Yes. But none of it has been of particular interest to my friends with the Justice Department.'

'I don't have to worry about building a case or following the rules of evidence. This is private. I have reason to believe that Charlie might be involved in something that he doesn't want the rest of the family to know about.' Rollie's eyes shifted over to me when I said it. 'You got any idea what that might be?'

Walter shook his head. 'No. I'm sorry. I know quite a bit about what the DeTillios are into, and the Gambozas, but really very little about the DeLucas.'

'Could be anything, Walter. Maybe he's cheating one of the other *capos*. Maybe he's ripping off Sal.'

Walter shook his head. 'I'm sorry.'

I sat back in the hard chair and crossed my arms and looked at him. 'Okay, forget that angle. I'll take any dirt you can give me.'

Walter closed his eyes and drew in deep on the Lark. 'There are maybe other people who might help you.'

'Like who.'

The smile. 'Mr. DeLuca often used an intermediary to acquire films featuring young women of color. I'm told that he had a taste for black hookers, especially those who had appeared in films and videotapes.'

Rollie said, 'Who told you this stuff?'

'A fellow named Richie. A sometime customer of mine. He spoke of Mr. DeLuca with great familiarity. He said they were associates.'

I said, 'Does Richie have a last name?'

Walter gave me sad and shook his head. 'I'm sorry.'

Rollie said, 'So the man likes kink with black chicks. Mob dagos been going for the dark meat since the speakeasy days in the twenties. Sal ain't gonna give a shit about that.'

'It's more than just a taste for the dark, Mr. George.' The smile, the cigarette glowing hotly. 'I'm told that his passion is short-lived, but that he pays very well. I would think that if anyone would know something, a person in that position might.'

'You got a name?'

'There was a woman named Angelette Silver, though she's no longer in the trade. I believe she works in a florist shop on 122nd Street, in Harlem.' The smile. 'But she may not be likely to help.'

'Why not?'

'Charlie uses them up rather quickly, you see. He can be quite a violent man.' Walter's eyes twinkled when he said it, as if somehow the knowledge of it was delicious. Then he shook his head sadly. 'Their parting wasn't on the best of terms.'

'But he pays very well.'

The smile. 'Yes. For every buyer there is a seller, for every seller, a buyer.'

Rollie said, 'Shit.'

I said, 'Walter, you in here ratting on the mob, aren't you scared they'll nail you?'

The smile, the Lark. 'I've always been willing to sell what no one else would sell, Mr. Cole. I find it quite' – the smile grew broader and the Lark glowed hotly – 'gratifying. Do be careful with Mr. DeLuca. He's quite mad, you know.'

'That's what they tell me, Walter. Thanks.'

'I hope this has helped you.'

'Sure, Walter. Maybe it has.'

Volpe opened the door and tapped his watch. 'The guys from the Bureau are here.'

Roland nodded, and then we went out into the hall, leaving Walter Lee Balcom sitting quietly at the table, smoking and smiling a gentle smile to himself.

CHAPTER 20

Out in the hall Rollie said, 'What's this business about Charlie being up to something?'

I told him what I had.

When I finished, he said, 'You figure Charlie's got his own private little nest egg growing down in Barbados.'

'That's what I need to find out. If he does, then I can use it to make him turn loose my client.'

Rollie nodded. 'What kind of money we talking here?'

'Forty, sixty grand at a crack during the last five months. Smaller money before.'

Roland whistled. 'That's serious crime. Sal wouldn't mind the nickel-and-dime stuff, postal scams, unregulated hijacking, that kind of thing, all the *capos* got something going, but fifty grand.' He shook his head.

'Could Charlie's crew be turning that kind of cash with nobody knowing about it?'

'No way. When these guys talk about family, they really mean it. Guys in Charlie's crew got brothers, cousins, uncles in all the other DeLuca crews. These guys get drunk together, they have barbecues. It'd be easier to keep a secret in a newsroom.'

'So if Charlie's got something going, he's keeping it from his own crew.'

'That's a pretty good bet.' Rollie looked thoughtful, then watched as a trim Chinese woman came out of the elevator and walked down the hall to a door with frosted glass. She had nice calves. When the door was closed, he looked back at me. 'Course, Sal might be the only other guy in the family who knows. Sal might be skimming a little off the top for Charlie 'cause it's his kid.'

'I thought about that.'

'And if Sal's in on it, you're screwed.'

I spread my hands. 'It's a position I'm accustomed to. Do me another favor?'

'Name it.'

'Can you check the JD files for anyone named "Richie" in the DeLuca family?'

'Sure.' Then he said, 'Elvis?'

'Unh-hunh.'

'What he said in there about Charlie being nuts, you remember that.'

I gave him a smile. *Dawn Patrol.* Errol Flynn courageous in the face of certain doom.

I left Rollie downstairs and took the elevator up to the lobby where I used a pay phone to get the number for the New York City Florists Association. The Florists Association told me that there were four flower shops on 122nd Street, two in Morningside Heights, one in Harlem, and one in East Harlem. They had no listing for an Angelette Silver as a licensed florist, and they couldn't tell me in which shop she might work. I copied down the names, addresses, and phone numbers of the four shops, thanked them, and hung up.

I got change at the little cigar stand they have there in the lobby, then went back to the phones and called Victor's Floral Gifts and asked to speak to Angelette Silver. A businesslike woman who sounded to be in her forties said that she was sorry, but no one by that name worked there. I thanked her, hung up, and called the Gilded Lily. A man with a heavy, masculine voice told me that he didn't know anyone named Angelette, but that he was certain he could meet my every need without her help. I thanked him and hung up and called

Rudy's Florist. Rudy didn't know anyone named Angelette, either, though he did know a guy named Angel.
Would that do? I said that I thought not. The fourth shop
was a place called Your Secret Garden. An older woman
with a soft southern accent answered.

I said, 'May I speak with Angelette Silver, please?'

There was an uncertain pause. 'You mean Sarah?'

There were voices in the background, then something
covered the mouthpiece, then a heavy male voice came
on. 'You got the wrong number. Nobody by that name
works here.' He hung up. Hard.

Hmm.

I picked up the Taurus from the parking garage, then
took Canal over to the West Side Highway, then went
north past the Village and the Lincoln Tunnel on my
way up to 122nd. Maybe I was on to something. Walter
Lee Balcom had put me on to Angelette Silver, who very
likely was living under the name Sarah, and maybe
Angelette Silver could connect me either to someone
named Richie or someone who knew what Charlie
DeLuca was up to. If I could just keep Charlie DeLuca
from killing either Karen Lloyd or me until I knew who
or what that was, all of this might work out. Stranger
things have been known to happen.

On the Henry Hudson Parkway at 86th Street, halfway
up the island and along the Hudson River, I spotted a
metallic-brown Chevrolet following me four cars back
and one lane over.

I swung south on Broadway, then east on 86th, then
south again on Columbus, but he stayed with me,
always four cars back, once gunning it through a red
light to keep his position. Pretty good. I wondered if it
was Ric.

An eight-wheel flower truck was parked on Columbus
in the right-turn lane at the corner of 76th Street. Traffic
was backed up and horns were blowing and people who

wanted to turn right had to work their way slowly around the truck. I turned right with them and slowed it down even more, staying hidden behind the flower truck until the traffic had cleared ahead of me. I goosed the Taurus half a block down, then threw it into park in the middle of 76th Street and was out of the car and walking back up the sidewalk when the metallic-brown Chevrolet came around the corner. It wasn't Ric.

The guy behind the wheel played it well. Traffic was backing up again and more horns were blowing and the other cars were putting on their blinkers and trying to get around the Taurus, so he put on his blinker and got into line to get around the Taurus, too.

I walked out into the street behind him and went up around his car and put the Dan Wesson in through the driver's side window. 'Surprise.'

He was a medium-sized guy in his early forties with a precise manner and a nice tan and thick hair. He kept both hands on the steering wheel, left in the ten o'clock position and right in the two o'clock position, just like they teach in driving school. He was staring at the gun. 'Jesus Christ, put that away. Where the hell do you think we are, Beirut?'

Around us, drivers were blowing their horns and a fat guy with a three-day stubble called us assholes and told us to get out of the street and nobody seemed to mind too much that I was holding the Dan Wesson. Just another story in the naked city.

'Take out the wallet very slow. If you jerk, I'll shoot you.'

He did it, still with his eyes on the gun. He said, 'I don't know what in hell you've got going on here, but it's not worth pulling the trigger.'

'We'll see.' I really know how to throw a scare into them.

I took the wallet and opened it. Nothing said MAFIA.

Nothing said HIRED KILLER. What I saw was a California driver's license in the name of one James L. Grady, address c/o James L. Grady Confidential Investigations, Los Angeles, California. I blinked at it a few times and then I blinked at James L. Grady.

James L. said, 'Will you stop pointing that goddamned gun at me now?'

I didn't stop pointing the gun at him. A pretty woman driving past in a white Mercedes gave us the finger. I said, 'Who hired you?'

'Peter Alan Nelsen.'

'Peter Alan Nelsen, the film director?'

James L. Grady gave me snide. 'Yeah. He said he hired you to find his ex-wife, but he figured you were stiffing him and he wanted to find out. I picked you up in Chelam with the ex and the kid, and I've been following you around ever since.'

'Ever since.'

'Peter came in last night. He's staying over at the Ritz-Carlton. He wants to see you.'

I stopped pointing the gun at him and he snatched back his wallet. A guy passing by in a red Nissan truck called me a shithead. So did James L. Grady.

CHAPTER 21

Peter Alan Nelsen had the Presidential Suite on the top floor of the Ritz-Carlton, overlooking Central Park. I followed Grady's Chevy to the curb, where we let a couple of guys who looked like they'd just mustered out of the French army have our cars, then we went inside.

James L. used a house phone and said, 'This is Grady. I'm in the lobby with Cole.'

He listened for a minute, then hung up and gestured with his chin. 'Elevator's over there.'

He stayed a half step in front as we crossed the lobby, looking very spiffy in his coat and tie, like a successful exercise-equipment importer or a high-end insurance executive. He didn't look like a guy who could follow me for a week without my noticing. If he did, I probably would've noticed him.

In the elevator, he leaned against one wall with his arms crossed and I leaned against another, and neither of us looked at the other. Invisible lines. The elevator was quiet and still and somehow made closer by the faraway hum of the electric motors. It was a long way up to the top floor. I said, 'How come I didn't make you?'

He shrugged, still not looking at me. 'I'm good at it. Also, I didn't have to maintain continual contact. Once I knew where you were staying and where the woman lived and worked, it was easy.'

'You didn't have to worry about losing me because you could always pick me up again.'

'Unh-hunh.'

I nodded. 'I put the plane ticket and the Ho Jo on plastic. There were the phone calls charged to my office number in L.A.'

'You weren't trying to hide. You didn't expect anyone to look.'

I stared at him for about twelve floors. 'Fed.'

Grady smiled. 'Secret Service. Fourteen years.' He finally turned and looked at me. 'I'm impressed you picked me up. I was back and I was loose. I don't get picked up even when I'm living in the other guy's shorts. You're good.'

I spread my hands. Maybe Grady wasn't so bad after all.

We got off at the top floor and followed the noise to the Presidential Suite. Nick met us at the door and gave me the big smirk, then jerked his thumb through the door. 'Inside, hotshot.' The Nickster.

Inside, a quadraphonic stereo system was blasting out Fine Young Cannibals, and the air smelled like Jiffy Pop popcorn and cigarettes. Peter Alan Nelsen was talking to a couple of guys in baggy suits out by the terrace, and a guy with a loud green tie was speaking into a phone by the bar. One of the guys with Peter was wearing a paisley ascot and was smoking a purple cigarette. Dani and T.J. were slouching on the palatial furniture, and a thin woman going for the Tama Janowitz look sat next to T.J. with her hand on his thigh. Dani gave me a little wave. There were open bottles of Absolut vodka and Jack Daniel's bourbon on the bar, and Nestlé's wrappers on the floor. Most of the Absolut was gone. It probably wasn't like this when the president was in residence. Grady frowned at the mess and gave disapproving. Nope, it wasn't like this with the president.

Peter saw us and turned away from the two guys by the terrace without excusing himself and said, 'Well, it's about goddamned time. Dani, turn off that shit and get these Broadway fruits out of here.' Broadway fruits. Always sensitive.

The guy with the ascot looked peeved. He said, 'Peter, we have the backers in place. If you'll agree to direct the play, we can be on the boards by next fall.'

Peter said, 'Nick, give Dani a hand with the fruits.'

Nick pulled the phone away from the guy at the bar, then pointed at the two guys by the terrace and showed them his famous thumb-jerked-at-the-door move. High verbal. The guy with the ascot said, 'I'm sure we can reach some sort of agreement,' but Peter wasn't listening; he was already over with me and Grady. Nick and Dani hustled the three Broadway people out. The Tama Janowitz went with them.

Peter said, 'Jesus Christ, you were supposed to find my kid and let me know. Instead, I gotta hire somebody to find you. I thought we were pals.' He looked hurt.

'There were things I wanted to find out and do before I called you in.'

'Like what?'

'I can't tell you.'

'Bullshit. I didn't hire you to do things. I hired you to find my kid. What're you trying to do, jack up the price?' Now he was giving me suspicious.

I said, 'If you had waited, I would've called. Karen needs to prepare the boy, and there are things going on in her life that she needs to straighten out. That's what's been taking the time.'

Peter grunted when I said it and looked interested, forgetting about the hurt and the pissed. 'You talked to her about me?'

'Yeah.'

'What'd she say? She excited?' He was leaning forward now, wanting to hear about himself.

'She's got a life here, Peter. She's scared that your

coming in is going to change that. You need to be sensitive to that.'

'Sure, sure. I'm sensitive. I'm caring.' He made a little hand move to show me how sensitive and caring he was. 'How about my kid? Is Toby okay?'

'Yes. He plays basketball. He seems happy.'

'Good, good.' Peter was moving around now, looking pleased with the way things were working out. Karen wouldn't be pleased, but there you go. 'So maybe you weren't trying to fuck me over. You were trying to smooth things out and that takes time. I can understand that.'

'Thanks.'

He gave me beaming. He was wearing a blousy white tuxedo shirt, black jeans, and black leather jump boots. The boots hadn't been polished in about three hundred years. 'I knew you were on my team. You're my kind of guy. We're two of a kind.'

I spread my hands. Two of a kind.

James L. Grady cleared his throat. 'You need me for anything else, Mr. Nelsen?'

Peter said, 'You got the address on my kid?'

Grady took a small spiral notepad from his jacket, tore out a sheet, and handed it to him. 'Yes, sir. Home and work addresses for the ex-wife.'

Peter gave the slip of paper to Nick without looking at it. 'Terrific, Grady. You're on the A list, just like Cole. A couple of A-team players.' He made another little hand gesture to Nick. 'Pay'm off, Nickster. Give'm something extra for the good work.'

Grady said, 'Just what we agreed to, Mr. Nelsen. I don't need extra.'

'Whatever.'

James L. started out with Nick, then turned back and looked at me. 'Good work finding the woman, Cole. I'll see you around.'

'Sure.'

He went out.

Peter strutted around the room, giving everyone more of the beam job. 'I'm excited. I'm jazzed. I'm ready for action.' He strode to the bar and picked up the phone. 'This is Peter Alan Nelsen. Have my cars ready in five minutes.' He hung up before whomever he had spoken to could answer, then he addressed the room. 'Everybody get ready. We're going to see my kid.'

I said, 'Peter, I know you want to see your son, but going out there like this isn't the way to do it. The boy doesn't know you're here.'

'I'll tell him.'

'He doesn't even know that you're his father. He needs to be prepared.'

Peter stopped grinning and frowned at me. 'What are you talking about? What does he need to prepare for? I'm not some kinda test.'

'Peter, think about it. The smart way is to take it slow. You don't want to screw it up with Toby before you begin.'

The frown got deeper. 'What are you saying? Are you telling me not to go?'

Dani said, 'Maybe we should let them know. It's not polite to just barge in.'

Peter said, 'Goddamnit, what's the big deal? He's my son, isn't he? She's my ex-wife, isn't she? How come everybody's turning against me?'

Dani said, 'Nobody's turning against you, Peter.'

I said, 'It's better if you wait. Let me set up a meeting with Karen.'

Peter suddenly made the big smile again and came over and pounded me on the back. 'You wanna set up a meeting, that's okay by me. Tell her Peter Alan Nelsen is back. Tell her I came three thousand miles to see my kid and I'm on my way. She's gonna be thrilled. The kid's going to be thrilled. Why wouldn't they?' He slapped me on the back again and then he told everybody he was going to take a leak and after that they would leave.

I said, 'But, Peter.'

He waved his hands. 'Trust me on this. I know people. I know the human heart. It's why I'm me.' Then he strode out of the room. Whistling.

I took a deep breath, let it out, then went over to where Dani was standing with the Nickster and T.J. The Nickster said, 'Hey, the guy's happy. Why you wanna piss on his parade?' Dani just looked at me the way you look at someone when you want him to help you.

I said, 'I'll call his ex-wife and let her know. There's a Howard Johnson's just off the freeway outside of Chelam. Neutral territory. Have him come there, to the restaurant. That's where she'll be.'

Dani nodded. 'I'll try.'

I strode out of the room, too, but I wasn't whistling.

CHAPTER 22

I went down to the lobby and used a pay phone by the men's room to call Karen Lloyd at the bank. It was not a call that I wanted to make. 'Yes?'

'It's me. Peter's in New York. He hired another detective who followed me to you. He knows where you live and he's coming out there now.'

She took a deep breath, then let it out with a soft hiss. 'My God. He's coming to Chelam now? Right now?'

'Yes.'

'We can't just spring it on Toby like this. Toby doesn't know anything. He'll be terrified. I don't want Peter coming to the house.'

'I've arranged for him to meet you at the Howard Johnson's. I'm leaving ahead of him so I'll be with you when he gets there.'

'That sonofabitch. Can't you stop him?'

'I thought about shooting him, but that seemed a bit drastic.'

'Not to me.' She didn't say anything for a while. 'Did you tell him about the DeLucas?'

'No. That's up to you, but he's going to know sooner or later.'

'That bastard.'

'Stay focused on DeLuca. We can talk to Peter. We can find a way to work it out.'

She said, 'Oh, that's shit,' and then she hung up. She didn't sound as thrilled as Peter had said she'd be, but maybe that was just me.

When I got to the Ho Jo it was four minutes after three that afternoon, bright and clear and smelling of autumn. Karen Lloyd and Joe Pike were sitting at a table in the front of the bar. Karen was wearing a maple pants suit and pale red lip gloss and she seemed calm and contained, but it was the kind of calm you feel in a hospital waiting room. This early, they were the only two people in the bar.

Karen said, 'Where is he?'

'A few minutes behind me. Did you meet Charlie?'

She gave me annoyed. 'No. I said that I wouldn't, didn't I?' She was holding a tall glass with something clear in it. 'I don't want to talk about that. All I can think about is Toby. I'll have to sit down with him tonight. I'll have to tell him about his father. It's all happening so fast.' She made a little head shake and had some of the drink.

'You may not want to talk about Charlie, but we need to. He's your more serious problem.'

'It doesn't feel that way.'

'It will.' I told her about Walter Lee Balcom and Angelette Silver. 'Did Charlie call to find out why you didn't show up?'

'No.'

'Did anyone who looked suspicious come into the bank, or watch you from a car, or follow you?'

'Of course not.'

I looked at Pike. He shook his head.

Karen said, 'You were watching?'

Pike nodded.

Even more annoyed. 'I didn't see you. I didn't know you were spying.'

Pike made a little head shrug.

Karen tapped at the table, then took more of the drink. Not a happy lady. Feeling the control slip away, but trying to make the best of it. 'All right. But I would think that your going to see Charlie and my standing up to him finally convinced him that I'm serious.'

Pike said, 'It's not over.'

Karen frowned at him. 'He can't want to make a stink about this any more than I. If I get in trouble, he gets in trouble. Isn't that right?'

I said, 'Guys like Charlie don't let it go.'

She made the little head shake again and closed her eyes. 'I'm sorry, but I just can't deal with this. I've got Peter to think about. I've got Toby. My God, how am I going to tell him that yesterday he didn't have a father but today he does?'

Pike leaned forward. 'Tell him you've got some good news.'

Karen closed her eyes again and said, 'Please.'

Four minutes later, Peter arrived. At first I thought that maybe Rommel and his Panzers were pouring through the pass, but then I realized it was Peter. Two black presidential stretch limos followed T.J. riding point on a candy-apple-red Harley-Davidson cop house special, T.J. in a heavy buckskin coat and World War I aviator's goggles, circling the parking lot and revving his engine as the two presidentials skidded in. Peter Alan Nelsen climbed out from behind the wheel of the first limo and the Nickster climbed out of the second. The waitress and the bartender went to the windows to look. Karen looked at them looking and chewed at her lip.

Dani and a couple of scared-looking guys in formal black chauffeur suits got out of the back of the first limo. Everybody could have easily fit into one, but why have one when you can have two?

I watched Karen Lloyd–once–Karen–Nelsen watch them and I touched her arm. 'It's going to be fine.'

'Of course it's going to be fine.' She took a sip of her drink.

Peter came in first, with Dani beside him and Nick

and T.J. sort of behind. Karen folded her hands neatly on the table in front of her and watched Peter the way you watch someone in the next yard, sort of detached. For a moment they looked at each other across the room, then Peter walked over and stopped at the edge of the table. 'Hi, Karen.'

'Hello, Peter.' Her face was without expression and she did not stand up.

I said, 'This is Dani. That's Nick and T.J.'

Everybody nodded and said howareyas. When Karen looked at Dani, Dani's big thighs jumped.

Peter sat down and Dani pulled up a chair from the next table. Nick and T.J. went to the bar. Peter looked at Joe Pike and said, 'Who's this?'

'Joe Pike. He has the agency with me. Remember?'

Peter looked back at Karen. 'It's been a long time, Karen. You look great.'

Karen nodded politely. 'Thank you.'

The waitress came out from behind the bar. 'What's everybody having?'

Peter said, 'I want a Budweiser. The guys at the bar, they're with me so give'm whatever they want.' He gestured at Karen's drink. 'What's that?'

'Vodka tonic.'

'Give her another.'

Karen said, 'No. Thank you.'

Peter said, 'You don't want another?'

'No. But thank you.' She pronounced the words slowly and carefully, as if she and the chair were in balance but the words might upset that balance. 'I'd rather do what we have to do, so that I can get back to the bank.'

Peter looked confused. 'It's over ten years.'

Dani said, 'I'll have a Perrier, please.'

The waitress eyed Peter past her order pad. She hadn't written anything down. 'You look like someone.'

I said, 'Bring the Bud and the Perrier, okay?'

The waitress put her hand on the side of her neck and rolled her eyes in recognition. 'You're the guy who makes movies. I saw you on *Arsenio*.'

Karen's jaw knotted.

The waitress said, 'You're Peter Alan Nelsen!'

Karen's jaw knotted harder and the corners of her mouth pulled down.

Peter nodded, turning on the smile. 'That's right. In the living 3-D.'

'Wow.'

Karen said, 'Oh, for Christ's sake,' and glared at the waitress. 'We're trying to have a discussion here, and you're not part of it.'

'You don't have to get snippy.'

'And you don't have to act like some sort of idiotic teeny-bopper. Just bring the drinks.'

The waitress gave Karen the ice treatment and went over to Nick and T.J.

Peter said, 'Jesus Christ, she probably just wanted an autograph or something.'

'She can get it later. I'm the vice-president and manager of the bank here, and I am a mother. I have responsibilities. I can't waste my time.'

Peter looked like a little kid who'd just been told to go to bed and didn't like it.

Karen said, 'I know you want to see Toby, but I'd rather you wait. He doesn't know that you're here and he doesn't know who you are or anything about you. Give me this evening to talk to him and then you can see him tomorrow.'

Peter liked that even less.

Karen said, 'If you come out now, you'll just scare him.'

Peter shook his head. 'Hell, what's he got to be scared of?'

I said, 'Any child would be scared, Peter. One day he's

comfortable with his life, the next a strange man walks up to him and says, hi, I'm your old man. Everything he knows changes, and everything becomes an unknown. Do you see?'

Peter frowned and sort of pooched out his lips. 'Whose side are you on?'

'The kid's. I'm also on yours and Karen's.'

Dani said, 'You've seen this kind of thing a lot, haven't you?'

I nodded. 'A couple of hundred times.'

Peter made a big deal out of sighing. Disappointed that he wasn't going to see his kid. 'Shit.'

Karen said, 'I'll tell him this evening, Peter, and that way he has the night to get used to the idea and maybe even excited about meeting you. Then you can meet him tomorrow. You can come to the house. If it goes well, the two of you might go to dinner. You could take him to Dasher's in Brunly. It's his favorite.'

'All right. Sure.' Peter was starting to nod, thinking that it sounded pretty good.

Karen said, 'One thing.'

'What?'

She looked at Dani, then at Nick and T.J. 'It would be less threatening if it were just the two of you.'

'Me and Dani?'

'You and Toby.'

Dani shifted uncomfortably in her chair. Peter leaned back and looked uncertain. 'I never go anywhere without the guys. What if I get mobbed?'

Karen flattened her hands on the table. 'You're not going to get mobbed in my home, believe me.'

Peter looked at me, even more uncertain. I nodded. He made a little shrug and then he looked back at Karen. 'Okay. That sounds fine. That sounds like you've got it all figured out.'

She gave him the flat, cool, vee-pee eyes. 'I do. I've

been figuring it out for the past ten years, so I'm good at it.'

Peter nodded again. 'Okay. If that's the way you want to play it. We can check in here. It'll be fine.' This wasn't Peter Alan Nelsen. The real Peter Alan Nelsen had stayed in the city and this was Mr. Reasonable, Peter Alan Nelsen's alter ego. Sure. That was it.

The waitress went through a little swinging door they have behind the bar and came back with a fat guy and a skinny black guy with a marcel. She pointed at Peter. Karen watched them for a moment, then said something under her breath and stood. She looked tired again, the way she had the night before when we were going through the bank records and Toby had come out. She said, 'Thank you for meeting me here instead of coming to the bank, Peter. And thanks for waiting to see Toby. If we continue to cooperate, I know this all will work out to the good.'

Peter looked surprised when she stood, and he took her forearm. 'Hey, where you going?'

Karen stiffened as if someone had thrown a switch and she didn't look tired anymore. She looked hard and bright and she stared at his hand without moving.

Peter said, 'What?'

Karen's eyes flicked up from the hand to Peter's left eye and held there. Locked on.

Peter gave embarrassed and let go her forearm. 'Sorry.'

Karen nodded once, giving him okay, then gathered her purse. 'I have work.'

'That's it? We don't see each other for ten years, and you have work? I've got a lot to tell you. I'll bet you've got questions.'

Karen shook her head and smiled at me. 'Do you see?'

Peter said, 'What's the smile?'

Karen held her purse with both hands and let out a deep breath and looked at him. She said, 'Peter, I'm not the same person you knew. I'm not a little bubblehead who wants to be an actress and is impressed when you talk about image density and emotional composition. I'm also not impressed by your success. I don't want your money.'

'Hey, who said you did?' Defensive.

'Because I'm not the same, I won't respond to you the way I used to. If I had never seen you again, it would've been fine. But you're Toby's father, and Toby has a right to meet you and know you and judge for himself. I'll work to that end, but don't expect anything more.'

Peter made a big deal out of spreading his hands. 'I don't understand this hostility.'

'Think about it.'

He said, 'Hey, I'm not looking to get you into the sack. We were married, for Christ's sake. That should mean something. We have a son.'

She stared down at him, her face without thought or consideration. 'No, we don't,' she said. 'I do.'

She brushed past me and walked across the bar and out the door.

Peter stared after her, his face sort of pinched and confused, and then he shook his head. 'I can't believe it. She didn't look happy to see me.'

'She wasn't.'

He looked at me. 'Maybe you were right. Maybe I should play this a little easier.' He was nodding to himself. 'You've seen this a lot. You know about this.'

'Sure.'

'Okay, you were right. Peter Alan Nelsen can admit when he was wrong and you were right.'

I spread my hands.

He suddenly leaned forward and looked hopeful again. 'This didn't go too badly between me and Karen, did it? Not for a first meeting?'

I shook my head. 'No,' I said. 'It went great. She could've shot you.'

CHAPTER 23

Pike and I had an early dinner, then went back to our rooms for a fun-filled evening of TV news and East Coast sports. Peter and Dani and Nick and T.J. took three adjoining rooms on the opposite side of the Ho Jo, but didn't join us for the dinner or for the sports. They left in both of the limousines. Taking advantage of the night life, no doubt.

Word of Peter's presence spread, and a news crew from a local television station came out and poked around. A tall thin woman was the on-camera talent. You could tell because she walked fast and every place she went, a short pudgy guy with a minicam followed. Seeking the truth. A few minutes after they got there, a carload of high-school kids cruised by, too. Running down rumors. The tall thin woman interviewed the high-school kids. Truth is where you find it. After that, everybody left. Not much news to be had sitting around a Ho Jo.

The next morning Karen Lloyd phoned me at seven-fifteen. Joe Pike was already gone. She said, 'I've spoken with Toby. Tell Peter to be at my home at four o'clock this afternoon.' Her voice sounded tired and strained, as if she hadn't gotten much sleep.

'How'd it go?'

'How do you think?' She hung up.

I called Peter Nelsen's room. On the fourth ring Dani answered. I told her about being at Karen Lloyd's at four. She said that she would tell Peter and then she asked if I would like to have breakfast with them. I said that I had things to do, but that I appreciated the offer. There was a little pause and then she said that it might go better this afternoon if I was at Karen's with them. I told her that I would be. She thanked me. She thanked people a lot. I hung up, showered, dressed, ate a short stack of Howard Johnson pancakes and two poached eggs, then drove back to the city to seek out Angelette Silver.

Your Secret Garden was a small shop on 122nd Street between a shoe-repair place and a Rexall Drug Store, along the eastern edge of Morningside Heights, just above the West Side.

As you go north through the West Side, climbing through the nineties and passing into the hundreds, white faces give way to Hispanic and black, and by the time I got to 110th, I was the only white guy around. I kept thinking of Natalie Wood and Richard Beymer, but no one was dancing down the streets singing *When you're a Jet*. I guess they didn't think much of George Chakiris.

A little bell rang when I went into the flower shop. Your Secret Garden was cool and humid and alive with the sights and smells of flowers and greenery and planting soil and soft classical music from tiny Bose speakers hanging from the ceiling. In the front of the shop there were cans of fresh flowers sitting on risers and a refrigerated cooler with glass doors showing ready-made floral arrangements. There was a little counter about halfway back with a workspace behind it where a black man and a black woman maybe in her sixties were building a flower arrangement. The black man was maybe five-eight, with the long arms and ropey neck of a guy who could've fought welterweight. An FTD sign sat on the counter.

In the front of the shop a slender black woman in her late twenties was arranging baby's breath in a can filled with daisies. She was wearing green pants and a light blue smock like orderlies wear. When the little bell rang, the man and the older woman in the back and the slender woman with the daisies glanced up at me and stared. The man gave me hard eyes for a time, then went back to working on his arrangement. Wouldn't see many white guys in here.

The slender woman came over and smiled. 'May I help you?' She was pretty except for a two-inch scar splitting the left side of her upper lip and two smaller scars cutting the brow above her left eye. They weren't old scars. A little name tag on her smock read *Sarah*.

I said, 'Hello, Angelette. My name is Elvis Cole. I need to talk to you about Charlie DeLuca.'

Her smile fell away faster than a sinking heart. She glanced at the man behind the counter, then back at me. The man was staring at us. He couldn't hear, but he knew something wasn't right. She said, 'You the police?'

I said, 'Charlie DeLuca's holding a woman I know. She wants out, and I'm trying to find a way to make him let go.'

She glanced again at the man behind the counter and made her voice low. The man stepped away from the flowers he was working with and wiped his hands on a gray cloth. She said, 'We don't talk about that. If you not the police, you better get out of here.'

'You were with Charlie, weren't you?'

Looking at the floor now. 'I was with a lot of men. William was in Dannemora and I had three kids to feed.'

'Sure. It must've been tough.'

She looked up, angry. 'William been out nine months and he's stayin' out. We both out. We got a man let us run this place.'

I nodded. The shop was a nice shop. Clean and fresh. Not like Dannemora. Not like walking the streets. I said, 'Charlie hurt your eye?'

'That's no never mind.'

175

'You know a guy named Richie?'

'I don't know nobody.'

William put his hands down on the cash register and gave me the jailhouse stare. The older woman came up behind him and put a hand on his right forearm that he didn't seem to feel. They couldn't hear us, but they knew what we were talking about. Funny, how that works. I said, 'My friend has a child, too, Angelette. She's got a life that she doesn't want to lose, just like you don't want to lose this life.'

William pushed past the older woman and came out from behind the counter carrying a two-foot length of galvanized pipe. Even with the smock you could see the strong forearms and the hard shoulders. Dannemora weight room. 'You better get on out of here, man. She ain't on the street no more and she ain't goin' back. She don't want nothin' to do with you.'

'I just want to talk to her.'

'You ain't gonna be talkin' to nobody with this pipe upside your head.'

I took out the Dan Wesson and cocked it and pointed it at him. I didn't like coming into their lives and I didn't like pulling the gun. But I didn't like what was happening to Karen Lloyd, either. I said, 'That's her choice, William. Not yours.'

The older woman made a low moaning sound and began to wring the gray cloth, rocking herself back and forth.

I said, 'Five minutes and I'm gone, Angelette. I won't bother you again.'

William stepped closer. Guess you been to Dannemora, you're not so impressed by the gun. 'I ain't saying it twice, Mister Man. There ain't no Angelette here. There ain't no bad things here.'

Angelette looked up at me for a time, then nodded once to herself, like maybe she'd seen something she could live with or couldn't live without. 'You got deliveries to make, William. Why don't you get to'm.'

William's eyes got wider and he pointed the pipe at me. 'He ain't nothin' here. He ain't the police. You ain't got to talk to him.'

She was looking at him steadily, and when she spoke, her voice was soft. 'He's trying to help his lady, William. What you gonna do, hit him with that pipe? You get violated, then what? You be back in Dannemora, where I'm gonna be then, makin' more dirty movies?'

'Don't you say that.'

'Workin' those streets again?'

'Don't you say that.' He blinked hard twice, then looked down at her as if it had taken a physical effort to move his eyes from her to me.

She said, 'Make your deliveries, William. When you get back, he'll be gone and everything gonna be just like it was before. Please, William.'

The older woman said, 'You better listen to her, William. You do like she say, now.' The older woman was still back behind the counter, looking scared and wringing the gray cloth and rocking.

William stared down at Angelette for a little longer, then the jailyard eyes softened and he turned and walked back behind the counter and through the little work area and out the back door.

Angelette watched him until he was gone, then took a deep breath and let it out, as if with his leaving some inner tension within her had been removed. 'It hurts him that I had to do what I did while he was away. It shames him.'

'He loves you very much.'

'Maybe.' She took another deep breath, then looked at me. 'My name is not Angelette. Angelette a street name.'

'Okay.'

'My name is Sarah Lewis.'

'Sarah. That's nice. Nicer than Angelette.'

She crossed her arms and made a sharp little laugh that was somehow hard and pained. 'Stop talkin' trash and tell me what you want.'

'I think Charlie DeLuca's up to something that he doesn't want the rest of the family to know about. If I can find out what it is, I can make him let go of my friend.'

'I ain't seen Charlie DeLuca since before William got out. That must be five, almost six months ago.'

'How'd you meet him?'

'On the street. That's the way he likes to do it, with the street girls. He see somethin' he likes in a dirty movie, then him and his bodyguards come up here and he gets some of it.'

'He always up here with the bodyguards?'

She laughed. 'Man, he don't take a pee without them bodyguards. Got this one creepy guy, all tall and white and skinny, look like a goddamn vampire.' Good old Ric.

'You hear the bodyguards say anything?'

She shook her head. 'No. They stay down in the car while we up in the room. You know.'

I said, 'A guy named Richie might know something. I think he supplies Charlie with the movies.'

She thought for a second, then shook her head. 'I don't know no Richie.'

'Did Charlie ever talk business with you?'

'Not the kind of business you talkin' about.' The older woman was working with the flowers, carefully turned away.

'He ever complain about anything to you, like what a crummy day it was, like how a big deal went bad?'

'Look, I know what you want, but it wasn't like that. Charlie takes a liking to a girl, he comes around a lot and he spends big, but he don't stay around too long. He never stayed with a girl longer than three weeks. He likes to hurt and you complain one time too much and then he beats the hell out of you and moves on.'

'He never said anything about what he does?'

'No.'

I said, 'You know any of his other ladies?'

'Just to see. You know, out on the street, walkin' around. We'd be on the corner, we'd talk about him.' She brushed at her mouth, past the big scar. 'It's pretty easy to tell who he been with.'

'You know who he's with, now?'

Her eyes flashed hot. 'How I know that? You think we stay in touch? You think Mr. Charlie send me love letters?'

'It's important, Sarah. Could you find out?'

She crossed her arms again and stared at me, maybe thinking she'd had enough of this, but then maybe thinking she'd come this far. She uncrossed the arms and went behind the little counter and used the phone. While she spoke, the older woman sneaked glances at me between a spray of lilacs.

Sarah Lewis put down the phone, then came back and said, 'He seeing some gal named Gloria Uribe. She lives over on 136th, up above a bar called Clyde's.'

'Thanks, Sarah. I appreciate the help.'

'Won't do no good, you talkin' with her, though. She'll be too scared to say anything, even if she knows more than me. Any girl with Charlie is that way.' Sarah brushed at the lip again, as if it itched. It was a bad scar, the kind that comes from a deep cut. When Charlie hit her, he had hit her hard, and probably more than once.

I went to the door.

'You really think you gonna find a way to put the hurt on Charlie DeLuca?'

'Yeah,' I said. 'I do.'

She squinted at me from the hurt eye, then made one

of the nods to herself again and opened the door. 'All right. You find a way to hurt him, you hurt him a little bit extra. You hurt him for Angelette Silver, you hear?'

The older woman had stopped pretending to work and was staring at me. I nodded at her, then looked back at Sarah Lewis.

'I was planning to.'

The older woman smiled and turned away, and I left.

CHAPTER 24

Clyde's was a knothole of a bar in the bottom of a four-story building that was mostly fire escapes and clotheslines. Three or four women in tiny red dresses and rabbit coats sat listlessly at the bar while a couple of guys in long coats leaned against a Pontiac out front laughing about something. One of the guys had a gap in his teeth like Mike Tyson.

I put the Taurus across the street in a bus stop, then walked back. The two guys kept laughing but watched me come. There were no more white guys up here than there were down on 122nd Street. If I were them, I'd probably watch me, too.

I went into a little open stairwell next to Clyde's and found the apartment-house mailboxes. *G. Uribe* was on box 304.

The guy with Mike Tyson's teeth looked in at me and said, 'Say, man, who you lookin' for?'

'Gloria Uribe. She around?'

'Naw, she workin'. She better be, she know what's good for her.'

'You her business manager?'

'Naw, man, she Haitian or Cuban or somedamnthing like that. They got their own people to take care of'm. I got somethin' on the fourth floor just as good, though. No waitin'.'

'No, thanks,' I said. 'My heart belongs to Gloria.'

He said, 'Shee-it, you the poe-lice, all right.' His buddy laughed and they knocked fists.

I gave him the okay-we-both-know-I'm-a-cop face. 'What's your name, homeboy?'

'Luther.'

'Luther, make a friend on the force. Gloria do a good business?'

'Fair to middlin'.'

'White guys?'

Luther nodded and winked at his friend. 'You sniffin' 'round 'bout that gangster with the big car. You from Organized Crime?'

'Maybe.' Maybe. Did Eliot Ness say maybe? 'Tell me about the big car. He here often?'

'Two, three times a week.'

'There any pattern to when he comes around?'

Luther gave me pained. 'Man, all these questions grinding my brain, you know?'

'Unh-hunh.'

I dug out a twenty and passed it to him. He didn't look impressed. 'Tha's pretty thin pickin's.'

'It's the budget crunch, Luther.'

'I hear that.' He made the twenty disappear. 'He came around twice last week. On Tuesday, then again Friday. Usually a Friday.' He looked at his friend and the friend nodded.

I said, 'What do the bodyguards do while he's with Gloria?'

'Shee-it, he ain't had his posse around in three months.'

I looked at him. 'He's been seeing Gloria Uribe for three months?'

'Hell, he been coming around longer than that.' Luther squinted at his friend again. 'What, four, five months now?'

The friend nodded, unh-hunh.

Luther looked back at me.

I said, 'He's been seeing Gloria Uribe for maybe five months, and when he comes, he comes alone?'

Luther frowned and gave me the heavy-eyelid treatment. 'How many times I gotta say it, a lousy twenty bucks.'

Luther's friend yawned and stared at something down the street.

I thought about it. In my business, you look for things that are out of the ordinary because out of the ordinary things usually mean clues. Sarah Lewis had said that Charlie DeLuca never stayed with a woman for longer than three weeks and that he never went anywhere without bodyguards. Of course, that was a long time ago and maybe Charlie had changed his ways. Maybe Charlie and Gloria were in love and all the getting together without bodyguards was to discuss wedding plans. Then again, maybe not.

I said, 'Luther, Gloria just a streetwalker, or does she do outcall?'

'She walkin' when times are hard. Things looking better, she be strictly outcall. You can tell when she outcall, 'cause her nose in the air.'

Luther's friend laughed like hell.

A white Caddie DeVille pulled to the curb and a slender, mocha-colored young woman in a tight dress and black-and-white cowboy boots got out. The Caddie's driver was an Asian guy in his fifties. She said something to him, then glanced at Luther and went into Clyde's. Luther frowned after her. 'I got business to tend to.'

'Thanks for the help, Luther. I appreciate it.'

'Just don't say nuthin' 'round that wop gangster. I don't wanna wind up on no pizza.'

'Sure, Luther. Count on it.'

Luther and his buddy disappeared into Clyde's.

I walked up the two flights to the third floor and down a short hall to 304 and knocked. No answer. Somewhere at the other end of the hall a baby was crying, and somewhere else a rapper was banging out a gangster line. Ice-T. *Drama*. No sounds came from within Gloria Uribe's apartment. I knocked again, then took out the wires I keep in my wallet and let myself in.

Gloria Uribe had a one-bedroom with a bath and a tiny kitchenette. The walls were discolored and paint was peeling from the ceiling, but it wasn't an unclean place. A tattersall sofa with a beaded slipcover sat opposite a Victorian china cabinet that had been polished a deep, purple mahogany. The kitchenette and the bath were neat and clean, and the bedroom was a spotless vision in pink: pink satin comforter, pink Princess telephone, pink lace pillows, pink walls and ceiling. She had even found a pink clock-radio, which sat next to the bed on a nightstand. The nightstand was brown.

I wanted to find her trick book. Streetwalkers don't keep them because they don't have regular customers, but call girls do. They use the book to keep track of their appointments and such details of their trade as client preference and past fees. If I found Gloria's trick book, I would know when Charlie DeLuca was with her and when he wasn't and what they did when they were together. I might even learn what was going on.

I started with the nightstand, then looked behind and beneath the bed and between the mattress and the box springs. I found two boxes of Softique tissues, one open, the other not, and a box of Trojan prophylactics, ribbed. I went through her vanity and a small chest of drawers with a forest of little knickknacks on top. Bottom drawer of the chest, there were a black snakeskin whip, a black vinyl body harness, two pairs of police-issue handcuffs, and a black rubber mask with a couple of little holes that I guess you were supposed to breathe through. Nice.

I looked through the rest of her bedroom and her closet and then I went into her bathroom. The trick book was wrapped in a freezer-strength Baggie and taped to the underside of her lavatory, along with a little vial of crack cocaine. It had taken me exactly eight minutes and forty seconds to find it. Cops probably do it in less.

I took the book out into the living room, sat on the couch, and looked through it. There were entries dating back ten months to the beginning of the year, and sure enough, exactly five months and one week ago, there was the first mention of Charlie DeLuca. He had seen Gloria on three consecutive days the first week they had met, then five times the following week. The notes were mostly abbreviations, but the abbreviations were obvious. I read them and tried to feel detached and professional, but all I managed was smarmy and embarrassed. None of the notes related to Charlie's business or to anything Charlie might've said about his business.

I looked through every day of every week up until the present and noticed that starting in the fifth week, whenever Charlie's name appeared, another name appeared, too. Santiago.

Hmm.

I flipped back to the beginning of the book again and this time went through looking for *Santiago*. His first mention was during that fifth week, with Charlie. Maybe Charlie had brought him along. I kept looking. Sometimes Gloria wrote the full name, sometimes she just wrote *S*. For the next few weeks, every time there was an *S*, there was also Charlie's name, but after that sometimes there was just the *S*. Luther had said that Charlie had been around last Tuesday and Friday, but there was no mention of him on those days in the book, just Santiago. Maybe Charlie didn't come around to see Gloria anymore and maybe that's why she didn't list him. Maybe he came to see Santiago.

Hmm, again.

Santiago was penciled in for tomorrow at four-thirty

in the afternoon. A Friday. Hmm. Charlie wasn't scheduled, but that was okay. Neither was I.

I closed the trick book, put it back in its plastic bag, then retaped it beneath the lavatory in Gloria Uribe's bathroom and let myself out. When I got down to the street, Luther and his friend were back leaning against the Pontiac. Luther grinned when he saw me, flashing more of the Mike Tyson teeth. I said, 'Luther, you know a guy named Santiago, comes around here sometime?'

Luther stopped grinning and shook his head. 'I don't want no part of that.' He pushed off the Pontiac and walked past me into Clyde's.

I looked after him, and then I looked at Luther's friend. Luther's friend shrugged.

I said, 'What was that all about?'

Luther's friend said, 'Santiago's her pimp. Few years ago, when she come here, Luther try to get her in his stable and Luther and Santiago have a thing. Santiago 'bout kill Luther. Stick him with an ice pick.'

'Oh.' Great. 'He run any other girls around here?'

'Nah. He been moving up. He some kind of Jamaican gangster now, and he doin' real well. Drives a nice car, wears a fine cut of clothes. I think Luther feelin' jealous.'

'Hunh.'

Luther's friend pushed off the Pontiac. 'I better see about Luther. You don't see about him when he get like this, he sulks.'

'Right. Thanks for the help.'

Luther's friend went into Clyde's.

It was two-forty-five. Still plenty of time to get back to Karen's by four.

I took my time walking back to the Taurus, remembering what Roland George had told me about the Italian mafia hating the Jamaicans and the Cubans and the Asians. Maybe I was on to something. Maybe this was a clue. Maybe if I could ferret out its true and hidden meaning, Karen Lloyd and Toby Lloyd and Peter Alan Nelsen could all live happily ever after. Just like in a movie.

For all of the drive back to Chelam, I wondered what Charlie DeLuca might be doing with a Jamaican gangster named Santiago. All I had to do was find out what.

CHAPTER 25

I got back to Karen Lloyd's home at twenty minutes before four that afternoon. Karen's LeBaron sat in the drive, but Toby's red Schwinn mountain bike wasn't leaning in its spot against the garage. I parked on the street to leave room for Peter. Karen answered the door in a long beige skirt and a sea-green top with a large ornate necklace that looked like something a Zulu chieftain might wear. Her makeup was freshly applied. She said, 'Thank God you're not Peter.'

'Yes. I've often thought that myself.'

'I'm trying to get the place straight.'

The carpet had been vacuumed and the magazines on the hearth tidied and the pictures on the mantel dusted and arranged symmetrically according to size, the largest frames centered around the Early American electric clock, the smallest at the ends. Pike was sitting at the table, sipping tea and staring at the world through his dark, expressionless glasses. I said, 'Where's Toby?'

Karen said, 'School. He wanted to stay home, but I said no.'

'Okay.'

'I told him that our lives weren't going to stop because of this. I said that we're still going to be the same people and live here and that he would go to the same school and still have basketball practice.'

I looked at Pike and Pike raised his eyebrows. I guess it had been like this all afternoon. I said, 'Consistency is important.'

'That's right. It is.'

She stood in the center of the room, left hand on her left hip and right hand under her chin, inspecting plant location and knickknack placement.

'Are you nervous?'

'Certainly not. I'm tense. That's different.' She glanced at the Early American electric, then at her watch. Whatever she saw there didn't agree, so she went to the mantel and added two minutes to the Early American. She straightened a copy of *Good Housekeeping* that was on an end table next to the couch, picked up a piece of thread from the rug, then went down the hall and into her bedroom. There was a quality of tension to the way she moved that I hadn't seen before.

Pike said, 'News crew came to the bank, sniffing around about what she was doing at the Ho Jo with Peter Alan Nelsen. She had the guard throw them out.'

'Ah.'

'She left early and came home. She's been cleaning all day.'

'She's scared. Someone who threatens her sense of identity is about to invade her home.'

'Awful lot of cleaning for someone about to invade your home.'

'The zen of housecleaning allows one to reach inner peace.'

Pike nodded again and sipped more tea. 'I've always found that to be true.'

I went into the kitchen, made a cup of coffee, then went back into the dining room and sat down with Pike. Karen came out of the hall, stared at the living room for thirty seconds, then went back down the hall. Zen.

I said, 'Charlie make contact today?'

Pike shook his head.

'I don't like it. Guys like Charlie don't let it go. They

freak out and try to teach you a lesson. He must be working something.'

Pike nodded. 'You get anything?'

I told him about Gloria Uribe and the Jamaican. Pike said, 'The mob doesn't mix with those guys.'

I shook my head. 'Nope.'

Pike said, 'Hmm.'

At eight minutes before four a black stretch limo came roaring up the street and pulled into the drive. I said, 'They're here.'

Karen came back down the hall and went to the window. The sea-green top had been replaced by an elegant black sweater and a small but tasteful string of pearls.

Car doors slammed and Karen stepped away from the window. She drew herself up and placed her hands at her sides. 'Damnit, I was hoping Toby would get here early.' She seemed pale, but maybe it was the light.

I said, 'Let's hide and pretend no one's home.'

'Very funny.'

I'm a riot, you get me going.

She stood in the center of the room and did not move until the doorbell rang. Then she looked at me and said, 'I will bet you twenty-five million dollars that the first thing he says will mark him as an asshole.'

'Why be defeatist?'

The doorbell rang again, and she walked to the door and opened it. Peter stalked in with Dani behind him. Nick and T.J. had been left at home. Peter said, 'Jesus Christ, you really live out in the goddamn sticks, don't you?'

Karen gave me the flat eyes. 'You see?'

The room felt smaller with them in it and the ceiling no longer felt high and peaked. Peter looked around like he was thinking of buying the place, and Dani stood to the side, sort of out of the way, one hand holding the other.

Karen said, 'Would either of you care for something? I have soft drinks and beer and I made iced tea.' The corners of her mouth were tight.

Dani said, 'No, thank you.'

Peter said, 'I'll take a brewski. You got a Bud?'

Karen went into the kitchen without saying anything.

Peter winked at me and smiled. 'She's doing okay, isn't she? If you'd known her back in L.A., you'd never believe it.'

I said, 'Peter. Go easy on that.'

He looked confused. 'What?'

Karen came back with a bottle of St. Pauli Girl and a glass and a napkin on a Dansk tray. Peter took the bottle but not the glass. 'You know I never use a glass.'

Karen said, 'I forgot.'

'Sure.'

Karen offered Dani a seat on the couch, then took one of the wingback chairs. I sat at the dining-room table with Joe Pike. Peter had some of the beer and went over to the mantel and looked at the pictures. It was five minutes to four and we were having just a fine ole time.

Peter said, 'Guess it was too much to hope you'd have a couple shots of me up here.'

Karen made her lips into a small hard rosebud.

'You know, for the boy.'

She looked out the window, then checked her watch.

Peter crossed the living room and sat on the other wing chair. He spread his legs under the coffee table and held the beer without drinking it. He said, 'I'm not trying to create a problem for you.'

Karen said, 'Of course.'

'I just want to know my son.'

'He should be here anytime.'

Peter nodded and drank some of the beer and didn't say

anything. Karen stared out of the window. Dani stared at the floor. Pike sat immobile, safely hidden behind the dark glasses. Maybe if I asked he would loan the glasses to me and I could pretend I wasn't here, either. I made a little face at him to see if he was looking, but he didn't react, so maybe he wasn't. Of course, he might be pretending that he wasn't. You never know with Pike.

At ten minutes after four Peter said, 'I thought the kid was supposed to be here at four.'

Karen leaned forward a fraction of an inch. 'Don't call him "the kid." His name is Toby.'

Peter spread his hands and nodded and stared off into space some more.

At fourteen minutes after four Karen's orange and white cat came out of the hall, walked across the living room, and sniffed at Peter. Peter reached down to pet it, then thought better of it and drew back his hand. Guess the scratches hadn't healed from before.

At twenty-two minutes after four Karen looked at her watch, then at the Early American clock, then frowned. Toby should've been home.

At twenty-eight minutes after four Peter put his hands on his knees and stood up and said, 'What the hell is this? Is the boy coming or not?'

Karen stood up with him and her nostrils were tight. 'He's having a hard time, Peter. He was nervous about meeting you. He didn't sleep well and he's scared.'

'What'd you tell him about me, that I eat rat turds?'

Karen made a hissing sound and went into the kitchen and picked up the phone. 'I'll call the school.'

Peter walked around in a little circle, then sat down again. Dani put a hand on his shoulder.

Six minutes later Karen came out, worried. 'They said he left forty-five minutes ago.'

I said, 'How long is the ride from school?'

'No more than ten minutes.'

Peter said, 'Jesus Christ, you think he ran away?'

Karen got her purse and her keys from the hutch in the dining room and went to the front door without saying anything. I got up with her, looking at Pike. 'I'll go with her. You hang here.'

Pike nodded, the black lenses moving just enough to catch the light.

Peter said, 'Hey, I'll come, too.'

Karen said, 'No,' and when Peter started to get up, Pike gently pushed him back down. 'Not this time.'

Peter said, 'Hey,' and tried to get up again, but Pike kept him in the chair, standing so close that Peter couldn't get the leverage to rise. Peter said, 'What in hell you doing?'

Dani stood and took a step forward, but I shook my head once and she stopped. Pike leaned down close to Peter, Pike's face maybe six inches from his, letting Peter stare into the glasses, and said, 'It's better if she goes without you.' Pike's voice was soft and even.

Peter squinted into the dark and stopped trying to get up. 'Sure.'

Karen was already climbing into the LeBaron when I got out the front door. Her back was stiff and her jaw was tight and she overcranked the engine, grinding the starter gears.

We drove to the school and circled the campus twice and then went into town and back out to the school. We took a shortcut that Karen thought Toby might've taken, but he wasn't there, either. We drove for over an hour and we saw no sign of him until we were heading back toward her house on a part of the road that was between two wide, flat fields overgrown with a heavy wild rye that was dying from the cold.

I said, 'Stop the car.'

She said, 'What?'

When the car was stopped, I got out and walked off the

road to Toby Lloyd's red Schwinn mountain bike. Its rear wheel was broken and its frame was crushed and the handlebars were bent backward and together so that the handgrips were touching and it looked the way a bike looks when it's been run over by a car.

I researched for Toby Lloyd in the high grass around the bike, but I couldn't find him.

Charlie DeLuca had finally made contact.

CHAPTER 26

Karen Lloyd got out of her car and ran to the edge of the field. When she saw the bike, her eyes got wide and she put her hands on the sides of her head and she yelled, 'Toby?' first scared and then angry, like maybe this was a bad joke and he would jump out and yell boo. She pushed past me into the rye and the timothy and the pumpkin vines, screaming her son's name and running one way and then another. 'Toby?'

I caught her and held her and she said let go and tried to pull away. I said, 'He's not there. They wouldn't hurt him. They want you on their side and they know that if they hurt him they'll lose you.'

'I want to find him.'

'We'll find him. We'll go back to the house and wait for Charlie to call.'

'Oh my God. What am I going to do?' She was breathing hard, as if her subjective reality had suddenly been hypered on to a higher plane. 'How could they do this? How could they know?'

'There's only one school here. They probably hung around until Toby started for home and then they picked him up.'

'But his bike.'

'I don't know.'

'Did they just run over him?'

'No.'

'My God. What did they do to him?' She turned and ran back to the car and I followed.

Five minutes later we knew.

Charlie DeLuca's black Lincoln Town Car was sitting in Karen's drive behind the limo. Ric was in the passenger's side with the window down and country-and-western music on the stereo. Reba McEntire. He still had the black Ray Bans and the black spiked hair and the deathly white skin. A brand-new red Schwinn mountain bike was leaning against the garage, the price tag still on the handlebars. Karen said, 'Oh, thank God.'

Ric peeled himself out of the Town Car as we parked. He was wearing a triple-layered black leather English jacket with an acne of metal studs. When the jacket pulled open you could see something stainless-steel and shining under his left arm. The ten. 'Let's go inside.'

Karen said, 'Is my boy all right?'

'Let's go inside. Charlie's waiting.'

Karen ran toward the door, and Ric and I followed.

Peter and Dani and Toby Lloyd and Charlie DeLuca were sitting in the living room, Peter and Charlie in the two wingback chairs and Dani and Toby on the couch. Charlie DeLuca was laughing at something that Peter was saying, and they were each holding a bottle of St. Pauli Girl. Toby was sitting on the edge of the couch, hands between his knees, staring at Peter with a kind of nervous curiosity. Joe Pike was standing against the wall by the fireplace, arms crossed and weight on one foot. When Ric came in, Pike put his weight on both feet but didn't uncross his arms. Charlie DeLuca smiled at us like he was everybody's favorite uncle and said, 'Here they are, now.'

Karen went directly to Toby and gripped his upper arms and looked him in the eyes hard enough to read something written on the inside of his skull. 'Are you all right?'

'Sure, Mom.'

'Did anyone hurt you? Or threaten you?'

The boy was looking confused and embarrassed. 'What do you mean?'

Ric nodded at Pike, took off his Ray Bans, and rubbed at his eyes. Guess one pair of dark glasses in the room was enough.

Charlie smiled at me. 'You're still here, hunh? I figured for sure you'd be back ridin' Dumbo, knew what's good for you.'

I gave him a little hand shrug. 'Maybe we didn't understand each other.'

Peter was smiling, like he had a joke. 'You're not going to believe why Toby's late, Karen. Go ahead, Charlie, tell her. Listen to this.' *Go ahead, Charlie.* Old friends.

Charlie settled back in the wing chair. 'I backed over his bike at school. Can you imagine that? I felt so terrible that I waited around until he came out so I could buy him a new one. Hey, a bike is like a horse, right? You're a kid, your bike is your best friend. I felt like such a dufus.' Dufus. Putting on the show for Peter, and Peter eating it up.

Karen stared at Charlie as he said it and then she looked back at her son. 'You went with this man to buy the new bike?'

'Well, yeah. Sure.' Talking fast and knowing that he was in trouble. 'We went to Quisenberry's. He said he wanted to pay for a new bike and he asked where they sold them in town and I showed him.'

Karen looked from Toby to Charlie and then back to Toby, then she slapped him so hard that it sounded like a .22 pistol fired indoors. 'Don't you ever go away with a stranger again!'

Toby's head snapped to the side and Dani gasped and Peter said, 'Hey! What'd you do that for?'

Karen said, 'Shut the fuck up.' Her face was white now, almost as white as Ric's, and she was trembling.

Toby looked scared. 'He knew you, Mom. I thought it'd be okay.'

Charlie said, 'Tobe, I'm afraid your mom's upset and she's got a right to be. It's my fault.' Good old Uncle Charlie. He looked back at Karen, and he didn't look so much like Uncle Charlie anymore. 'All of this never would've happened if I hadn't come all the way here from the city for a meeting, and you know what? I'm stood up. I'm left hanging. I need this, right? To be insulted like this?'

Peter nodded, in perfect agreement with his new friend Charlie. 'Hey, I get a clown working on a picture does that, I set him straight.'

Charlie smiled. 'That's right, Pete. Sometimes you just gotta set people straight.'

Peter nodded again and shot a wink at his son.

Karen said, 'Toby. Go to your room and close the door.'

Toby's face darkened, but he went out. When he was gone, Karen turned to Charlie and said, 'You bastard.'

Peter gave surprised. 'Jesus Christ, Karen, the guy's apologized fifteen times. Toby's okay.'

She didn't look at Peter. Her eyes stayed with Charlie and her chest rose and fell and the skin at the corners of her mouth turned a sort of purple color under the makeup.

Charlie said, 'Believe me, I know how she feels. You warn kids about strangers, but kids are still kids, right? They make mistakes. I know how I would feel if anything happened. You wouldn't want anything to happen, would you, Karen?' Giving it to her slow.

Karen shook her head. 'No. I wouldn't want anything to happen.'

I said, 'We get the drift.'

Ric said, 'No one asked you.'

I said, 'Did anyone ever tell you you look like Herman Munster?'

Charlie's eyes made a slow-motion move from Karen to me, then he got up from the chair and walked over. A vein pulsed in his right temple. He said, 'Some guys never get it, Ric. Some guys, you tell'm and tell'm, they never get it, and they end up in trouble.'

I nodded. 'Some guys, trouble is a way of life.'

Peter was giving confused. 'What are you guys talking about?'

Charlie took another step closer. He was maybe six inches from me, red-faced and snorting, staring with eyes that were now dead and fishlike, and you could see how he got the name, Charlie the Tuna. 'You got brain damage from too much sun? You wanna go over the top right now?' His voice was a sort of a hiss.

Peter said, 'Hey, this doesn't need to get out of hand.'

Ric said, 'It's cool,' and came up behind Charlie, putting a hand on either shoulder, working him just like he had worked him with Joey Putata, whispering, talking until the snorting and the pulsing had stopped. Keeping Sal DeLuca's kid in control of himself. I wondered if they paid him extra for this.

Peter said, 'Hey, Charlie, you all right? You want a glass of water?'

The deep-sea eyes submerged and Charlie made a little move that stopped Ric. Charlie stepped back and picked up his coat and Ric held it open so that Charlie could work into it. Charlie said, 'I'm fine, Peter. Just a little misunderstanding, that's all. Misunderstandings happen.'

Peter said, 'Hey, sure.' Everything okay now.

Charlie looked at Karen again, then buttoned his coat and went to the door. 'It was a pleasure to meet you, Peter. Christ, you know *Chainsaw* is one of my favorite pictures. I bought a videocassette. Seventy-nine ninety-five. I musta seen it – what? – over a dozen times, Ric?'

Ric said, 'A dozen.'

Peter said, 'You'll never have to buy another. Give Karen a call and let her know your address. I'll send you tapes of all my movies.' He hoisted the St. Pauli Girl and made a little salute.

Charlie smiled. 'I'll give Karen a call.' Then he looked back at Karen and shook his head. 'C'mon, Ric.' Ric opened the door and they left.

Joe Pike peeled himself away from the wall and went across to the window and looked out.

Peter said, 'Jesus, I don't know why you had to make such a big deal about it, Karen. Toby's fine.'

Outside, a car door opened, then closed. Toby yelled 'Bye' from his room. Watching out his window. An engine started. A car pulled away. Pike drifted back to the wall.

Karen went through the dining room and into the kitchen, closing the door quietly after her.

Peter said, 'What's her problem?'

I left them in the living room and went to the kitchen after Karen Lloyd. She was standing at the sink, staring through the garden window at her backyard. There were little clay pots on the shelf in the window for growing herbs. Some of the pots were planted, but some of them weren't.

She said, 'The man came to my home. He actually came to my home. He was threatening my child.'

'Mobsters will do that.'

She stared at the backyard some more, and I thought she was going to cry, but she didn't. Every tendon in her body was standing out. I *will* change my life. I *will* maintain control. You had to admire it. She said, 'Oh my God, what am I doing to us? What if they had hurt my son?'

200

I reached out and touched her back. She didn't pull away. I said, 'They didn't and they won't. Charlie wants you on his side. He hurts the boy, he knows he's lost you.'

She nodded, thinking about that but not believing it. 'I want you to watch out for him. Will you do that? Will you and Mr. Pike stay with us until this is over?'

'Yes.'

She turned away from the window and looked at the door to the living room. 'I'm going to have to tell all of this.'

'I don't see any way around it.'

She closed her eyes and looked tired. 'Christ,' she said, 'that's going to be worse than dealing with Charlie.'

CHAPTER 27

I left Karen Lloyd in the kitchen and went back out into the living room. Toby had come back and was sitting on the couch with Peter. Pike was gone. Outside, probably. Peter said, 'You want to come visit me in California?'

'Sure.'

'Hey, you come out,' Peter said, 'I'll make the studio send their jet. They got this jet, it does nothing but fly jerks to places they don't need to go. The studios are scared shitless of me. I got a house in Malibu on the beach. Johnny Carson lives a couple doors down. So does Steven Spielberg and Sly Stallone and Tom Hanks. We can hang out. Won't that be great?'

'Unh-hunh.' Maybe meaning Spielberg and Stallone, maybe meaning the jet. Dani was smiling and nodding at how wonderful it would all be. Every boy's adventure come true.

Outside, I could see Pike on the driveway, palms together over his head, standing on one leg. Tree pose. Seeking focus and balance and escape from chaos. Peter said, 'What's your favorite car?'

'What do you mean?'

'I mean, what's your favorite car? You see TV, you see cars driving around, you look at magazines. You gotta have a favorite car.'

'I kinda like red cars.' He had never thought about it.

Peter spread his hands and beamed. 'Hey, you come out, we'll get a red car to drive around. How about that?'

Toby made a face like his father was speaking Venusian. 'You'll buy a car because I'm there?'

'Sure. You're my son. We'll buy a fuckin' helicopter, you want.'

Toby sort of giggled, maybe for the helicopter, but more likely because Peter had used the F word.

Peter said, 'Dani, go get the thing.'

Dani grinned and went out to the limo and came back with a couple of good-sized boxes. Peter said, 'Open'm up, champ.' Champ. Just like Ward Cleaver talking to the Beave.

Toby opened them. The boxes contained a top-of-the-line JVC professional videotape camera, a turbo-charged videotape player and electronic editor, some blank tapes, and copies of all of Peter Alan Nelsen's movies. I figured the setup would retail out at about thirteen grand, excluding the movies. Toby said, 'Wow.'

Peter patted him on the leg. 'Now you can make your own movies. Just like your old man.'

'Will you show me how?'

'Bet your ass.' Peter leaned forward and ruffled his hair. 'You're Peter Alan Nelsen's kid, and things are going to be different from now on. Your life is going to undergo *enormous* improvement.'

What a thing to say to a twelve-year-old.

Peter said, 'Whatever you want, it's yours. Anything you wanna do, we'll do it. I'm thinking about buying a couple of motorcycles so we can go riding together. Would you like that?'

'Yeah!'

When Karen came out of the kitchen, Toby said, 'Look at what Peter gave me.'

Karen didn't like it much. 'It looks expensive.'

Toby said, 'We're gonna get motorcycles. We're gonna go riding together.'

203

Karen didn't like that at all. 'Motorcycles are dangerous, Peter. Toby is too young.'

Peter said, 'I'll get'm a trail bike. We won't ride on the
street. We'll ride in the woods.'

Karen's jaw clenched and her eyes went hard. 'That's
not the point. Toby lives here. Toby lives a certain way
and too many expensive gifts will distort his values.'

I said, 'Tobe. Peter and your mom have to talk. Why
don't you go outside for a little bit.'

Peter said, 'The boy and I were just getting to know
one another.'

Karen said, 'I know, but this is important. You can get
to know each other after.'

Toby went out the front door and pretty soon there
was the *thump thump thump* of the ball on the drive.
Karen looked at Dani. 'Could we have some privacy?'

Dani flushed and said that she'd keep Toby company
and went out.

Peter said, 'What?'

Karen sat on the couch and tucked her skirt under and
stared at the man she had married when she was
seventeen years old and lived with for fourteen months.
Then she took a sharp, quick breath and told him about
her involvement with the mafia. No preamble.

Outside, the deepening twilight was purple and chill
and punctuated by the bounce of the ball and an
occasional laugh or word. I could see Dani and Toby and
most of the drive, but not the hoop. Someone would
shoot the ball and the ball would arc up, but then it
would be gone, passing from my line of sight. It didn't
matter. You could tell if they made it or not by their
faces and the sounds they made and by how the ball
rebounded. If someone ran to one side or the other, the
ball had caromed off the side of the hoop. If someone ran
fast straight ahead, they had lofted an air ball and it was
rolling into the garage. If the ball gently came back to

them or they trotted forward to the hoop, they had made a basket. You didn't see the event, you saw the results of the event. I had read a book on modern astronomy which had said that both Neptune and Pluto were predicted long before they had ever been seen because of peculiarities in the orbits of the other outer planets. It made me think that planets weren't so very different from people. Seeing what happened around them was enough to tell you where they were and what they were.

When Karen Lloyd was finished, Peter looked at me and said, 'Is this for real?'

'Yep.'

He stood up and gave impatient. 'No. I mean, is this really real? This guy who was here, Charlie, he's a criminal, he's in the *mafia*?'

I said, 'It's really real, Peter.' Something only someone in show business would have to hear. 'The DeLucas are one of the largest mafia families in New York. I've talked to Charlie about letting Karen out of the setup, but he's said no.'

Peter made a big deal out of looking around the room before he looked back at Karen. He was grinning, like this wasn't really real after all, like maybe we were clowning around. 'You're in the mafia.'

'No. I'm not in the mafia. I'm involved with the mafia.' Her voice was edged. The edge hadn't been there a few minutes ago.

'Does the boy know?'

The jaw knotted again. 'Stop calling him "the boy." He has a name.'

'Jesus Christ, all right. Toby. Does Toby know?' Now Peter was giving us irritated.

'No. This is illegal, Peter. What I'm doing is against the law. You don't tell a child something like that.'

I said, 'This is why I didn't call. We were trying to get this straightened out before I brought you in.'

Peter said, 'Jesus Christ.'

'If Karen goes to the police, she'll have to cut a deal with the states and the feds. She can do that, and her testimony will put Charlie and probably Sal away, but then she'd have to go into witness protection.'

Karen said, 'We'd have to change our names. We'd have to move and go into hiding. I won't do that to Toby or to me.'

Peter said, 'But the guy's here threatening our kid.'

I said, 'Charlie did what he did today to get a message across. He won't do anything else if Karen makes the pickups that he tells her to make and continues to launder the money.'

Karen said, 'I've asked Elvis and Mr. Pike to move in here until this is over.'

Peter blinked at me. Surprised. 'I didn't know you were staying here.'

'I wasn't staying here. I'm going to stay here *now*.'

Peter frowned, thinking about it and not liking it. 'How long is this going to take?'

I told them about Gloria Uribe and the Jamaican named Santiago, and that maybe Charlie was going to meet with Santiago sometime tomorrow.

Peter was shaking his head. 'You're gonna follow him around and hope you see a connection? Christ, that could take years.'

'It's what we can do.'

Peter went to the window. Outside, Toby passed the ball to Dani, who shot and missed. She laughed when she missed and said something that I couldn't understand. Peter said, 'All right. If that's the way things are, that's the way things are. I'll take care of it.' He was looking sort of pleased with himself.

Karen said, 'What do you mean, you'll take care of it?'

Peter made a little no-big-deal gesture with his right

206

hand. 'I'll talk to the guy. I'll pass a little cash and smooth him out. I'll take care of you, Karen.'

The skin beneath Karen's right eye began to jump. 'You'll take care of me.' Her voice was soft.

'Sure. We don't need all this running around and following.'

I said, 'Peter, this isn't some mid-level union fixer looking for a payoff.'

'I know what this guy is.' Annoyed.

I said, 'No, you don't. This guy is a professional nut case who made his bones when he was sixteen years old by killing a man. This guy is not going to do what you want because you're from Hollywood. He's *capo* of the largest crew in the DeLuca family, and one day he's going to be boss of all the other *capos*. If he wants to pal around with people from Hollywood, he'll buy a studio.'

Peter leaned toward me, giving me the Donnie Brewster treatment. 'And I'm telling you I can smooth this guy out. I come three thousand miles and find out the mafia got my family, I know what to do. I'm Peter Alan Nelsen.'

Karen leaned toward him. 'We're not your family.'

Peter's face went red and he blinked behind the thick glasses. 'Hey, I'm just trying to help. I'm just trying to take care of the boy. All this following around and waiting, something could happen. Someone could get hurt.'

Karen said, 'Elvis knows how to do this. If you come barging in, you'll mess it up.'

Peter rolled his eyes and made a big deal out of waving his hands. 'That's right, that's right. I don't know anything.' He looked at me, and then he looked at Karen, and then he shook his head. Mr. Incredulous. 'You got no idea how lucky you are. There must be four hundred million women out there wish they had been married to me. You oughta wake up and take advantage.'

Karen's face went very white and a small dimple appeared below the corners of her mouth, and she said, 'You arrogant sonofabitch. Get out of my home.' You could hear her breathe.

Peter slammed out of the door. Outside, the ball stopped bouncing and the voices grew hushed.

Neither of us said anything for a time, and then Karen went to the window and looked out. She lifted her hands and looked at them and said, 'My God, I'm shaking.'

I nodded.

She put one hand in the other and held them down, looking again at whatever was on the other side of the glass. 'I guess I'll have to let him own me a little while longer, won't I?' I didn't know if she was talking about Peter or Charlie, but maybe it didn't matter.

'Yes,' I said. 'I guess you will.'

She nodded. 'Okay. If that's what it takes, I can do that.'

'You're doing fine.'

'I'm surviving.'

'Sometimes that's enough.'

'No,' she said. 'It used to be. But it isn't anymore.'

CHAPTER 28

Karen Lloyd put out blankets and pillows and towels for Pike and me in a little spare room that she used as a home office. There was a couch and a desk in the little room, and just enough floor space for one of us on the couch and one of us on the floor. Pike said he'd take the floor.

We drove back to the Ho Jo, got our things, and checked out. The waitress who had always wanted to visit California was in the lobby when we paid. She said that she hoped she would see us again soon. I said anything was possible. By the time we got back to Karen Lloyd's, Peter and Dani were gone, Toby was in his room, and Karen had gone to bed. Twenty minutes after seven. Guess it had been a rough day all the way around.

At nine-forty-two the next morning Pike and I cruised past Clyde's Bar on 136th Street, Pike's head moving slightly to check out the fire escape, the alley, the street, the people. Luther and his buddy weren't around, and neither was their Pontiac, but maybe sixty or seventy thousand black people were on their way to work or school or doctor's appointments or the market. Pike said, 'Be tough to maintain a low profile around here.'

'Maybe we could do the stakeout in blackface.'

Pike's mouth twitched.

I felt as obvious now as I had before, but neither was the first time I had felt that way. The first time had been in 1976, not long after I had left the Army, walking with a man named Cleon Tyner in Watts. It was a feeling that everyone was staring at me, even though I could see that they were not. When I told Cleon, he said, now you know what it's like to be black. Cleon Tyner had died in Beverly Hills ten years later, shot to death by an Eskimo.

I said, 'Gloria Uribe is on the third floor, 304, up two flights of stairs, on the east side of the building.'

'What time is Santiago coming?'

'Four.'

'Let me out.'

I pulled to the curb, let him out, and drove around the block. My third time around, Pike came out from the alley and slipped into the car. He said, 'Maintenance entrance in the back next to an old coal chute, but no way up to the third unless you come through the lobby. You can get up the fire escape in the alley, but a guy coming here for business wouldn't use it. Thirty-foot drop to the roof from the next building.'

'So anyone who comes or goes is going to come or go through the lobby.'

Pike nodded. 'We try to hang around here all day, everyone on this street is going to know it. So will the woman.'

I turned south on Fifth and dropped down Central Park toward the Village. 'We can pick up Charlie. If Charlie doesn't come, it doesn't matter if Santiago shows up or not.'

Pike grunted and settled back in the seat. 'Let's do it.'

I pulled to the curb by a pay phone, called information, and got the numbers for the Figaro Social Club and the Lucerno Meat Company. I called the social club first and asked if Charlie DeLuca was there. A guy with a voice like a rusty gate said no. I called the meat plant and said, 'Charlie's office, please.' A woman came on and I told her that my name was Mike Waldrone and that Charlie's dad Sal had said that I should call and could I speak to him. She told me that he was on the other line and asked if I wanted to hold. I said no thanks, hung up, and went back to the car. 'Meat plant,' I said. 'Piece of cake.'

Twenty-eight minutes later we parked the Taurus just off Grand around the corner from the meat plant, walked back to a fruit shop with a little juice bar in the window, ordered a couple of papaya smoothies, and sat down to watch for Charlie DeLuca. Elvis and Joe go hunting in the city.

Econoline vans and eight-wheel delivery trucks came and went and guys in stained smocks loaded and unloaded packages of meat. At nineteen minutes after ten Ric the Vampire came down the sidewalk carrying a little white bag and took it into the meat plant. Danish, no doubt. At eleven-fifty-one Charlie and Ric came out and got into the black Town Car. Charlie was wearing a three-thousand-dollar Johnson & Ivers topcoat and climbed into the front seat. Pike and I hustled back to the Taurus and followed them northwest up across the Village to a little café two doors down from Foul Play Bookstore on Abingdon Square. Charlie went into the restaurant and Ric stayed in the car. In the café, Charlie met three other men, also in Johnson & Ivers topcoats, and sat in the window where they laughed and talked and read racing forms. Power lunch, no doubt. Who will we rob today? Who will we kill?

An hour and ten minutes later Charlie came out and got into the Town Car, and he and Ric drove to the Figaro Social Club, *members only*. Ric went in with him this time, instead of staying in the car. Shoot a little pool, drink a little espresso, hang out with the other wiseguys. They still hadn't cleaned the front door.

Neither Charlie nor Ric came or went for the next two hours and twenty-five minutes. A couple of old men hobbled in and another old man hobbled away, and strong younger men with broad backs and sturdy necks drifted in and out, but Charlie never moved. Probably weren't a lot of command decisions to be made at a meat plant, anyway.

At ten of four Pike said, 'Maybe it's a pass.'

At four Pike said, 'We can forget the Jamaican connection.'

At six minutes after four Pike said, 'You wanna check on this Santiago guy, anyway?'

At eleven minutes after four Charlie DeLuca came out and got into the black Town Car, and Pike said, 'He's alone.'

I looked at Pike and gave him Groucho Marx eyebrows.

Charlie pulled away from the curb and went up Bowery to Fourteenth, then across to Eighth and uptown past the theater district and the porno parlors and the street hustlers and a guy carrying a placard that said TRAVIS BICKLE WAS RIGHTEOUS. Heading north. Maybe north to Morningside Heights and Gloria Uribe and a guy named Santiago, but maybe not. He could always turn off to New Jersey.

This time of day the streets were crowded with cars and yellow cabs, and the cars and the cabs accelerated and swerved and stopped without regard to lanes or reason. Yellow cabs roared past the pedestrians who lined the street corners, some speeding up the closer they came to the warm bodies, others veering sharply across traffic, passing within inches of other cabs and cars, and nobody bothered to slow down. Everyone drove as if they were in Beirut, but that made it easy to follow him. In the chaos that was the approaching rush hour, we were just another random particle.

Pike loosened his .357 in its holster.

We stayed north on Eighth for a long time and then Charlie turned off Broadway onto Eighty-eighth and then over to Amsterdam, and suddenly we weren't going toward Morningside Heights and Gloria Uribe anymore. Pike said, 'Change of plans.'

'Unh-hunh.'

Charlie DeLuca pulled to the curb in a No Parking zone on Amsterdam Avenue. A young guy maybe thirty with a rat face and pimples and two sweatshirts came out of a doorway carrying a white, legal-sized envelope and got into the Lincoln. The Lincoln pulled away and we followed. Less than two blocks up Amsterdam the Lincoln again pulled to the curb and the pizza-faced guy got out. He closed the door as soon as he was out and walked away without looking back. He didn't have the envelope. The Lincoln started up Amsterdam again.

Pike said, 'Let me have the kid.'

I jerked the Taurus to the curb and Pike was out of the door before the Taurus stopped moving. I gunned it back into traffic and stayed with Charlie up Amsterdam into Morningside Heights and finally to Clyde's Bar. Well, well.

Luther and his friend had shown up and were leaning against their Pontiac. Luther didn't look happy. I drove around the block four times before I found a place to park and then I went back to see Luther. Luther smiled nastily when he saw me and said, 'Figure I be seeing you again. The Godfather roll up around five minutes ago. He upstairs now.'

'I know. How about Santiago?'

Luther nodded, slow, maybe remembering the ice pick. 'Yeah. He up there, too. So's the woman.'

'What's Santiago wearing?'

'Camel hair coat. Hat with a little pink feather in the band. Boots with these real skinny heels.'

'Great, Luther. Thanks.'

Luther gave me the slow nod, considering. 'You really a cop?'

'Luther,' I said, 'I am the right hand of God.'

Luther nodded again, and the nasty smile came back. 'If you plannin' on smitin' the sinners, I be glad to help.' He pushed back his long coat and showed me a little Rossi .32 snub-nose stuck in his pants. He remembered the ice pick, all right.

'Strictly surveillance this time around. Any smiting will have to come later.'

Luther shrugged and closed his coat. 'I be here.'

I went back across to the Taurus. Six minutes after I got settled Charlie and a tall black man in a hat with a pink feather and a camel overcoat came down and got into the Lincoln. When they passed Luther and his buddy, the tall black man said something to Luther and laughed. Ice-pick joke. Luther slid his right hand under his coat and watched the tall black man with sleepy eyes until he was in the Lincoln. It was going to take more than an ice pick the next time.

I followed the Lincoln down to 135th Street, then east across the island to Second, then straight down Second to the Queensboro Bridge and across the bridge into Queens.

We worked our way down off the bridge into an area of row houses and basketball courts and four- and five-story residential buildings. The sidewalks were crowded and most of the faces were black or brown, but not all of them, and many of the signs were in Spanish. The Lincoln pulled to the curb outside of a little coffee shop named Raldo's Soul Kitchen, and Charlie and the tall black guy went inside.

I looped around the block and parked in front of a barbershop, then walked back to Raldo's and looked in through the window. Charlie and the tall black guy were sitting at a booth with a shorter black guy and another white guy. The white guy looked sort of working class and the black guy looked like a fashion-row closeout with small eyes. Charlie handed the white envelope he had gotten from the guy on Amsterdam to Santiago, and Santiago handed it to the other black guy. Chain of command. I went back to the Taurus and waited.

Sixteen minutes later Charlie DeLuca and the two black guys and the other white guy came out of Raldo's and walked to a green Jaguar Sovereign parked up the block. The black guy with the small eyes opened the trunk and took out two brown-paper grocery bags and gave one of the bags to Charlie and the other to the working-class white guy. Charlie's bag was bigger and looked like it weighed more. As soon as they had the bags, the white guy went to a brown Toyota Celica and Charlie came back to his Lincoln and the two black guys got into the Jaguar. Nobody shook hands and nobody said so long, but everybody looked happy. Also, everybody went in different directions.

Portrait of the detective in crisis. Stay with Charlie or go after the black guys or the guy in the Toyota? Staying with the black guys would be hardest, and if they made me so soon after their meeting with Charlie, they'd tell him, and he might get scared and stop whatever he was doing. I went with the white guy in the Toyota.

We drove north to the Long Island Expressway, then east to 678 and then south through the heart of Queens to an exit that said Jamaica Avenue. Two blocks east of the Jamaica Avenue exit, the brown Toyota turned into a little parking lot next to a bright, modern cast-cement building with a sign that said BOROUGH OF QUEENS POLICE.

He parked in an empty spot next to a Volkswagen bug and got out with the brown-paper bag. He opened the Toyota's trunk, tossed in the bag, then took out a cop's blue-on-blue NYPD uniform and a gray gym bag. He closed the trunk, then carried the uniform and the gym bag into the station house.

I sat in the Taurus in the Borough of Queens Police

parking lot for a very long while until a couple of cops with thirty years on the job gave me the bad eye, and only then did I drive away.

Amazing what you learn if you just wait and watch.

CHAPTER 29

I called Rollie George from a pay phone outside a Korean market and gave him the license numbers off the cop's Toyota and the Jaguar Sovereign. I told him that one of the black guys might be known as Santiago, and I asked him to get me anything on them that he could.

Rollie grunted. 'I don't like we got a cop in this. Maybe he's undercover.'

'Maybe.'

'Yeah.' He didn't say anything for a minute, but there was a lot of breathing. 'You know, Elvis, I haven't asked who you're working for.'

'I know.'

After a while Rollie said, 'Okay. I'll run these and get back to you.'

'Thanks, Rollie.'

He hung up without saying good-bye.

By the time I got back to Karen Lloyd's, the sun was settling comfortably in the trees to the west and the arctic air had made its predicted move down from Canada, dropping the temperature and clouding the skies.

Joe Pike was sitting in one of the wing chairs with the cat in his lap and Karen Lloyd was making noise in her kitchen. I had the car, but Pike beat me back. One of life's imponderables. I said, 'You made good time.'

'I followed the kid with the pimples to an apartment building on Broadway and 96th Street. Name on the post drop was Richard Sealy.'

'Aha. Richie.'

'Un-hunh. I called Rollie a little bit after you. He'll run a make.'

There was more noise from the kitchen. Heavy glass tumblers set hard on a counter. 'You been here long?'

'Long enough.'

More noise. Drawers slamming shut. I looked toward the noise, but Pike didn't. 'Everything okay?'

'Nope.' Pike's mouth twitched.

Karen Lloyd came out of the kitchen with a bucket of Kentucky Fried Chicken. Her mouth was narrow and tight, and she took short, quick steps. She said, 'We're having the Colonel. I want you to come here and look at this.' She put the Colonel on the table and went back through the kitchen toward the garage. I looked back at Pike. 'You get it like this, too?'

Pike's mouth twitched again.

I went back through the kitchen. Karen was standing in the laundry room at the door to the garage with her arms crossed. The door to the garage was open. 'Look at what that bastard did.'

I thought she meant Charlie DeLuca, but she didn't. A gleaming new blue and white Yamaha snowmobile was parked next to her LeBaron. 'It's going back. I told Peter about the gifts. I thought we had it straight, but this is what I find waiting for me when I got home with Toby.' No questions about the mafia. No *Did you discover what's going on?* No *Did you find out where he gets the money?* No *Are we going to get out of this alive?*

I said, 'That louse.'

She turned red. 'It's not an appropriate gift. Toby's too young.'

'Sure.'

'It's dangerous. Can't you see that?'

'It's not as dangerous as motorcycles, and I don't think

it'll skew your son's values if he gets a nice gift from his father.'

She shut the door on the garage. 'I wouldn't think that you'd understand.'

Karen went back into the kitchen and put out the rest of the things she had brought from the Colonel and then she called Toby to the table. He came out sulky and silent. She asked him what he would like to drink and he said nothing. She asked him if he wanted rolls and the cole slaw and he said no. She asked him if he wanted a breast or a thigh and he said he didn't care. Sore about the snowmobile, I guess. Pike made himself a cheese sandwich and ate as if he were alone.

We were most of the way through the chicken when the white van that said WKEL-TV turned into the drive and the tall, thin woman got out. The weenie with the minicam got out with her. When Karen saw them coming through the big front window, she said, 'Oh, Jesus Christ.'

I said, 'Would you like me to get it?'

Karen shook her head and went to the door. 'No, thank you. This is my house, and my problem.'

The doorbell rang just as Karen opened the door. The tall, thin woman tried to step in past Karen, but Karen wouldn't get out of the way. The tall woman gave a nice local-news on-camera smile and put out her hand. Karen didn't take it. 'Hello, Ms. Lloyd. Janice Watkins, WKEL-TV. I do local color and human interest, and I was fascinated when I heard that Peter Alan Nelsen, the filmmaker, is your husband.' Janice Watkins seemed neither to mind nor notice that Karen hadn't taken her hand. Probably used to it.

Karen said, 'You've made some sort of mistake. I'm not married.'

The smile didn't falter. 'Ex-husband, then. I know how that is, I've got two.' She chuckled. Establishing rapport.

'I'm sorry, Ms. Watkins. I don't know what you're talking about.'

A corner of the smile gave way. 'Peter Alan Nelsen and his entourage are staying at the Howard Johnson's.'

Toby craned around the bucket of chicken, trying to see. Pike pushed the bucket out of his way.

The thin woman said, 'You've been seen with him. So has your son. Everyone is saying that Toby Lloyd is Mr. Nelsen's child and that Mr. Nelsen has journeyed across the country to find him.' *Journeyed.* She was working up the human-interest angle, all right.

'I've never been married to Peter Alan Nelsen and I don't know what you're talking about.'

The smile faltered. 'You weren't?'

'No.'

'Is Peter Alan Nelsen the boy's father?'

'No.'

Janice Watkins blinked. She tried to peek past Karen to see if Peter Alan Nelsen was lurking inside. I waved at her.

Karen Lloyd said, 'You've interrupted our meal. Do you mind?'

Janice Watkins narrowed her eyes. 'Ms. Lloyd, I have this information on very good authority.'

Karen Lloyd leaned toward Janice Watkins. 'Ms. Watkins, chew a used rubber.' Then she slammed the door.

Toby was staring at his plate when Karen came back to the table. His face was red and her face was tight and pale. When she picked up a piece of original recipe, her hand trembled and she put it back down.

Toby said, 'Why did you tell'm he wasn't my dad?'

Karen lifted the piece of chicken again and this time took a small bite. She didn't answer. After a while Toby got up, took his plate into the kitchen, then went down the hall to his room.

Karen Lloyd put down her chicken and said, 'Shit.'

At seven-fifty that evening the doorbell rang again and this time when Karen answered, Peter Alan Nelsen came in without Nick or T.J. or Dani. He said, 'I've been thinking about this and I've got a way to make everybody happy.' Toby must've seen the limo, because he came out of his room.

Karen stiffened as if someone had injected her with Super Glue and said, 'He can't keep that thing.' First words out of her mouth.

Peter started to say something, but then he didn't. Showing restraint. 'I'm not a dope. I know I'm here at a bad time. You're trying to straighten out this thing with the DeLuca people, and you've got me here, and you've gotta be worried about Toby. Lemme lighten the load for you. How about I take Tobe back to L.A. with me until you guys get this worked out?'

Toby said, 'Yeah!'

Peter looked from Karen to me and then back to Karen. He spread his hands. 'Toby'll be safe, and I'll be out of your hair, and you can take care of what you need to take care of. When it's done, you can give me a call and Toby and I will come back and we can work out our family situation.'

Toby was giving it the ear-to-ear. 'Great! Can I meet Sylvester Stallone?'

Peter said, 'Sure.'

Karen said, 'No.'

Peter frowned. 'No, he can't meet Sylvester Stallone, or no, he can't go to L.A.?'

Karen went back to one of the wing chairs and sat down. Her knees were together and so were her hands. 'He has school. He has basketball.'

I said, 'It might make things easier.'

Peter said, 'Jesus Christ, Karen, it won't kill him to miss a few days of school.'

Toby said, 'I can get Miss Garrett to give me the work. I won't fall behind.'

'No.'

Peter said, 'What do you mean, no?'

'It would be too disruptive. Who knows how long this is going to take?'

I said, 'I think it's a good idea.'

Karen flashed the hard eyes at me. 'Nobody asked you.'

Peter rolled his eyes and looked at the ceiling. 'Hey, am I being an asshole here or what?' Getting loud.

Karen said, 'Watch your language in front of my son.' They were starting to shout.

Peter gestured wide with the arms the way he had when I'd first seen him, reading the riot act because a couple of executives had been trying to fob off a TV guy on him. 'Hey, Karen, a *mobster* was here with *our son*. Do you remember that?'

Karen pushed up out of the chair and made a shooing gesture to Toby. 'Toby, I want you to go to your room.'

Peter said, 'Lemme take the kid back to L.A. He'll be safer there than here. You think I won't bring'm back?'

Pike stuck his fingers in his ears.

I said, 'Peter, maybe now isn't the time to talk about it.'

Peter whirled around and glared at me. 'I'm Peter Alan Nelsen and I'm tired of fooling around.' He wheeled back toward Karen. 'If you played it smart, I could set you up. You wouldn't have to worry about a thing and you could do whatever you want. You could even be an actress again. I'm Peter Alan Nelsen, and I could make you a star.' Like she was still nineteen and always would be.

Karen Lloyd put her hands on her hips and laughed at him. 'You arrogant asshole.'

Toby started crying and yelled, 'Why won't you let me go with him? Why are you being like this? You're gonna make him go away and I hate you!' He ran down the hall and slammed his door.

Pike still had his fingers in his ears.

Peter was giving us confused and frustrated, as if he were trying to explain that two plus one equals three and Karen just couldn't get it, and the frustration was giving way to suspicion, like maybe she got it but was pretending she didn't because something was going on. He squinted at me, then back at her, and then he nodded and made an oh-I-get-it smile and said, 'You're fucking this guy.'

Karen Lloyd slapped him. It was a hard, quick shot that took him off guard and backed him up. I stepped in between them, taking his wrists and keeping his hands at his sides and pushing him backward. Karen yelled, 'You piece of shit. You rotten piece of shit. Why'd you have to come back? Why couldn't you leave us alone?'

Peter jerked away from me and threw a punch that seemed to float down from heaven. I stepped outside of it, then stepped back in very close and pushed him up against the door and told him to relax. He tried to bite me and then he tried to butt me with his head, and when he did, I punched him once in the stomach. He made an *urp*-ing sound and went down onto his hands and knees and threw up on Karen Lloyd's beautiful bleached-oak floor. I hadn't wanted to hit him, and I was glad the boy wasn't there to see it.

Peter stayed on all fours, head hanging down, and made little burping noises. 'I'm sick.'

Pike said, 'Take deep breaths.'

Karen stood by the mantel, holding herself. Pike went into the kitchen and came back with a roll of Scot towels.

Peter took the deep breaths, then staggered to his feet and shook his finger at me. 'Goddamnit, you're fired.

You're off the fucking payroll. I'm gonna make sure you never work again.'

I said, 'Clichéd, Peter. I expected more originality from the King of Adventure.'

Peter burped some more and then he lurched out the front door. In a minute the limo pulled away and Pike held out his hand. 'I'd better make sure he gets home.'

I tossed Pike the keys and he left.

Karen Lloyd and I stood without moving in the now quiet house, and I said, 'Peter's idea was good.'

She shook her head.

'It's smart to get the boy out of the picture. It's smart if Peter's gone, too. It would give you more room.'

She shook her head again. 'If he wanted to help, he could just leave. He doesn't need Toby. This is just more of the same old Peter Alan Nelsen bullshit. Peter wanting everything his way.'

'Karen,' I said, 'think about it. They've threatened your life. They made a move on your son. Falling behind in history doesn't rate with getting him out of here. Do you see?'

She made a little blowing move with her mouth and then she crossed her arms and sat on the edge of the hearth, leaning forward so that her elbows touched her knees. She gave me a short glance, and then she looked at the floor, and then she uncrossed her arms and put a hand on either side of her head and squeezed, like maybe she was trying to keep her head from bursting. She said, 'I'm not crazy. I am not crazy. *I'm not crazy.*'

'Nope,' I said. 'You're scared, but it isn't Charlie DeLuca who scares you, though it should be.'

She shook her head and closed her eyes. 'I'm too tired to argue.'

I said, 'This is your house. You bought the couch and the table and the wood in the fireplace. You secured the loan for your car. You buy Toby's clothes, and you've made a good life.'

She shook her head some more.

'But now comes Peter, and you're scared that it won't be yours anymore. You'll be the woman who was married to Peter Alan Nelsen, and Toby will be Peter's son.'

She stopped shaking her head.

'You're scared of losing yourself.'

Two tears squeezed out of the inside corners of her eyes and ran down her cheeks. 'You sonofabitch.' She might've been talking to me, but maybe not.

I said, 'Don't think about Peter. Think about Charlie. Charlie is who you have to focus on. Charlie can hurt you and Toby a lot worse than Peter.'

She brought one hand up and rubbed at the tears but still did not open her eyes. 'Do you think I'm stupid?'

'No.'

'It sounds so stupid, worried about losing myself. It sounds weak and silly, like something one of those idiot *Cosmo* feminists would whine about. I don't want to be weak. I don't want to be stupid.'

I made a shrug. 'Pride isn't male or female. It's human.'

'I'm a vice-president at the bank. I have a real estate license and I am a certified financial planner and I've been president of the PTA twice and vice-president of the local Rotary.' The tears were coming harder.

'Unh-hunh.'

'I have a B.A. in finance. I am Toby Lloyd's mother. I will not lose those things.'

'No. You won't.'

'I will not lose who I am.'

'I won't let you.'

She opened her eyes and looked at me.

'Saving selves is one of my best things.'

She rubbed at the tears again and then she put her face in her hands and sat very still. I guess she wasn't convinced.

I used the Scot towels on the floor, then put them in a white plastic trash bag and took the bag out and put it into a blue garbage can in the garage. It seemed twenty degrees colder than it had been at dusk, and the north wind rattled tree limbs and dead leaves and pushed dark shapes across the lawn. Thunder rumbled many miles to the east, a winter storm moving with the front. When I went back inside, Karen Lloyd had gone to bed.

I turned off most of the lights and went down the hall to the room where Joe Pike and I were bedding. Karen Lloyd's room was at the end of the hall in the back of the house, and Toby's room was across from Karen's, in the front. Both of their doors were closed, but I could hear them crying, she in her room and he in his. I felt a very great urge to knock and say the word or make the touch that would make them feel better. I went into my own room and I closed the door.

You do what you can, but you can't do everything.

CHAPTER 30

When I woke the next morning, the sky was dark with clouds and the air was as cold as the edge of a hunting knife. The snow above us waiting to fall was a physical thing, heavy and damp and alive with turbulence.

Toby was sullen and Karen was unhappy and nobody said very much as we went through the house and prepared for the day. Karen drove into the office early and I took Toby to school. Pike stayed at the house, waiting for Roland George to call. Neither Toby nor I spoke on the way to school, but when I dropped him off I told him to have a good day. He didn't answer. It was as if the bad feelings and restless, logy sleep had carried over into wakefulness.

At nine-forty-two that morning Roland George called. I took it in the living room. Pike picked up in the kitchen. Roland George said, 'The Jag you saw is registered to a Jamaican named Urethro Mubata. Came up here in 1981. Fourteen arrests, two convictions, assault, armed robbery, like that. He's mostly in the dope business.'

'Not exactly a good-will ambassador.'

'Unh-unh. He did eight months at Rikers for possession with intent and another fourteen at Sing Sing for attempted murder. When he was at Ossining, he did cell time with a man named Jesus Santiago, another Jamaican. Santiago served out, but Mubata's on parole.'

'Santiago in for pimping?'

'That's it. Sorta curious how this guy Mubata got the forty grand for a new Jaguar when his employment of record is being a busboy at Arturo's Tapas Stand in Jackson Heights.'

Pike said, 'What about Sealy and the cop?'

'Sealy is a hype, registered in the methadone program at St. Vincent's. He's a nobody with a string of minor busts, mostly hijack and street boosting, run a little policy, steal a few stereos, that kind of thing.'

'Is he part of DeLuca's crew?'

'It's not in the files, but it's possible. The guy's a drop of pus, but he's a known associate. Hard to figure, though. Hype like this, Charlie DeLuca shouldn't be having anything to do with him.'

Pike said, 'He shouldn't be having anything to do with a police officer, either.'

'Yeah.' Something hard came into Roland's voice. 'The officer in question is employed by Kennedy Airport Security. He is not undercover.'

'Okay.'

I hung up. Joe Pike came into the living room from the kitchen and said, 'I make it for a hijacking setup. Something coming into Kennedy.'

'It sounds right, but why's Charlie sneaking around? He gets a tip that something worth stealing is coming in, he uses the Jamaicans to pull the heist, then they split the take with him. Big deal. Why does he want to keep it from Sal?'

'Because he doesn't want to split the money.'

I thought about it some more and shook my head. 'It's not a world breaker. Charlie shows a little initiative, he makes a few extra bucks. What's Daddy going to do?'

Pike said, 'There's the hype.'

I nodded. The hype didn't figure. You want to keep secrets, you don't do business with a hype. 'Maybe

Charlie doesn't have a choice. Maybe, whatever he's doing, he can't do it without the hype.'

Pike grunted. 'Makes you wonder what he's got going, that he can't do it without a hype.'

I said, 'Yes, it does. Maybe we should ask the hype and find out.'

'What if the hype won't cooperate?'

'He'll cooperate. Everyone knows that a hype can't keep secrets. They have low self-esteem.'

We put on our coats and our guns and made the drive into Manhattan in less than fifty minutes.

We parked by a subway entrance near 92nd Street and Central Park West, then walked two blocks to an eight-story gray-stone building with painted windows and a lot of crummy shops on the ground floor and a fire escape.

Pike said, 'Third floor in the back. Three-F.'

We entered the lobby of the apartment building between a place that sold discount clothing and a place that sold donuts. The lobby had a white and black linoleum floor, circa 1952, probably the last year it had been waxed, and someone had scotch-taped a little handwritten sign that said *out of service* to the elevator. Someone else had urinated on the floor. You watch *Miami Vice* or *Wiseguy*, the criminals always live in palatial apartments and drive Ferraris. So much for verisimilitude.

We walked up the two flights, then down a dingy hall past a stack of newspapers four feet tall, Pike leading. An empty plastic Cup•A•Soup was lying on its side atop the newspapers. Three-F was the third apartment on the left side of the hall. When Pike got to the door, he stood there a moment, head cocked to the side, and then he shook his head. 'Not home.'

'How do you know?'

Shrug. 'Knock and see.'

I knocked, then knocked again. Nothing.

Pike spread his hands.

I said, 'Why don't we be sure?'

Pike shook his head, giving me bored.

There was only one lock and it was cheap. I let us into a studio apartment that was just as attractive as the rest of the building. Bags of fast-food wrappers and potato-chip empties in the kitchenette, stacks of the *New York Post* and the *National Enquirer* along the walls, paper cups packed with dead cigarettes by a throw-pillow couch, and the sour smell of body odor and wet matches. Nice. No Richard Francis Sealy, though. Maybe Pike could see through walls.

We went back down to the mail drop in the lobby. Most of the little mailbox doors had been jimmied – junkies looking for checks – and most of the boxes were empty. The top box had a little plastic sticker on it that said: *Sal Cohen, 2A, mgr.*

We went back up to the second floor and found 2-A. I knocked hard on the door three times. Somebody threw a series of bolts and then Sal Cohen scowled out at us from behind what looked like eight security chains. He was little and dark, and he had a Sunbeam steam iron in his right hand. He said, 'The fuck you're knocking so loud?'

New York, New York. The attitude capital of the universe.

I said, 'Richard Sealy in three-F, he's a pal of ours. He was supposed to meet us here and he's not around.'

'So what?' Mr. Helpful.

'We're movie producers. We're going to produce a movie and we want him to be the star. We thought you might know when he'd be around so we could get him in on this.'

Sal Cohen blinked at me and then he blinked at Joe Pike. 'Yeah?'

'Yeah.'

Sal smirked. 'What bull. I know cops when I see'm.'
Pike walked away down the hall.

I stepped closer to the door, lowered my voice, and tried to look furtive. I have never in my life met a cop who looked furtive, but there you go. 'Okay,' I said, 'we're on the cops. We need your help in locating Richard Sealy so that we might topple the organized crime structure in our city.'

He said, 'You find him, you get me the eight months' back rent the little bag of shit owes.'

'You got any idea when he'll be around?'

'No.'

'You know where he works?'

'That lazy sonofabitch, work? If he worked, he wouldn't be eight months back on the rent. None of these lazy bastards work.'

'You know where he spends his time?'

'Look down at Dillard's. He's always down there, shooting pool and trying to buy dope, else he's running around with those crazy Gamboza bastards.'

'Gamboza bastards?' Pike came back and stood next to me.

Sal nodded and squinted out at us. 'Yeah.'

'As in the Gamboza family?'

'Yeah.' More squinting.

I said, 'Richard Sealy hangs out with the DeLuca family.' Sal laughed, and it came out like a series of sharp hacks. 'Hey, you just fall off the lamebrain truck, or what? I run this building thirty-five years. Those fucking Gamboza bastards grew up right over there on Wilmont Street and so did Richie Sealy. They useta throw rocks at the niggers and steal their money, the little bastards, Richie Sealy and Nick and Tommy Gamboza and that nut case Vincent Ricci. Jesus Christ, the DeLucas.' More of the hacking laugh. 'Richie's about as close to being a Gamboza as you can be without the blood. Why else you think I gotta put up with a junkie eight months back on his rent? I heave him out, those bastards would cut out my heart and fry it in a pan.'

I said, 'But how does he fit in with the DeLucas?'

Sal squinted at me past the security chains like I was a new release from Bellevue. 'He don't. Nobody around here got anything to do with the fucking DeLucas. The Upper West Side is owned lock, stock, and short hairs by the Gamboza family. DeLucas got lower Manhattan. This look like lower Manhattan to you?'

I was seeing it. 'Sonofabitch.'

Sal Cohen said, 'No wonder this city's down the toilet, fucking cops like you.' Then he slammed the door.

Joe Pike and I walked down the flight of stairs and out onto the street and looked around at deepest, darkest Gamboza country. Nary a DeLuca in sight.

'Well, well, well,' I said. 'Now I'm beginning to see why Charlie's keeping this secret.'

Pike nodded.

'The Delucas and the Gambozas hate each other, but they have an agreement. They're supposed to be standing together against the foreign gangs.'

Pike's mouth twitched. 'Doesn't look that way, does it?'

'Nope.'

Pike's mouth twitched a second time. Hysterics, for Pike. 'You think whatever these guys are stealing at Kennedy, it's something that would make a lot of people mad?'

'I've got some guesses.'

Pike nodded again. 'Let's go down to Dillard's and see if your guesses are right.'

CHAPTER 31

You had to walk up a long wooden flight of stairs to get to Dillard's. The stairs were dark and the finish was worn off the center of each tread. A sign at the bottom of the stairs said DILLARD'S POOL & BILLIARDS, LADIES WELCOME. Another sign said NO MINORS, UNDER 21 NOT ALLOWED.

We went up the stairs and into a big room with a high ceiling and maybe twenty tables and a splintered floor that went pretty well with the stairs. A dozen kids in black leather jackets over white T-shirts shot pool and smoked and sucked on red cans of Coca-Cola as if this were still 1957, only most of them had long shaggy hair or buzz cuts. Pool cues like prison bars stood upright on racks against the walls, and fluorescent lights on the ceiling made everyone look dead. One of the lights flickered. A sixty-year-old bald guy with knotty arms sat behind a short bar where you could get beer or soft drinks. He was reading a copy of *Sporting Times*. I didn't see any ladies and no one except the guy behind the bar looked over sixteen. I didn't see Richie Sealy, either. Pike said, 'I'll check the back.'

Pike went across the big room and into a little alcove where a couple of signs said *restrooms* and *exit*. I walked over to the guy behind the bar.

He watched me come over the top of his paper and squirmed around on his stool. Nervous. I said, 'We're looking for Richard Sealy. Is he around?'

The old guy glanced toward the rear of his place, where

Pike had gone, then back to me. He didn't fold the paper or put it down. 'You guys with the cops?' First Sal Cohen, now him. Maybe if we let our hair grow.

I said, 'Richard Sealy.'

More of the nervous. 'Look, I'm straight now, okay? I did the nickel and I'm good at my parole and I live straight, so whatever Richie's got going, I don't know.' He shot little glances at the kids and kept his voice down, hoping no one would hear. They probably thought he was tough, and he didn't want them to know he wasn't.

I gave him a hard cop look like I'd seen Robert Stack give in old *Untouchables* reruns. 'We just want Sealy.'

In the back, a fat kid with glasses laughed too loud and then a gray metal door that said GENTLEMEN opened next to a pay phone and Richard Sealy came out. He was wearing the same two sweatshirts and the same fingerless gloves and he was smiling. Thirty-five years old and he was hanging out with kids.

The old guy said, 'No shooting.'

I looked at him. Life at the Longbranch.

Pike came out of the back as Richie went over to a green table where a couple of kids were shooting eight-ball. Richie grabbed a pack of Marlboros off the edge of · the table, lipped out a cigarette, fired up, then bent over to line up a shot. Someone had taped a poster of Heather Thomas in a bikini onto the wall. Heather looked okay.

Pike moved along the far wall past the pool cues and came up behind Richie. When he was ten feet from Heather Thomas, I walked over and came up from the near side. 'Hey, Richie.'

Richie let out a cloud of the Marlboro and looked at me. 'I know you?'

'Sure.'

Richie squinted through the smoke and rubbed at the

inside of his left arm. He looked sleepy. 'Where I know you from, Gino's?'

I said, 'Let's take a little walk. We got something to talk about.'

Joe Pike came up from the other side and stood very close to Richie without expression. The kids shooting eight-ball stopped and looked over.

Richie glanced at Pike, then me. 'What the fuck? I don't know you.'

'Come on.' I put my hand on his arm. 'We've got mutual friends.'

'Hey, I'm in the middle of a game here.' Eyes flicking faster now, Pike to me, Pike to me.

I went in closer until we had him sandwiched and made my voice quiet. 'Tommy Gamboza sent us, Richie.'

Surprised. 'Tommy wants to see me?' Almost a little excited, like maybe Tommy had sent us around to tap him for the secret order, like we'd drive somewhere and he'd get to take the blood oath to become part of La Cosa Nostra.

'Yeah.' I took him under the arm and pulled him toward the stairs. Pike looked back at the kids and told them that the game was over.

Richie said, 'Hey, if Tommy wants to see me, how come he didn't come himself? How come he didn't send Tony or Frankie to get me? I don't know you guys.'

'We're imported, Richie. Vegas.' You say Vegas, they know it's bad.

He jammed on the brakes, pulling up short. You see how it is with Vegas? 'Hey.'

I leaned close and whispered in his ear. 'The Gambozas know you're selling them out to Charlie DeLuca.'

Richie Sealy's knees went weak and he sort of slumped. If I hadn't been holding his right arm he would've gone down the stairs like a runny egg. 'Oh, Jesus,' he said. 'Oh, Jesus.'

We took him down the stairs and around the corner into a little alley that smelled of grease and ammonia and put him into the wall against a metal dumpster. I held his collar and Pike patted him down and came up with a sharpened screw-driver and two ten-dollar packs of white powder. Pike opened the bags and poured out the powder. I said, 'Don't you know this stuff is bad for you, Richie?'

'I don't know what you're talking about. I don't know anything about Charlie DeLuca. I swear to Christ on my mother's life.' These junkies.

I said, 'Richie. The Gambozas know. Vincent Ricci saw with his own eyes. Are you calling Ricci a liar?'

'Hey, no way, but, you know, like maybe he made a mistake –'

I jerked his collar once. 'Knock off the shit.' Elvis Cole, Professional Thug.

Richard Sealy started to cry.

I said, 'The Gambozas know that something is going on, but they don't know what. You know how they hate that bastard Charlie DeLuca. You know what Tommy thinks.' I didn't know what Tommy thought, but if the blood between the DeLucas and the Gambozas was as bad as Roland George had said, whatever Tommy thought couldn't be good.

'Yeah. Yeah, I know.'

'Okay. They told us, give him one chance. They said, if he comes clean with you, let him live, but only if he comes clean and gives the whole thing.' I looked at Pike. 'Isn't that what they said?'

Pike nodded.

I looked back at Richie. 'You hear that?'

Richie was sobbing. A ribbon of mucus ran down

across his mouth and along his chin. He said, 'I can't say anything. I can't.'

I slapped him. 'You made fools out of those guys, you moron. Ricci, Tommy, the Gamboza brothers. They grew up with you. They loved you like family and you have made them look like turnips, and you have done this with the help of Charlie DeLuca. Can you imagine how this makes Tommy and Nickie feel?' Elvis Brando. One step away from the Great White Way.

Richie Sealy was nodding and shaking his head at the same time and his eyes looked like dried apricots. He said, 'Jesus Christ, we're talking Crazy Charlie DeLuca. Charlie the Tuna. Charlie will kill me. He'll cut out my eyes, for Christ's sake, can't I make it up to Tommy another way?'

I shook him and said, 'Moron. You're worried about Crazy Charlie. Why do you think the Gambozas brought us in for this?' I looked at Pike again. Pike reached behind his back and brought out a twelve-inch Buck hunting knife. It was so bright you could shave in the reflection.

Richard Sealy tried to backpedal away, but the dumpster was there. 'Okay,' he said. 'Okay. Whatever you want.'

'What do you and Charlie have going?'

'I tell him when some of the dope shipments are coming in through Kennedy.'

'Gamboza dope.' There it was.

'Yeah. Sure.'

'What about the Jamaicans? What about the cop out in Queens?'

'Jesus Christ, Tommy knows everything.'

I pulled Richie close. 'Tommy knows all and sees all.'

Pike sighed and looked away.

Richie said, 'Charlie sells the information to the

Jamaicans. The Jamaicans hijack our stuff and sell it and then they give Charlie a piece.'

'Is this DeLuca family, Richie, or is this just Charlie? If it's family, we're talking war.' War. Mario Puzo, eat your heart out.

'I don't know, but I think it's just Charlie. Charlie's the guy turned me. He came to me and said he'd cut me in and I could have all the smack I wanted. It was Charlie's idea. You gotta tell Tommy that.'

'Sure.'

'I don't never see anyone else.'

'So Charlie is violating the agreement the DeLuca family made with the Gamboza family. He's in business with the Jamaicans to steal from another family and Sal doesn't know.'

'No. Sal doesn't know. Jesus Christ, Sal would have a fit. Tommy should know that. Sal, that old gumbah.'

I looked at Pike and Pike looked at me. Pike said, 'What do we do with him?'

Richie said, 'Hey, I come clean. You said I come clean, Tommy said you should let me off.'

Pike said, 'He tells Charlie we know, it's over.'

Richie said, 'Hey, I won't tell Charlie nothing. I swear to Christ.' He was crying again.

I looked into Pike's flat dimensionless glasses and saw little reflections of myself. Pike waited. I turned back to Richie and pulled him close again. 'Here's what you're going to do. You're going to walk out of this alley and go to the Port Authority bus terminal and you are going to take a bus to Miami. You will not speak with Charlie DeLuca or the Jamaicans or anyone else about this, do you understand?'

'Yes.'

'If you do, Tommy Gamboza swears that he will find out. If you do, the entire Gamboza family will seek you out no matter where you might hide, and we will kill you. Do you understand?'

'Yes.'

'Get out of here.'

He ran out of the alley, knocking into a garbage can, then bouncing off a wall, then disappearing around the corner and into the street.

Pike said, '"Seek you out"?'

'Too dramatic?'

Pike frowned.

Everybody's a critic.

CHAPTER 32

Karen Lloyd gave me confused. 'He's stealing from other criminals?'

'Yes.'

'How can you go to the police with that?' She was leaning against the front edge of her desk at the bank with her arms crossed. Pike and I were sitting in the two chairs opposite. It seemed colder in Chelam than it had in New York, but maybe that was because it was later and the damp clouds and the cold air pushing down from Canada had gained greater purchase over the woods and the fields and the small clean buildings.

I said, 'We won't go to the police. We'll go to Charlie. He isn't just stealing money and hiding it from his father and the other *capos* in his own family, he's stealing from another family in direct violation of a treaty that the DeLucas made with the other families.' I gave her what Rollie George had given me, how the families had divided up territory and crime, and how nobody much liked it but everybody had been living with it. 'Until now.'

She nodded, seeing it as a banker would see it, IBM and Xerox negotiating a market arrangement. 'All right. He's violating a trade agreement.'

'Yeah. Only he's got more to worry about than the Securities and Exchange Commission. If the Gambozas found out that Charlie DeLuca was stealing from them in collaboration with the Jamaicans, they'd kill him and they'd probably try to kill Sal, too.'

Karen blinked at Pike, then at me. 'Does Sal know?'

'Probably not, but it doesn't matter. If he doesn't know, it makes things cleaner because we only have to deal with Charlie. If Sal's in on it, then we have to deal with him, too. A little more complicated, but the outcome is the same.'

She wet her lips, getting anxious with it, thinking it through and seeing the potential, but unwilling to commit until all the *i*'s were dotted and the *t*'s crossed. She shook her head. 'Even if he goes along, we'll still know. Charlie's going to think that. He's going to think that the only way to keep himself safe is to kill us.'

I said, 'He'll think about it, but we'll set things up so that he can't. We'll bring in Rollie George. We'll make sure that other people know what we know, and we'll prove it to Charlie so that he knows it, too. If he kills us, he gets screwed. Do you see?'

She wet her lips again and made a very small nod, still thinking it through. 'We go to Charlie, we say that he has to let go of me or we tell the Gambozas.'

'Yes.'

'We tell him that people we trust know, too, so that if anything happens to us, the Gambozas will still be told.'

'Yes. If we die, he dies. We make this deal, it's a deal we honor forever. We can't change our minds. Do you see?'

She nodded again, stronger. 'Of course. When are you going to do this?'

'I'll call Rollie this evening and maybe drive down to the city to talk with him. He knows people in publishing and on the cops we can trust. We'll have to get together with them and set up what we know and how to prove it to Charlie. It'll take a couple of days.'

'And then we do it.'

'Yep. We do it.'

She wet the lips again and looked at Pike, then me. 'What if it doesn't work?'

'If it doesn't work, we go to the Gambozas and you go in to the cops for witness protection. It isn't what you want, but it's the best hand we've got.'

She made a hissing sound and her eyes sort of fluttered for a moment, but then she nodded. 'Yes. I believe it's the best we can hope for, too.' She went around behind her desk and sat with her fingers laced in front of her, very much like she did the first time I came into her office. Businesslike. 'I've thought about what you said last night. I've decided that you're right. It would be best for everyone if Toby went back to California with Peter until this is resolved.'

'Okay.'

'Peter can take Toby as soon as possible. I'd like him to be in California before we meet with Charlie.'

'All right. I'll stop by the motel and set it up.'

She nodded tightly. 'Thank you. I'll tell Toby when I see him after school.'

Pike and I drove to the Howard Johnson's looking for Peter, but the limo was gone. We went in to the front desk and asked if they knew when Mr. Nelsen would be back. They said they didn't, but that his friends were in the bar and that they might know. We went into the bar.

Nick and T.J. were sitting at a little round table, drinking Heinekens and eating hamburgers. Nick said, 'Hey, look, it's Mike Hammer and his sidekick, Tonto.'

T.J. laughed with his mouth full.

I said, 'Where's Peter?'

Nick said, 'Peter said you're canceled, pal, so he's taking care of business himself. We don't need you anymore.'

I said, 'What do you mean, Peter's taking care of business?'

'He got tired of waiting around. He and Dani went to straighten out the wop.'

'He and Dani went to see DeLuca?'

'Yeah.'

'When?'

'A little while ago.'

Pike moved next to me.

'Where?'

Nick gave me the smirk. 'Hey, fuck you. It's not your business.'

Pike stepped in close, took out his .357, and touched it to Nick's upper lip. 'Tonto wants to know.'

Nick stopped smirking and T.J. stopped laughing. Nick said, 'Some meat place. He got the address from the operator.'

Pike and I ran out of the Ho Jo and pushed the Taurus hard back along the state road to the expressway and then down to Manhattan.

We were half a block from the meat plant when a brown Nissan Sentra nosed out of the parking lot and into the street. Two guys I hadn't seen before were in the front seat and Ric was in the back with Dani and Peter. Peter's head was sort of lolling to the side.

Pike said, 'We get the chance, we take them in traffic.' He took out his Python and held it in his lap.

I let the Sentra make its first corner, then I jerked the Taurus around and caught up to them going east on Canal to climb the Manhattan Bridge across the East River to Brooklyn.

The bridge was electric with late-afternoon congestion as thousands of cars raced for home before the bridge gridlocked. If the bridge was locked now, what we were trying to do would be easy, but the bridge wasn't locked. Traffic coursed and bumper-to-bumper cars weaved from lane to lane, cutting each other off, hitting their brakes and making it hard to keep the Sentra in sight. Pike rolled down the passenger window and climbed out to sit on the door, but it didn't help. Eight cars ahead of us and two lanes over, the Sentra took the second exit ramp over the Brooklyn shore and that's where we lost it.

Pike said, 'Off-ramp.'

I blew the horn and cut in and out between three cars and knocked the bumper off a green Dodge station wagon, but I kept going.

We jumped across the two right lanes and hit the off-ramp in a skid and followed it down in a great looping arc over factories and waterfront and chain-link fences and bridge supports, Pike standing as tall as he could in the window, trying to spot the Sentra, finally yelling, 'Got it.'

The Sentra was below us in a U-Stor-It yard under one of the on-ramps leading back to Manhattan. The two guys were out of the Sentra's front seat and Ric and Peter and Dani were getting out of the back. One of the guys from the front was wearing a red leather jacket with very wide shoulders. The other had a gun out. Revolver.

We came off the ramp at the rear of the storage yard on the wrong side of a ten-foot chain-link fence. I said, 'Faster to go over it.'

We went up and over and came out between two corrugated-metal storage sheds eighty yards away as Ric took out the stainless-steel ten, pointed it at Peter, and said something to the guy with the revolver. Peter was standing with his hands up the way he'd had actors stand in his movies. Eighty yards away, you could see that his face was white and his eyes looked scooped out behind the thick glasses. Dani was maybe a half step in front of him. Peter said something to Ric and put out his hands, maybe saying please don't shoot, and Ric raised his gun to eye level and Dani went for him. I yelled, but it didn't do any good. Ric's gun popped once and the right back quarter of Dani's head blew off. Then I had the Dan

Wesson out and Pike had his .357 and we were firing at them, eighty yards away, me screaming at Peter to get down, but Peter standing there, still with his hands up.

The guy with the revolver went down.

Ric ran toward the Sentra, firing as he went, and the guy in the red jacket pulled out a black automatic. Bullets slapped into the little corrugated sheds around us with the sound of hammers hitting garbage cans and left silver streaks on the tarmac where they hit and bounced into a concrete bridge support. The guy in the red jacket fired fast, *bapbapbap*, and then he went for the Sentra, too. I shot him in the back. He fell in through the Sentra's front passenger window as Ric roared away, fishtailing into storage sheds and a boat trailer, and then through the far gate.

When the Sentra was gone, the storage yard was still.

We got to Dani as fast as we could, but there wasn't anything to do.

Peter said, 'He told that guy Ric to kill me.' He was talking fast and there was a knot below his left eye, like maybe someone had hit him there. His hands were still in the air. 'Just like that, he said kill'm. I said I'm Peter Alan Nelsen. I said you can't kill me. He said, you wanna bet? And then these guys were bringing us out here and they were gonna kill me.' Me. Me and I.

I stood up. 'Dani.'

He was hopping from foot to foot, confused and squinting at me. 'What?'

'They killed Dani.' I said it carefully, each word distinct.

He gave me more of the confused and said, 'What?' Pike was squatting next to her body and I was standing over her, and Peter and I were talking about her, but he hadn't looked at her and he hadn't said anything about her. He said, 'I told'm you can't do this to me. I'm Peter Alan Nelsen.'

I went over to him and said, 'Put down your hands.'

He put down his hands.

I punched him in the chest with my right hand. He fell backward and landed hard on his butt and said, 'Hey, what did you hit me for?' Surprised.

I grabbed him by the hair and lifted him as high as I could and I hit him in the face. His nose popped with a little spray of blood and I hit him again. He started to cry. I said, 'Who's lying right there? What's her name?'

'Dani.' He still wouldn't look at her.

'Look at her.'

'No.' Blubbering now.

I knotted his hair between my fingers and turned his face toward the body and pointed at her. 'Look at her.'

He clenched his eyes tight. 'No!'

I slapped him hard on the left side of his face two times and then I dug my fingers at his eyes, prying them open. I said, 'Look at her, you sonofabitch. Dani's lying there and not you. They killed Dani. Do you see her? They didn't kill you.' Peter covered his face, peering out from between his fingers at what was left of the woman who picked up his candy wrappers. I said, 'Do you see her, Peter?'

He coughed out a great whooping sob. 'Dani.'

I let go of him.

He rocked forward and crawled toward her body. 'It's my fault,' he said. 'Oh God, it's my fault.'

I didn't say anything. I was breathing hard and something sharp throbbed behind my right eye.

Peter sat on his knees next to her, and touched her muscular arm, and cried all the harder. It made me feel ashamed.

Pike came up behind me. 'Ric will go to DeLuca. Things will happen fast now.'

'Yes.' I took a deep breath and let it out. 'Peter?'

'What?' He didn't look at me.

246

'Did you tell Charlie that we were on to the Jamaicans?'

He nodded, still not looking at me.

'Did you tell him we knew about the secret accounts?'

Another nod.

It felt cold and damp and ready to snow. Above us, the roadway vibrated with cars and trucks and thousands of people. Around us was a city of millions. We'd fired maybe fifteen high-velocity pistol rounds, yet no one came.

Pike said, 'Charlie will panic. He'll do the first thing he thinks of and that means he'll come for us and for Karen and the boy. He won't want anyone around who knows about the accounts or the Jamaicans.'

I looked down at Dani. 'We'll have to leave her.'

Pike said, 'Yes.'

I lifted Peter Alan Nelsen to his feet. He didn't look at me or at Pike and he didn't resist; he stared at Dani's body.

I said, 'Did you hear? Did you understand?'

Peter nodded.

'All right.'

Pike took Peter by the arm and led him back to the car.

I took off my G-2 jacket, ripped my name out of the inside collar, and put it over Dani's head. Then I followed after them.

CHAPTER 33

I stopped at the Texaco station in Chelam and used the pay phone to call Karen Lloyd at the bank. I had to pull off the shoulder rig and the Dan Wesson and leave them in the car. No jacket. The old guy in the hunting cap was still sitting in the hard chair and the old retriever was still lying on his piece of cardboard. The retriever wagged his tail when he saw me.

I told Karen that something had gone wrong and that she should pick up Toby from school and go home. She wanted to know what. I told her that I was at the Texaco station and would tell her when she got home. I said, 'Are the printouts of the DeLuca transactions at your house or at the bank?'

'The bank.'

'Bring them.'

At ten minutes of four we parked in Karen Lloyd's drive and went into the house. Karen was in the living room, looking nervous, and Toby was with her. Peter was sort of slack-jawed and distant and walked as if his knees were stiff. They stared at him. Karen said, 'What's wrong?'

'Plans have changed.'

Peter said, 'They killed Dani.'

'What?'

Peter went to the couch and Joe Pike went past them down the hall to Karen's study.

I said, 'You guys are going to have to go away for

tonight. Maybe a couple of nights. Throw whatever you need into a bag.'

Karen started to ask another question, then looked at Toby. 'Tobe. Do what he says. Go pack an overnighter.'

Toby took a couple of steps back along the hall, then stopped.

Joe Pike came back with his duffel bag and took out a 12-gauge Winchester autoloader and a box of Remington Long Range Express shotgun shells. Number 4 buck. The autoloader had an illegal 14-inch barrel and a pistol grip in place of a stock. When Karen saw the shotgun, she said, 'Oh my God. What is happening here?'

Pike took a Browning .32 automatic in an ankle holster out of the bag and showed it to me. 'You want the backup?'

'Yes.'

He handed it to me and I put it on. I made sure the safety was off.

'*Tell me what happened*!'

I told her. I told her that at about the time Pike and I had been in her office, explaining what we had found out and what we were going to do with it, Peter and Dani had gone to see DeLuca and that now Dani was lying beneath an on-ramp to the Manhattan Bridge in Brooklyn. When I said the part about Dani, Karen's face went gray and she said, 'You stupid sonofabitch.'

Peter looked at the floor.

I pulled my pants leg down to cover the Browning and Karen said, 'What are we going to do?'

'It's not just Charlie anymore, but there's still maybe a way to do this without the cops. Before, we had it contained and we could have worked it so that we were dealing only with Charlie, but now that's different. We shot two DeLuca soldiers. One of them is dead and the other might be. Charlie's going to have to explain where the dead guys are and how they got dead.'

'So what will he do?'

'He'll hit us. He'd rather lose the laundering setup than risk the other *capos* or the Gambozas finding out what he's been doing.'

Karen said, 'Maybe we can talk to him. Maybe we should call him.'

'It's past that.'

'What can we do?'

Pike said, 'Sal.'

Karen looked at Pike, then me.

I nodded. 'Sal's our only way out. Charlie's thinking he's got to end it. He's got to get all of us before we send up the flare. So we go to Sal and we lay it out for him just like we were going to lay it out for Charlie. Sal won't want the Gambozas or the other families to find out what Charlie has been doing any more than Charlie.'

Karen nodded, maybe looking hopeful. Toby had worked his way back to the living room and she had her arm around him. He was staring at Peter.

'Did you bring the account records?'

She got them out of her purse in the dining room and gave them to me.

I said, 'Joe will stay with you. Does Charlie know about May Erdich's place?'

Karen shook her head. 'I don't think so.'

'Go there. If they come here looking for you tonight and don't find you, they might get the idea to look around. They'll check the Ho Jo, so don't go there. Get a room with May Erdich. If it goes okay, I'll come to May's when it's done.'

'All right.'

Maybe Peter could feel the weight of Toby's eyes. He looked up and he said, 'I got her killed. I'd make it better if I could, but this is what I've done.'

Toby turned and ran down the hall.

Peter Alan Nelsen, the King of Adventure, put his face in his hands and sobbed like a baby.

I borrowed Pike's coat and pulled it on. It was a little big, but it fit well enough. I folded the account records and put them in the right outside pocket.

Karen said, 'Peter.'

Peter's shoulders shook and what you could see of his face looked red and splotched.

Karen said, 'Goddamnit, Peter, we don't need to listen to this.'

Peter cried harder.

Karen crossed her arms and looked out the window, and then she walked over to Peter Alan Nelsen and put her hand on his back. Peter gulped air and made a deep, racking sob and hugged her around the hips and cried into her skirt. Karen Lloyd stared at the ceiling and patted his back.

I walked out of the house and climbed into the Taurus and drove hard through the falling darkness all the way down to Manhattan and Sal DeLuca's.

CHAPTER 34

Sal 'The Rock' DeLuca had three adjoining brownstones just east of Central Park on 62nd Street. One block in from the park a homeless woman with two children was building a little hut out of cardboard against somebody's front gate while a wino staggered by and offered her a drink. The wino didn't look where he was going, tripped over something, stumbled around in a wide orbit with a lot of hand waving, then fell onto the cardboard and threw up. The homeless woman kicked him in the balls. Anywhere else in America, East 62nd Street was a place you'd avoid after the sun went down, but not in New York. In New York, people paid millions to live on East 62nd Street. There were trees on East 62nd. The French Embassy was around the corner.

Charlie DeLuca's black Lincoln Town Car wasn't around, but a couple of guys in a maroon Mercedes were. If Sal knew what Charlie was up to with the Jamaicans, I figured that Charlie would come to Sal first for damage control. If Sal didn't know, then Charlie would charge straight out to Chelam and try to end it before Sal found out. The black Town Car not being around was a good sign, but maybe Charlie had come with somebody else. He even might've taken a cab.

I made the block twice, then parked on Fifth and walked back, trying to figure a way to see Sal without getting killed. The two guys in the Mercedes watched me as I walked past.

The homeless woman and her children were huddled

in their little cardboard house and the wino was sitting with his back against the building, holding his crotch with one hand and his bottle with the other. I made a big deal out of weaving as I walked and stopped a couple of times as if I had to steady myself and then I sat down next to the wino and studied the block. There were no fire escapes to creep up and no alleys to slip within and no second-story landings to leap to in a single bound. There were only the two guys in the Mercedes and another guy hanging around on Sal the Rock's top step. Phoning for an appointment probably wouldn't work.

The wino burped softly and gingerly fingered his crotch.

I said, 'Pretty nasty shot she gave you.'

He nodded ruefully. 'Women have been my ruination.'

'Is there any wine left in your bottle?'

The wino lifted the bottle and looked at it forlornly. 'Alas. *Non.*' Our breaths were fogging in the cold night air.

'May I have it?'

He placed the bottle carefully on the sidewalk. 'My world is yours to share.'

I picked up the bottle and wobbled across the street.

The two guys in the Mercedes and the guy standing on the top step watched me, but it was the guys in the Mercedes I was worried about.

I leaned against one of the trees for a while and pretended to drink, then continued along the sidewalk until I came to Sal DeLuca's. When I got to Sal's, I sat on the bottom step.

The guy on the top step said, 'Beat it, rummy.' He was a little guy with a squinty face.

I mumbled something and hugged the bottle.

'Hey, asshole, I said beat it.' He pounded down the steps and grabbed me by the back of the jacket and tried to lift me. When he lifted, he pulled me to him and I

253

pushed the Dan Wesson into the soft flesh beneath his ribs. I said, 'If you give it away, you die first.'

He stopped moving and stared directly into my eyes.

I said, 'Take me up the steps. Walk like you're helping me. We're going inside. Do you understand?'

'Yes.'

'Is Sal DeLuca in there?'

'Yes.'

'Is Charlie DeLuca in there?'

'No.'

'Who else is in there?'

'The old man. Vito and Angie. The staff.' I didn't know who Vito and Angie were, but it didn't seem to matter.

'Let's go.'

We went up the steps, walking close so that the gun was hidden between us.

Halfway up, the passenger side of the Mercedes opened and one of the guys got out. 'Hey, Freddie.'

I dug the gun into Freddie's side a little harder. 'Tell'm you're getting me something to eat.'

Freddie told him.

The guy at the Mercedes laughed and called Freddie an asshole.

We went up the rest of the way and Freddie let us into a long marble entry with a high ceiling and ornate stairs. The house was quiet. I said, 'Take me to Sal.'

'You gotta be crazy.'

'If I was crazy, I'd have said take me to your leader.' I gave him another prod.

We went down the long entry, then through a living room that looked like it was maybe a hundred years old and then into a wood-paneled den with a fireplace. Sal DeLuca was sitting with a couple of well-dressed guys close to his age, the two guys on one couch and Sal on another, facing each other across a little table. Vito and Angie. They had hard, lined faces, and one of them had a

254

gray mustache, and both of them looked at me with the sort of mild curiosity you reserve for a strange dog with a skin rash. *Capos*. Mafia executive material.

Sal looked surprised. 'What do you want?'

Then Sal saw the gun.

Sal DeLuca was in his early sixties and maybe five ten but he was very wide, with the sort of muscular density that allows great strength. He would've been very strong when he was younger, and he was probably very strong now. They don't call you Sal the Rock because you're wuzzy. He had a round face and protruding eyes and a wide mouth and fleshy lips, sort of like a frog's. He was wearing a deep blue smoking jacket. The last guy I'd seen in a smoking jacket was Elmer Fudd, but I didn't tell him that. Instead I said, 'Two of your soldiers were killed today in Brooklyn. I'm the guy who killed them. Charlie DeLuca is partnered with a Jamaican gangster named Jesus Santiago. No one knows it yet, but they're stealing dope from the Gamboza brothers.'

The guy with the gray mustache said, 'Hey.'

The other guy said, 'You gotta be outta your fuckin' mind.'

Sal DeLuca didn't say anything, but when I mentioned Charlie, something cold flickered in his eyes and I felt scared.

I said, 'I wanted you to find out first, Sal. I didn't want it to get around before you knew.' I lowered the Dan Wesson.

Sal said, 'Vito.'

The guy with the mustache hopped up and took the gun. Vito. I said, 'There's a .32 on my right ankle.' He took that, too, and put both guns on the little table between the two couches. Sal picked up the Dan Wesson with his left hand, felt its weight, and then he looked at me and nodded. 'You got balls, I'll give you that. What's your name?'

'Elvis Cole.'

'That's a stupid fucking name.'

'Better than Elvis Jones.'

Sal made up his mind about something and leaned back in the chair, still holding the Dan Wesson. 'Okay. You got fifteen seconds to tell me something that will save your life.'

CHAPTER 35

Sal said, 'Freddie, you wait in the hall.'

Freddie looked nervous. 'He had the gun, Sal. I couldn't help it.'

'Wait in the hall.' The cold thing still alive in his eyes. Freddie went out into the hall.

Angie said, 'Sal, you don't believe this shit, do you? Guy comes in like this, a stranger?'

Sal made a little hand move. 'So now he has to prove it.'

I said, 'Take something out of my right front pocket?'

Sal nodded.

I took out the computer sheets and gave them to him. 'What the fuck is this?'

'Transaction records of your money-laundering operation through the First Chelam Bank. You remember Karen Lloyd?'

Sal nodded again.

I glanced at Vito and Angie. 'You want to do this alone?'

Sal said, 'You're not from New York. Where you from?'

'California.'

He made a little head move, like that explained it. 'This is my brother Vito. This is my cousin Angie. We're family here. You understand family?'

'Yes.'

'Say what you came to say.'

I walked them through the eight accounts. I showed

them how the deposits in Charlie's private account went from nickel and dime to the mid-five figures starting about five months ago, when Charlie had met Gloria Uribe and through her fell in with Jesus Santiago. I told them that Charlie had turned a Gamboza hype named Richie Sealy and that the hype fed information to Charlie about incoming Gamboza dope shipments and that Charlie then sold the information to the Jamaicans so that they could hijack the dope. I told them about following Charlie to Queens and the meeting that I had witnessed between Charlie and the Jamaicans and the cop from Kennedy airport. I told him about Peter and Dani and what had happened in Brooklyn under the Manhattan Bridge. I spoke slowly and carefully and I gave them names and addresses and times of day.

When I was finished, nobody said anything. Angie was chewing at his upper lip and Vito was staring at the fireplace. It was a long time before Sal moved or spoke, and when he did it wasn't to me. 'Vito, we hear anything about the Gambozas getting ripped off?'

Vito shrugged, not wanting to commit himself. 'Something about maybe some niggers took down a load of Gamboza dope. Who listens? We got no financial interest in dope anymore. We gave that up to the Gambozas.'

Sal shook his head. 'We traded with them, Vito. We gave them our piece of the dope for their piece of the labor.'

Angie said, 'Hey, Sal, this mook's talking about your kid, for chrissake. I think he's fulla shit.'

Sal went over to the fireplace and stared at the dead coals, already knowing it was true. He said, 'We got somebody in the coroner's over in Queens?'

'Yeah.'

'Check it out.'

'Jesus Christ, Sal. It's Charlie.'

'Check it out. Who's running the nigger whores for the Gambinos?'

'Marty Rotolo.'

'Call'm. Find out about this Gloria Uribe.'

Vito picked up the phone and punched in a number and spoke in a voice that was difficult to hear. He spoke for a few seconds, then hung up, but he stood with his hand on the receiver, not moving for maybe five minutes. Sal moved less than Vito. The Rock. When the phone rang, Vito picked it up and listened without saying anything. When he finished with that call, he made two more and then put down the phone and turned back to Sal. 'They found a woman's body when they found Carmine. Under the Manhattan Bridge.'

'Dani,' I said. 'Her name was Dani.'

'Stevie says Charlie's catting around with the Uribe woman. He said the Gambinos don't know anything about her because she's Jamaican. She's mixed up with some other Jamaican named Jesus Santiago.'

Sal made a soft hissing sound, steady and high-pitched, as if some core of deep pressure within him had been tapped. Angie said, 'Jesus Christ, Sal.'

Sal went to the door and told Freddie to come in. 'Find Charlie and tell him I want to see him.'

Freddie glanced at me. 'Sure, Sal.'

'Don't tell him anything else, Freddie.'

'Sure, Sal.' Freddie left.

Sal went back to the dead fireplace and looked at me. Calm. Like I hadn't just told him these things about his son. The Dan Wesson was almost hidden by his thick left hand. 'Okay. So maybe you're not full of shit. What do you want?'

'Karen Lloyd.'

'And if I don't want to give her up?'

'I give Charlie to the Gambozas.'

Angie gave with, 'So what? So we give a shit about the fuckin' Gambozas.'

I shrugged. 'Play it out that way. The Gambozas will kill Charlie for showing them up and then they'll move on you, and probably the rest of the families will, too. Everybody had an agreement and the DeLuca family broke it.'

Angie said, 'Bullshit,' and threw up his hands.

Vito didn't throw up his hands. Vito stood slow and easy, and went over to Sal. 'Not bullshit, Angie. He's right.' Vito stared at Sal when he said it and Sal stared back at him. 'Charlie's selling out another family to do business with an outsider. The fuckin' Jamaicans, for Christ's sake. Our word won't be shit. The families will turn their backs on us.'

Sal nodded.

'The family comes first.'

Sal looked at his brother, and the cold thing was suddenly very bright and alive. 'You don't have to tell me what's what, Vito.'

Vito spread his hands.

No one said anything more to me. Angie went out and came back with coffee and hard cakes, and the three of them sat on the two couches by the fireplace, drinking the coffee and eating the cakes in silence. I wasn't offered anything and I wasn't spoken to. After a while I went to an overstuffed chair across the room and sat down. Vito made more calls, and a couple of times big men knocked and looked in and would start to say something in English, but when they saw me they would switch to Italian. Angie went out twice and Vito went out once, but Sal didn't go out at all. He sat and stared, and I was glad he wasn't staring at me.

We sat like that in Sal DeLuca's den for almost six hours.

At ten minutes before five the next morning, Freddie

came in with Charlie and Ric. Charlie's hair was mussed and his collar was open and he looked anxious, like maybe he had been looking for someone and he hadn't been able to find them. Ric still looked like a vampire, all hard bones and white, leathery flesh. Charlie was saying something about why the hell this couldn't wait until morning when he saw me and you could see the fear jolt through him like a galvanic shock. He scrabbled under his coat for his gun, but Vito slapped the gun out of his hand.

Sal said, 'Freddie, close the door.'

Charlie said, 'That's the sonofabitch killed Carmine and Dante.' Trying to cover, doing a lot of arm waving and loud talking, as if the loud talk might convince Sal and Vito and Angie that whatever I'd said was lies. 'He's trying to force us outta the bank. Jesus Christ, what's he doing here?'

Sal's left hand snapped out and caught Charlie beneath the right eye. It was a hard shot and it caught Charlie by surprise. He yelled, 'Hey!'

'Shut up and listen to this.'

Charlie shut up. Ric settled back against the bookcases and watched, choreographing the dance in his head, seeing himself move fast and perfect.

Sal looked at me again for the first time since he had sent Freddie away to find Charlie and said, 'Tell him.'

I went through it for Charlie just like I had for Sal. The more I said, the more Charlie fidgeted, moving from foot to foot and picking at his hands and visibly sweating. The more Charlie moved, the more Sal didn't move. When I finished, Charlie said, 'This is bullshit. This is *merda*. Whattaya listening to this guy for?' He looked at Angie. He looked at Vito. 'Uncle Vito. Hey, Angie. Who's family here?' He looked back at his father. 'Whattaya listening to this guy for?'

Sal put the blank, frog eyes on his son and said, 'I

listened because I got no doubt in my heart that you would do this, and watching you now, I know you did.'

'Whattaya talking about? That's horseshit.'

Sal hit Charlie with the back of his right hand so hard that Charlie staggered backward. Vito looked at Ric, and Ric made a little head move, saying he wasn't in it, and Vito nodded.

Charlie was taller than Sal, and younger, but where there was something flabby and mean about Charlie, in Sal it was hard and vibrant, even at sixty-five. The Rock. 'You're a piece of shit, Charlie.' What Charlie had said to Joey Putata. Charlie tried to cover up, but Sal slapped him again and again, steady, rhythmic shots. Sal held my Dan Wesson in his left hand and slapped with his right. 'You double-crossed the fuckin' Gambozas. You made the family into liars, and you ain't even got the balls to admit it. Be a man, Charlie. Face me and tell me that you've done this horrible thing.'

I looked at Ric again, but Ric didn't seem to be watching or hearing. His eyes were flagging closed and his head was gently bobbing in time with some dark music.

Charlie stumbled into a chair, trying to get away. His face was purple and ribbons of snot leaked down across his mouth. 'It's not true. I dint do nothing. I swear I dint.' Like a little kid.

Sal said, 'I gave them my word, Charlie. This family made peace with the other families and you've broken it. You understand that? You know what that costs?'

Charlie scrambled away from the chair and covered up against the wall. He said, 'Please, Daddy.'

Sal grabbed Charlie by the throat and shook him. 'I keep hoping you'll come around, but that day is never going to come, is it? I put you in business, I make it easy for you, but you're always gonna be a fuckup.'

Charlie slipped out of Sal's grip and fell to the floor,

then tried to crawl away. Sal hit him harder, grunting with every blow.

Vito looked embarrassed and Angie looked confused and I wished I wasn't there seeing it. Sal followed his crawling son around the room, hitting him until Charlie ended up on his side, curled into a ball behind a heavy leather chair. Sal stood over him, breathing hard and hitting and saying, 'Be a man, be a man,' until finally Vito said, 'Jesus Christ, Sal,' and went over and pulled him away, lifting Sal DeLuca off his feet and talking to him and calming him down. Moving the Rock.

Then it was over. Sal stood in the center of the room, the Dan Wesson at his side, breathing hard and watching his blubbering adult child for what seemed like forever. Maybe violent insanity ran in the family.

He shook his head and seemed to see me again, as if for a time I was gone but had now returned. 'Okay,' he said. 'Karen Lloyd walks. Is that what you want?'

'Part of it. There's something else.'

'What?'

'The woman who died in Brooklyn.' I looked at Ric. 'He pulled the trigger. I want you to give him up to the cops.'

Ric moved the steel-girder shoulders and peeled himself away from the bookshelves, the leather jacket falling open.

Sal looked at Ric and then looked back at me. 'I ain't never gave one of my people up to the cops and I never would. My guys know that.'

Ric made a little smile.

'That's the deal, Sal. Take it or leave it.'

Sal the Rock DeLuca shook his head. 'No cops.' He raised the Dan Wesson, aimed it between my eyes, then turned and shot Ric once in the chest.

Ric saw it coming and yelled, 'No!' and tried to move, but the slug caught him. It pushed him back into the bookshelves and then his heels slid out from beneath him and he fell to the floor.

Charlie made a gargling sound and whimpered.

Ric tried to get up, but his feet kept slipping.

Sal shot him again.

Ric clawed under his jacket and came out with his gun.

Sal shot him twice more, smoke from the caps rolling across the room like smog spilling through the Glendale Pass into the San Fernando Valley.

There were shouts in another part of the house and the sound of men running and then someone was banging on the door. Freddie came in first.

Sal was as calm as if he had taken out the trash. 'Freddie, get a couple of those big plastic bags and take care of this.'

Freddie swallowed and stumbled backward out of the room.

Sal looked down at his son and then looked at me, his eyes empty and bottomless. 'Good enough?'

I nodded.

'Okay, you got what you want. Now I get what I want. The Gambozas must never know. What we speak of here stays here, buried forever. Will you bury this? Will you keep my kid safe?' Sal and Karen Lloyd, each worried about their children.

I nodded again. 'We bury it. We keep everyone safe.'

Vito said, 'We got loose ends, Sal. Other people know.'

Sal said, 'We'll take care of the loose ends, Vito.' He looked back at me. 'You want anything else?'

'No.'

'Then it's a done deal. Get the fuck out of my sight.'

264

CHAPTER 36

I walked out of Sal DeLuca's brownstone to a fine powder of snow on the streets and the sidewalks and the cars parked at the curb. The air was cold and the Manhattan skyline to the east was clear and pink in anticipation of the rising sun. To the west and the north, though, the clouds were still heavy and dense and promising more snow. The drunk was gone, but the little cardboard house remained, quiet and white in the early morning light. Cars belched fog-breath out on Fifth and 62nd, and men and women in heavy coats walked fast along the sidewalks, leaving gray trails. Somewhere there was music playing, but I didn't hear the notes clearly and couldn't make out the song. I slipped a twenty-dollar bill into the little cardboard house and went back to the Taurus.

I drove across Central Park, then up through the city and the Bronx and Yonkers and White Plains. I drove slowly and listened to a pretty good classic rock station that played a lot of John Fogerty and CCR. *Run Through the Jungle*. Nothing like a little Creedence Clearwater Revival at six in the morning after spending the night with the Godfather. Four miles above White Plains, I pulled into a rest stop overlooking a lake and started to shake. I shook for what seemed like hours but was probably only a couple of minutes. I let the motor run and the Taurus's heater pump on high, but I wasn't shaking from the cold.

A tan and white RV was parked broadside to the view,

and had probably been there all night. A man and a woman in their sixties came out with coffee cups and went to the rail, looking out at the lake. They watched the lake for a while and sipped the coffee and held hands. When they turned and came back to the RV, the woman gave me a friendly smile. The license plate on their little mobile house said *Utah*.

At a quarter to ten I parked on the street in front of May Erdich's house. Toby and Joe Pike were standing in brown leaves and snow, tossing a beat-up Wilson football, and Peter was sitting on May's front step, watching them. Peter looked cold.

Karen Lloyd came out of the front door as I went up the walk.

I said, 'It's over.'

She shook her head, like maybe I was lying. 'You got Charlie to go along?' Pike and Toby stopped throwing the ball. Toby ran over to stand by his mother.

'Sal. Charlie doesn't have anything to do with it anymore. It's Sal, and Sal says you're out of it. Charlie will do whatever Sal says.'

She gripped one hand with the other. 'I can stay at the bank?'

'Yes.'

'No more Charlie? No more deposits?'

'It's over, Karen.'

Peter smiled and crossed his arms but stayed on the front step.

Karen came down the steps and hugged me and then she hugged Pike. She started crying, holding us tight and digging her fingers into our shoulders as if only by holding us here could it be real. When she did it, Peter looked at his feet.

Karen let go and stepped back, smiling and crying and thanking us. She said, 'Can we go back to the house?'

'Sure. Any time you want.'

266

Peter looked up and said, 'Karen, I'm glad. I couldn't be happier.'

Karen smiled at him, then looked at her son. 'Tobe. Let's get our things. Let's say bye to May.'

They went into the house together. Inside, there was movement and warmth and the pounding footsteps of Toby running down a long hall.

Peter uncrossed his arms and pushed away from the top step. He said, 'I've gotta get Dani. I want to bring her home and take care of her.'

I nodded. 'The police will have questions. We'll have to figure out what to tell them.'

He made a little shrug. 'I'll tell them the truth. She died saving my life because I'm a jerk.'

Pike said, 'You can't.'

Peter looked at him.

I said, 'I gave my word to Sal that we wouldn't let what Charlie was doing get out to the Gambozas. You tell the cops or *People* magazine or anyone else you know how Dani died, the Gambozas or someone who works for them will put it together. When they do, the deal with Sal will be over. He'll come for you.'

'I don't care about me.'

'He'll come for Karen and Toby.'

Peter pursed his lips and looked at the ground. He didn't like it, but he was learning to live with things that he didn't like. He said, 'It makes me feel like I'm cheating her.'

'You are, but it's all we can do. Do you understand?'

He pursed his lips some more, but he nodded. The front door opened and Toby brought out his overnighter, put it on the porch, then went back inside and closed the door. Peter watched him. 'They think I'm full of shit.'

I didn't say anything.

'I'm thinking I've gotta get back to L.A. I've got the

picture going into production soon. There's no point in me staying around.'

I stared at the house for a while. My back hurt and my neck was stiff and I wanted to go to bed. 'You shouldn't have come back here expecting them to think of you as husband and father. You could've earned that, perhaps, but you didn't think in terms of earning. You thought it was your right. You demand what you want and you get it, usually, and that makes you think that you can get whatever you demand.'

'I didn't come out here wanting to fuck it up.'

'I know.'

'I wanted this to work out. I wanted them to be a part of my life. There are empty places.'

'Maybe the way to look at it is that you should've worked to be a part of their lives and hoped to fill the empty places they have.'

Peter pressed his lips together and looked at the ground, like maybe there was something interesting there. Elm leaves, dried and brittle in the cold. 'Shit. I've gotta go.'

He walked across the leaf-strewn yard and got into the limo and drove away. There was still a little snow on the windshield when he left.

Pike and I waited at the Taurus until Karen and Toby came out. Karen was smiling and said, 'I feel like a celebration. Would you like to have a late breakfast? On me, of course.'

'Whatever you want.'

We went to the Chelam diner and sat in a booth and had eggs and sausage and pumpkin pancakes and home-fried potatoes, but it wasn't much of a celebration. There was a curious letdown feeling between us, as if there were unresolved business still at hand. When Toby was finished, he got up and played a video game. *Space*

Command. A guy with a ray gun trying to kill thousands of little bugs. Karen watched him uneasily.

I said, 'At loose ends?'

She nodded. 'Does it show?'

I said, 'There's a lot to think about. There's still Peter in your life.'

She nodded again. 'It's that, but it's more than that, too. It's as if a very large object has moved across the sky, but only we've seen it. These other people here in the diner, Joyce Steuben at the bank, no one else in town has seen it.'

I nodded. It's always like that.

She said, 'I don't know what I'm going to do. I thought I did, but now I don't.' She turned away from her son and looked at me. 'I fought so hard to keep what I have here in Chelam and at the bank. Now that I've got it, you know what keeps coming to mind? Maybe I can get a better job closer to the city or up in Boston. Maybe I can find a better high school for Toby. Isn't that crazy?'

I made the same little shrug for Karen Lloyd that I had made for Peter Alan Nelsen. 'Not crazy. It wasn't a choice you could make before. Now you're free to make any choice you want.'

She sort of smiled at that and looked back at her son. 'Yes, I guess I am.' Then the smile became a little laugh that was light and open. It was the first time that I had heard her laugh.

After a while Joe and I went to the Taurus and Karen and Toby went to her LeBaron and the four of us drove back to her house beneath gray skies expectant with snow. We went inside and packed our things while Karen made phone calls and Toby dug around in the kitchen for something to eat. Twelve years old, and you're always hungry. When my bags were packed, I called United and booked two returns on a flight they had leaving from Kennedy at six-forty that night. When I

269

told Pike the time, he said, 'Didn't they have anything sooner?'

At twenty-four minutes after noon the black limo turned into the drive and Peter Alan Nelsen came to the door. Karen let him in. She said, 'I thought you had gone back to Los Angeles.'

Peter said, 'I want to start over. I know that me coming here is going to create problems for you, and changes, and I want to do what I can to help you through them. I don't want you and the boy to think I'm an asshole. I want Toby to get to know me, and I want to get to know him, and I want to work out things like visitation and holidays and getting together. I want to pay child support, but only if that's okay with you. Can we talk about this stuff?'

Karen Lloyd said, 'Oh, shit.'

Peter said, 'Please.'

Karen Lloyd made a little whistle and tapped her right hand on her thigh and looked at the television. The television was not turned on.

I said, 'Sounds pretty good to me.'

Karen shook her head and frowned.

Peter said, 'C'mon, Karen. *Please.*'

I said, 'For Christ's sake, meet him halfway.'

Karen crossed her arms and the frown grew deeper. 'We'll see.' Give'm an inch.

The phone rang and Karen Lloyd went into the kitchen and answered it. When she was gone, Peter said, 'What do you think?'

I spread my hands. 'We'll see.'

Karen came back and said, 'It's a man named Roland George.'

I left them to stare at each other and went into the kitchen. Rollie came on with a tight, clipped voice. 'You heard?'

'What?'

'On the news ten minutes ago. Sal DeLuca was shot to death in his health club, four in the head, close range, sometime around ten this morning. You know anything about it?'

'I think it was Charlie. If it was, I think he'll want us next.'

I hung up and went back into the living room and told Karen and Peter and Joe Pike. When I told them, Peter said, 'You mean the sonofabitch is coming back here?'

'Yes.'

Karen said, 'I knew it couldn't be this easy. I knew it wasn't over. What are we going to do?'

'Get into town where there's people. When you and Toby are safe, Joe and I will see what we can do with Charlie.'

Karen called Toby and we went quickly out the front door and into her LeBaron. I told Peter to get in the back and I told Karen that I would drive. Neither of them objected.

Toby said, 'Is it those men again, Mom?'

We pulled away from her house and went down the clean new tarmac street and turned onto the main road toward Chelam. It was twenty-eight minutes after noon.

We had gone about two miles when they found us.

CHAPTER 37

. They came up behind us in two cars, a green Dodge station wagon and the black Town Car, just as the snow began to fall.

Pike saw them first. 'Behind us. Turned out from a side road, maybe a half mile back.'

I pushed Toby's head down. 'Get on the floor. Make yourself as small as you can and wrap your arms around your head.'

I pushed Karen down on top of him.

The Town Car pulled into the left lane and the wagon stayed in the right and they came on hard. Pike reached under his jacket and took out his .357.

I pressed the LeBaron's pedal to the floor, but the Town Car inched closer and then there were gold specks flashing around it and something hit the rear of the LeBaron two times, *bam bam*, like rocks thrown by a kid hiding behind a tree. The right rear tire blew and Karen Lloyd made a sharp gasping sound and Toby said, 'What was that?'

The LeBaron nosed up and I swung us to the right, and then we were off the road and bouncing across an untended pumpkin field, ripping through weeds and a barbed-wire fence and a couple of white birch saplings. I gunned the engine and forced the LeBaron across the field, sideways half the time and near out of control, until the flat right rear dug into the loam maybe three hundred yards from the road and the LeBaron wouldn't go any farther. I said, 'Everybody out.'

The station wagon and the Town Car skidded to a stop on the road and doors banged open and eight men pushed out, five of them with shotguns. Charlie DeLuca had been driving the Town Car and Joey Putata was one of the guys in the wagon, but I didn't recognize anyone else. Ric was conspicuous by his absence. No one now to keep Charlie calm, no one to rub his back and say the quiet things and keep Charlie DeLuca among the land of the sane. Sal the Rock had learned that. Charlie was certifiably, stark-raving, bad-to-the-bone out of control.

I shoved the driver's side door open and fell out, then pushed my seat forward and pulled Karen and Toby out after me. Pike went out the passenger's side and the .357 boomed twice. Peter followed Pike, and then the five of us were crouched down among the pumpkins behind the LeBaron.

Two of the guys up on the road started blasting away with their shotguns, but then someone did a lot of arm waving and they stopped. Three hundred yards with shotguns was silly.

The little pumpkin field was maybe five hundred yards on a side, bordered to the east and the west and the south by thick stands of birch and elm and maple trees. Behind us to the south there was a little ramshackle feed shed that looked to be maybe a hundred years old. I squatted down next to Karen and said, 'Does anyone live around here?'

'Maybe a couple of miles that way.' She pointed southwest.

'Is there a road behind us?'

She scrunched her face, trying to think but not having an easy time of it. 'There must be. Some kind of farming road.'

Toby said, 'Yeah, there is. It's a utility road. Dirt.'

'How far?'

'Maybe a mile and a half. It's on the other side of all

273

these fields. It comes out by this little airport where the crop dusters fly, but there won't be anyone there. They close it down in the winter.'

Pike said, 'If we can get there, maybe we can make a farmhouse.'

The snow fell harder, swirling and piling up in little white pockets on the LeBaron and on the pumpkins, thick enough in the air to make the men on the road indistinct and shadowy. Two of the shadows went off to the left and two of them went right and four of them started off the road directly for us. Classic pincer move. Probably taught that at the mafia academy.

I said, 'They're going to try to envelop us, faster guys moving out on the flank, the other guys coming slow up the middle to drive us toward them.'

Pike said, 'Unh-hunh,' and opened the duffel. He took out the shotgun and a cartridge box and began filling his pockets with the shells. Twenty-five rounds in the box, but he found places for all of them.

Peter was squatting next to Karen and behind Toby. He had put an arm around Karen's shoulders without thinking about it. Or maybe he had. He said, 'Maybe we could dig in here and hold them off.'

Pike shook his head. 'Not with twenty-five rounds.'

I duck-walked to Karen and Peter and knelt close to them. Their faces were white and their eyes were squinty and drawn. 'We're going to have to split up. Pike and I will go out to the flanks. You guys move straight back across the field and try to get to the farm road. Do you understand that?'

They both said, 'Yes.'

'Stay low and run as fast as you can just like you've seen people do on television. Try to keep the car between you and the four guys coming across the field. They're coming slow because they know we have guns, so you'll have time. Work your way to the feed shed and get behind it, and then work your way to the woods using the shed as cover.'

Peter nodded and Karen said, 'Yes.'

'Don't stop until you get to people. Then call the police.'

Karen wasn't looking into my eyes. She was watching my mouth, getting every word. Hanging on by her fingernails.

Peter said, 'I don't want to run off. I want to do something.'

'You are doing something. You're helping this woman and your son get to a safe place. That's your job.'

Peter glanced down at the woman that he used to be married to and their son, and he nodded. 'Sure. Okay.'

I turned to Toby. 'Tobe, you think you can find the road through the woods?'

'Sure. You just keep going south.'

'Okay. You get to the road, which way to the airfield?'

'East.'

I looked back at Karen and then at Peter. 'Do it.'

Karen said, 'They're going to kill us, aren't they?'

'They're going to try. But Joe and I won't let them.'

Her eyes were big and darting. She held tight to Toby's arm. 'How can you stop them? There're eight of them and we're trapped here in the middle of nowhere with them.'

Pike chambered a round into his shotgun. 'No,' he said. 'They're trapped with us.'

I gave Karen a little nod and then she crabbed away, holding on to Toby's shirt with her right hand, crouched low and stumbling through the frozen weeds and the pumpkins. Peter followed close after them.

Pike said, 'How many rounds you got?'

'Just what's in the gun.'

He gave me disapproval.

'I know,' I said. 'You can't take me anywhere.'

275

He handed me the .357, butt first, then gave me a little leather pouch with three speed-loaders. Be prepared.

'You ready?'

'I'm ready.'

'Let's do it.'

We fired six quick rounds at the four men coming across the field, then Joe broke left and I broke right, moving low and fast, and then he was behind me and gone.

The snow was a glistening powder across the field, piling up in little mounds that scattered without sound as I moved. Charlie DeLuca saw us break, and the three guys with him opened up, firing with the shotguns and their pistols, still better than two hundred yards out. Panic shots. I guess they hadn't expected us to try to outflank the flankers. Charlie yelled something at the guys who had gone into the woods, but with the snow and the wind and the distance you couldn't make out what he was saying. Pellets rained on the field around me and a great orange pumpkin exploded, but I didn't stop and I didn't look back. I stayed low and moved hard and wondered if the guys in the woods were making better time coming my way than I was making going theirs. Then I didn't think about it anymore and pretty soon I was in the trees.

I moved twenty yards into the tree line and stopped between two white birch to listen. If the flankers had moved fast, maybe they were already behind me. They weren't. Thirty yards upwind toward the road, limbs snapped and dead leaves crunched and it sounded like the Fifth Marines were on the march. City kids come out to play. This deep in the trees, you couldn't see the field. They didn't know Karen and Peter and Toby were falling back and they didn't know Pike and I had moved into the tree line. Out in the field, the pistols and the shotguns had stopped firing and Charlie was yelling, but I couldn't hear what he was saying. If I couldn't hear, the flankers couldn't hear. They were making so much noise that even if Charlie had been understandable, they wouldn't have heard.

I moved deeper into the trees and found a place beside a fallen elm and waited. In the woods the snow fell only slightly, caught higher in the tree canopy by dead leaves and vines and branches. Some of the earlier snow had melted and the water had leached down the trees, making their bark feel velvety and damp and enhancing their good smell. Except for the coming of the flankers, it was quiet. Calm. The natural state of the woods.

Joey Putata and a guy in a blaze-orange hunting jacket pushed their way through a tangle of vines hanging from a dogwood tree. The guy in the orange jacket had heavy sideburns and the kind of coarse virulent beard that had to be shaved three times a day and a little hat with a feather in the band. Joey Putata was carrying a 12-gauge Mossberg slug gun and the guy in the orange had a Ruger Redhawk .44 Magnum revolver. Joey's eyes were still black and green from the beating Charlie had given him, but here he was, tramping through the woods. Some guys are stupid all the way through. The guy in orange ducked down under a branch but didn't duck far enough. The branch knocked his hat off and a slug of fresh snow fell down his back. He said, 'Sonofabitch,' and then they stopped.

Joey Putata said, 'You think we're far enough?'

The guy with the hat said, 'How the fuck I know? Let's go that way and see if we can find Tony and Mike.' Tony and Mike must be the other flankers.

From a very long way off there were two quick *booms*. Joey got excited and said, 'Maybe we got'm.' When he said it, he shoved the guy with the hat, and the guy with the hat turned sideways and saw me. I shot him once in the chest. The .357 slug hit him square in the sternum like an express-speed brick and punched him back into the vines. I said, 'Hey, Joey. Don't you ever learn?'

Joey brought up the Mossberg, but he didn't bring it up fast enough. I shot him once in the neck and then I was moving back toward the field.

When I came out of the tree line, Pike was running toward the LeBaron. Charlie and the other three guys were gone and so was the black Town Car.

Pike said, 'He took off a couple of minutes ago, heading away from town.'

I came up next to Pike and reloaded the .357. 'He's betting that the others are making for a road behind us and he's gone to look for it.'

Pike cocked his head. 'I don't figure he's looking. I figure it's the side road he came at us from and he knows just where it leads.'

'Great.'

We set off south across the field, running side by side past the little feed shack and falling into an easy rhythm. When we made the woods, it was easy to see where Karen and Toby and Peter had passed. The damp mat of dead winter leaves was kicked up and branches and small winter-dead saplings were broken.

The narrow dirt utility road was less than a mile in from the main road, closer than Toby had thought. We came out of the trees and went east, pounding along as the road cut through the woods, striding in tandem and feeling the cold air cut into our throats. There were foot tracks and fresh tire tracks in the snow, but the tire tracks didn't necessarily belong to Charlie's Town Car. They could have been anything. Pike said, 'I see it.'

The road broke out of the little section of woods and cut across flat white fields of pumpkins and squash and winter truck. Half a mile farther down the road, there was an orange wind sock flapping in the wind and a utility shed and a corrugated-metal hangar. If the wind sock wasn't orange, we would never have seen it against the snow. A couple of Piper Pawnee crop-dusting planes were next to the hangar, tarped and tied down, as winter-dead as the leaves.

The black Lincoln Town Car was parked by the utility shed and people moved between the planes.

We hadn't come out of the woods in time. Charlie DeLuca had them.

CHAPTER 38

Pike and I picked up our pace, running on either side of the road, our breath great white plumes in the snowy air. We ran hard until we drew close, then we throttled back, trading speed for quiet as we moved up to the hangar. The shadow shapes we had seen when we came out of the woods were gone.

Charlie's Town Car was parked at a skew outside the corrugated-metal hangar, already collecting little pockets of snow on the windward side. The two Pawnees were on the field side of the hangar, and, before them, a couple of rusted water mules used for aviation gasoline and pesticides. Somewhere upwind, Karen Lloyd yelled and there was a single sharp *pop*, pistol, but the wind and the snow carried away the sound.

Pike said, 'They'll be in the hangar or in the fields behind the planes.'

We went to the hangar, looped around the corner, and saw them through a dust-streaked window built into a door. Karen Lloyd was on her knees, crying, and Charlie DeLuca was holding Toby by the hair, pointing a Browning .380 automatic at his right temple. Toby was crying, too. He was probably crying because he was scared, but he might've been crying because a fat guy was hitting Peter Alan Nelsen in the face and knocking him down. He would hit Peter and knock him down, and Peter would get up and go after him again. The fat guy was thick through the middle and the hips and the shoulders and the back, sort of like an overstuffed sausage, but it was hard fat. There wouldn't be a lot of stamina, but there was plenty of mean. Peter kept trying to get to Charlie, but the fat guy kept beating him up. Karen was yelling something about doing whatever Charlie wanted if only he'd stop. It was hard to hear them through the glass.

I touched Pike's shoulder and pointed past them to the big sliding doors at the back of the hangar. The doors were open.

Pike nodded, and we slipped under the window and took one step toward the field when the two other guys who'd been with Charlie DeLuca came around the corner. One of them was tall and the other wasn't. The shorter one had a dead cigar in his mouth and what looked like a .32 revolver in his right hand. The taller one was grousing about the cold, and neither of them knew we were there until they saw us. Joe Pike hit the shorter guy with an outside spin kick that sounded like it broke his neck. The taller guy said, 'Hey,' and fired what was maybe a Rossi .38 into the ground, and I shot him high in the chest. Blood squirted out in a little geyser, and he looked down at it and then started pressing on the blood, trying to make it stay where it was. Then he fell over.

Inside, there were the sounds of fast movement and Karen screamed something and there was the peculiar high shriek that only young children can make. Someone started shooting and bullets slammed through the side of the hangar, well wide of us, and then the shooting stopped.

We looked in through either side of the window in time to see Charlie drag Toby through the hangar doors. Karen followed them. Peter was lying on his side and the fat guy kicked him twice, then took a blue revolver from under his jacket. He pulled Peter's head back and put the revolver into Peter's mouth. Pike shot him in the top of the left shoulder with a load of number four. The fat guy fell backward and Pike shot him again.

We ran back between the two Pawnee crop dusters just as Charlie came around the hangar with one arm locked around Toby Lloyd's neck, looking for us. The Browning .380 was pressed under Toby's ear. Charlie's face was bright red and there were veins standing out on his forehead. He was checking the roofline. Batman and Robin always come down from the roof. He screamed, 'You're mine, you sonofabitch. I'm gonna cut out your fuckin' guts and fry'm in a pan!'

Karen came around the corner behind them, tears washing her face, her hands tight and clawed. She wanted to run to Toby, but she was scared if she did the nut with the gun would kill him. She yelled, 'Toby!'

Charlie DeLuca dug his pistol so deep under Toby's jaw that Toby shrieked again and wet his pants. Charlie yelled, 'I'm gonna kill him, you chickenshit motherfuckers, you don't come out here. I'm gonna blow his fuckin' eyes out.'

I glanced at Pike. Pike's flat black lenses were locked on Charlie DeLuca, the shotgun resting easy along the Pawnee's metal wing strut. Pike's a better shot than me. Maybe the best I've ever seen. I said, 'He's going to do it. He's going to kill the boy.'

'Yes.'

I gave him the .357 and took the shotgun. 'Can you make the shot?'

Karen screamed, 'Help him, please. Somebody help!'

Pike said, 'I can make the shot, but not with his gun on the boy that way. He could jerk when he dies.'

Karen screamed, 'Toby!'

Peter stumbled out of the hangar and said, 'Let go my kid, you fat fuck!' There were cuts over both eyes and his nose was broken and his lips were split. There was so much blood on his face that he looked like he was wearing makeup. 'I'm Peter Alan Nelsen, and I will kick your fat fucking ass!'

Karen screamed, 'Peter! No!'

Charlie DeLuca smiled and swung the Browning toward Peter and said, 'Kick this.' Then he fired once.

Peter fell down, and Karen and Toby screamed, and I stepped out from behind the Pawnee and yelled, 'Charlie!'

Charlie DeLuca swung the .380 back toward me, pulled the trigger, and something tugged at the top of my shoulder. Then I felt something solid wash past me from behind and there was a loud noise and the back of Charlie DeLuca's head blew out like a big rig tire filled with red paint. Pike's Python. Charlie was dead before he started to fall.

Toby kicked away from what was left of Charlie DeLuca and ran to Peter, yelling, 'Daddy! Daddy!'

Blood was spilling from the top of Peter's left thigh, but he made it to his knees and dragged himself over to Charlie DeLuca and started punching the body. If Peter could get up, I figured I should get up, too. I did okay at it, but my ears were ringing and my shirt felt wet. I looked down and opened my jacket and saw that my shirt was turning black from the top down. Then Pike was there, peeling back the shirt. 'Doesn't look bad. Caught it across the top of the trapezius.'

'Sure.'

Pike went over to Peter, took off his belt, and wrapped it tight around Peter's leg. Then he came back to me and used his sweatshirt as a compress on my shoulder. I burned where the bullet had torn through the muscle and there was a tingling feeling, but it could've been worse. Peter blinked at his leg and at Charlie DeLuca and then he grinned at me. 'We got the bastard. We got him.'

'Yes,' I said. 'We did.'

He began to laugh. 'It's over.'

Karen was laughing then, too. Nervous and scared and letting off the tension by laughing. 'Yes,' she said. 'God, yes.'

Karen came over and hugged me. Toby helped Peter to his feet and they came over and hugged me, too.

Some days, I guess you're more huggable than others.

CHAPTER 39

We left the bodies at the airport and went into town to see Chelam's only doctor, a young guy with a beard and glasses name of Hocksley. Karen Lloyd drove.

The doc was good about it. He practiced out of his home just four houses down from May Erdich's place, the kind of guy who wanted to know his patients and bring babies into the world and watch them grow. Idealistic. You know the type. When he cut off my shirt and Peter's pants, he whistled and said, 'Man, I haven't seen anything like this since I left the Bronx General ER.'

'Hunting accident.'

'Sure.'

He swabbed us down and cleaned us out, then put in a couple of stitches and gave us each two injections, something clear to fight infection and something white to fight tetanus. He also gave us some orange pills for the pain. He said, 'Don't suppose I should call the police about this.'

I said, 'Mind if I use your phone?'

I called Rollie George and told him where I was and what had happened. While I told him, the doc crossed his arms and listened and absently stroked his beard. When I hung up, he said, 'Think I should maybe go take a look?'

I shook my head. 'It won't do any good.'

He looked at Peter. 'You look familiar.'

'I've got one of those faces.'

We left the doctor, dropped Toby with May Erdich, and drove back to the little airfield. The snow had stopped falling but not before a gentle skin of white had been pulled over the road and the airplanes and the bodies in the field. Joe Pike and I unshipped the tarps from the two Pawnees' engine cowlings and covered Charlie DeLuca and the three guys who'd died with him and then we sat in the LeBaron to wait.

A couple of Connecticut state cars got there first, followed by a plain blue sedan with somebody from the Connecticut AG's office. They came in the right way, without the sirens or the lights, and I liked them for it. The guy from the AG's office walked over to us and asked who we were. I told him my name and Joe's, but I didn't mention Karen or Peter, and he didn't ask. He said that he had been told something about bodies at another location. I told him how to get to the pumpkin field and that there were two bodies on either side of the field in the woods. He nodded and went back to the uniform cops, and then he and a car full of the uniforms drove away to take a look. Twenty minutes later a tan car with an FBI emblem on the side door and a white Ford from the New York State Attorney General's office pulled in just ahead of a gray Cadillac limousine. Two guys got out of the FBI car, and a bald guy and two women got out of the N.Y. car. Rollie George and his dog got out of the limo. The law student was driving. Everybody except the bald man smiled when they saw Rollie and shook his hand and told him it was good to see him. Nothing like palling around with a big-time novelist at a murder scene.

Karen said, 'Shouldn't we be out there with them?'

'No. We sit and wait and see what they say.'

They went as a group to the spot between the two airplanes and lifted the tarpaulin and looked at what was under it. Maxie sniffed at Charlie's body and lifted his leg and Rollie had to pull the dog away. One of the women laughed. They stood over the bodies for a long time, sometimes glancing back to the car, but mostly not. Everybody seemed in agreement with what they were talking about except the bald guy. You could see it in his face. He made sharp gestures and once he pointed at our car. They talked some more, and then Rollie George walked over to us and bent down by the driver's side window. He gave Karen the sort of reassuring smile your grandfather might give, and if he recognized Peter, he didn't say anything. He leaned close to me and said, 'Can we have the bad cop?'

I said, 'Yes. If my people don't get named and don't have to testify.'

He nodded. 'It looks like there's more than one officer involved. It looks like there might be several with Kennedy security who took part.'

I nodded back at him. 'I sort of figured that.'

Rollie smiled at Karen again and then he and Max walked back to the little group around Charlie DeLuca's body. There was more talk and the bald guy liked it even less and made more of the sharp gestures until one of the women he had ridden out with said, 'Oh, shut the fuck up, Morton.'

The feds and the people from the two AG offices came to the car for Pike and me and walked us around the site asking us questions. Most of the questions were about Charlie DeLuca and the Jamaicans and the cop I had followed to the Queens precinct house. I didn't mention Charlie DeLuca's secret account, or that he was doing something that Sal didn't know about, or the Gambozas. The Jamaicans probably didn't know whose dope they were stealing and neither, probably, did the cop. If they did, and if they told, that was between the DeLucas and them. You do what you can.

When the AG people were finished with their questions, they brought us back to the car. None of them looked at Karen Lloyd or Peter Alan Nelsen, or spoke to them. It was as if they weren't there. One of the women and one of the feds went with a couple of Staties to the pumpkin field. They weren't gone long. After they got back, there was more talk and then Roland George came back to us. He said, 'I think we've done about all we can do here. You can go now.'

Karen Lloyd said, 'Is that all?'

'Yes, ma'am.'

'You don't need to question us? You aren't going to take us in?'

Peter said, 'Karen.'

Rollie George smiled and walked away.

Karen looked at me. 'They're keeping us out of this? Even with people dead?'

'Yes. Start the car and let's get out of here.'

We drove to Karen Lloyd's house in silence and parked in the drive beneath the basketball hoop until Peter had his story straight. The people from the AG's office were going to release Dani's body to him with no questions asked, but he would need to know what to tell Nick and T.J. and the press. Peter Alan Nelsen's bodyguard had been murdered and there would be questions. He was going to have to lie, and he was going to have to maintain the lie for the rest of his life. He said, 'I can do it.'

Karen said, 'You'd better.'

He frowned at her and then he got out of the LeBaron and got into his limo and drove away. Karen watched him go. 'Do you think he can?'

I nodded. 'Yes. He's learned a lot.'

'I hope.' She let out a sigh. 'I hate this. I hate it that once you let someone into your life, they're part of your life forever.'

I said, 'Part, maybe, but not all. You're still you. You're vice-president of the bank. You're twice president of the PTA. You're a Rotarian and a member of the Library

Committee. Maybe, without having gone through what you went through with Peter, you wouldn't be any of those things. Maybe you would be less.'

She turned and looked at me, and then she leaned across and kissed me, and then she turned in the seat and kissed Joe Pike. She said, 'I'll do what's best for Toby. I've always been able to do that. What happens now with the DeLucas?'

I looked out the window at the house and the basketball hoop and Toby's bike leaning against the garage wall. Then I looked back at her. 'I don't know. Sal and Charlie aren't running the family anymore. They'll have a new boss.'

She made her lips into a little rosebud and then she nodded slowly. 'Do you think he'll try to make me keep doing this?'

Pike leaned close to her and patted her arm. 'Go live your life. You let us worry about that.'

Karen Lloyd took a deep breath, let it out, and got out of the car.

CHAPTER 40

Pike and I collected our things, said our good-byes, and drove down to the city where we took a fourteenth-floor room at the Park Lane Hotel on East 59th Street. It was a nice room with a view of Central Park.

We took turns in the shower, then dressed and walked to the Museum of Modern Art on 53rd. They call it MoMA for short, which is dumb, but they had Vincent van Gogh's *The Starry Night*, which is anything but. Score one for New York. I had always wanted to see it, and now sat for the better part of an hour staring into its depths and textures. Pike said, 'I know how he felt.'

'They say he was mad.'

Pike shrugged.

We walked up to West 71st Street and had an early dinner at Victor's Café 52. Cuban food, which rivaled and in some ways surpassed the excellent fare found at the Versailles on Venice Boulevard in Los Angeles. I had the chicken steak and black beans. Pike had the white bean soup and fried plantains. We both had beer. Score two.

It was still light when we finished, so we walked across the three long blocks of Central Park, past the lake and Bethesda Fountain and something that called itself the Boathouse Café. The café was closed. People were jogging and riding bikes and a couple of kids were flying a model airplane. No one seemed about to do crime, but the mounted police were in high profile. After the sun went down, it might be different. I asked Pike, 'Are you afraid?'

He shook his head.

'Would you be afraid at midnight if we were alone?'

He walked a moment. 'I have the capacity for great violence.'

I nodded. So did I. But I thought that I might still be afraid.

Pike slipped his hands into the pockets of his parka and we walked past a smaller pond where an older man and a couple of young girls were sailing a model sailboat. A man and a woman decked out in serious biking apparel were standing with a tandem bike, watching them. We stopped and watched them, too, and I wondered how deeply into winter the pond could venture before it would freeze. The brisk fall wind carried the boat well across the pond. Pike said, 'Elvis?'

'Yeah?'

'I remember being afraid. I was very young.'

We watched the old man and the girls and the boat, and then we left the park and walked down to the brownstones that used to belong to Sal DeLuca. There were no limos at the curb or thugs hanging around the stoop. There was a black bow on the door.

Joe stayed on the corner at Fifth Avenue and I went up to the door and rang the bell once. In a little bit Freddie opened the door and looked out at me. His face was flat and without expression. 'Yeah?'

'You hear about Charlie?'

'We heard.'

'I'm at the Park Lane.'

'Swell. Have a party.'

'Tell Vito. Tell Angie. I'll be there until this is squared away.'

Freddie gave me the patented tough-guy sneer. 'We got no business with you.'

'That's where you're wrong. Tell Vito and Angie. The Park Lane.'

The next morning there was a three-inch article on page six of *The New York Times*. It reported that a prostitute named Gloria Uribe and a man believed to be her pimp, one Jesus Santiago, were found shot to death in a warehouse in lower Manhattan. Authorities had no leads as to the circumstances of their deaths. In a separate article on page eighteen a Jamaican national and known drug dealer named Urethro Mubata was found murdered in the front seat of his late-model Jaguar Sovereign in Queens. His throat was cut so deeply that the head was almost separated from the body. Police speculated his death to be the result of a drug deal gone sour. The *New York Post* reported that Richard Sealy, a drug addict, had been found dead in a Port Authority men's room with multiple fractures of the head, neck, both arms, and left leg. Guess junkies don't rate the *Times*.

Loose ends were being tied.

Two days later, in the afternoon, I was walking down Central Park West across from the Hayden Planetarium when a blue Cadillac Eldorado pulled up beside me. Pike was maybe forty yards back and across the street. Vito DeLuca opened the door and looked out at me. 'Get in.'

I got in. Freddie was in the front seat, driving. Vito was in back, alone. Vito said, 'I'm *capo de tutti capo*. You know what that means?'

'You're Marlon Brando.'

Vito smiled, but there was something hard and tired in it. The weight of responsibility. 'Yeah. You killed a lot of our guys.'

'Charlie's people.'

'Some of the *capos*, they don't like it. They think something should be done.'

'What do you think?' Out the window, past Vito, I

could see Joe Pike moving closer, talking to a guy who was selling Middle Eastern food from a little cart.

Vito looked out the window but saw only people on the street. 'I think Charlie came very close to bringing dishonor to the family. He was my nephew, my blood, but Sal was my brother. Sal knew how a man acts. You behaved like a man behaves. These guys, they talk about California and granola and Disneyland, I say, Christ, he put ten of our guys in the ground. If he was Sicilian, I'd kiss him on the mouth. He could be a made guy.'

'What about Karen Lloyd?'

Vito turned back and looked at me. He said, 'Sal DeLuca was *capo de tutti capos*, and when he spoke, he spoke for the family. The DeLucas honor their word. *Capisce?*'

'Charlie wouldn't.'

'Charlie's dead.'

I nodded.

'She's out. She will never be seen by DeLuca family eyes again. The DeLuca family will always honor that.'

He put out his hand and we shook. When we shook, he squeezed my hand hard, so hard that it cut off the blood. More than one rock in the family. He said, 'The agreement works both ways. Does the woman know that?'

'Yes.'

'Does her husband? The movie guy?' Peter Alan Nelsen, the movie guy.

'Yes. I'll be responsible for them.'

He nodded. 'That's right. You will. For the rest of your life.'

He let go of my hand and I got out of the limousine and walked across the street. Joe Pike and I went back to the hotel, called Karen Lloyd at her bank, and told her what Vito DeLuca had said. We checked out that afternoon.

CHAPTER 41

October moved into November, and three weeks later, on a pleasant Sunday afternoon, I was on my deck grilling salmon steaks and Japanese eggplant for Cindy, the beauty supply distributor, and Joe Pike and another woman named Ellen Lang. Ellen Lang had been a client once, several years ago, and since then she and Joe Pike have seen each other, time to time. She had a deep tan, and when she laughed there were dimples high on her cheeks. Laughter came easier to her now than in that earlier time.

Joe Pike and Cindy and Ellen Lang were inside, making salad and garlic bread and mint tea, when the phone rang. Someone inside answered it, and Ellen Lang came out and said, 'There's a call for you. It's Peter Alan Nelsen. The director.'

I said, 'Wow. Maybe this is my big break.'

She said, 'Oh, you.'

Ellen stayed with the salmon and I went inside and took it in the kitchen. On the counter next to the sink, Pike sliced the long French bread and put it on a tray while Cindy watched him. Cindy had soft auburn hair and expressive brown eyes. I liked watching her watch Pike's precise moves.

Peter said, 'They're coming out to visit.'

'Karen and Toby?'

'Yeah. He's got a week off for Thanksgiving and I asked'm to come out.'

294

'Great.' I already knew, because Karen had called and told me.

'She doesn't want him traveling alone, so she's coming, too.'

'Even better.'

'She's not coming by herself. She's bringing some guy.' She had also told me that.

'She's got a life, Peter. That's a good thing. Why don't you get a date and the four of you can go out one night. Leave Toby with me.'

'I know. I know.' He didn't say anything for a little bit. 'Listen, when they're out, I'm gonna bring Toby to the set, take'm to Disneyland, that kind of thing. You think you could sorta be around some of the time? At first.'

Pike finished cutting the garlic bread and Cindy took it outside. She wriggled her eyebrows as she passed and gave me a yum-yum smile. She smelled of daisies. Yum, all right. 'Sure, Peter. Not the whole time. But if you need me around at first, sure.'

'Hey, thanks. I really appreciate that. I really do.' He sounded relieved. 'I'm out at the Malibu house. You wanna come out?'

'I've got company.'

'Another time, okay? You ever wanna come out, you don't even have to call. Just come.'

'Sure.' Elvis Cole, detective to the stars.

I hung up and Pike said, 'What's up?'

'Karen and Toby are coming out and he's scared. Growing up is a scary time.'

'He asks you a lot. Maybe he should try growing up without you.'

'He calls me less now than he once did. He'll call me less still. He's getting there.'

Pike nodded. 'Yeah. I guess he is. Karen getting any chaff from the DeLucas?'

'Vito's been good at his word. All of the DeLuca

accounts through the First Chelam Bank have been collapsed and the funds in the Barbados accounts have mysteriously vanished.'

'So she's free.'

'Yes. She's as free as you can be when you've got the memories she has, but, like Peter, she's getting there, too.'

Outside, Ellen Lang moved the fish to the side so it wouldn't overcook and Cindy put the garlic bread in the center of the grill. Pike washed off a yellow pepper, cored it in the sink, then sliced it into thin rings. Each ring was uniform, no thicker or thinner than any other ring. When the pepper was cut, he added the rings to the large salad that had already been built and we took it out to the deck.

Ellen Lang says that if you stand on my deck and close your eyes, with a breeze coming up the canyon to blow across your face, it's easy to imagine that you're flying free through the sky, over the city with Tinkerbell and Mark and Wendy, off to Never Land to find the lost boys.

I haven't told her, but I've always thought that, too.

New Orleans
2005

MONDAY, 4:28 A.M., the narrow French Quarter room was smoky with cheap candles that smelled of honey. Daniel stared through broken shutters and shivering glass up the length of the alley, catching a thin slice of Jackson Square through curtains of gale-force rain that swirled through New Orleans like mad bats riding the storm. Daniel had never seen rain fall up before.

Daniel loved these damned hurricanes. He folded back the shutters, then opened the window. Rain hit him good. It tasted of salt and smelled of dead fish and weeds. The cat-five wind clawed through New Orleans at better than a hundred miles an hour, but back here in the alley—in a cheap one-room apartment over a po'boy shop—the wind was no stronger than an arrogant breeze.

The power in this part of the Quarter had gone out almost an hour ago; hence, the candles Daniel found in the manager's office. Emergency lighting fed by battery packs lit a few nearby buildings, giving a creepy blue glow to the shimmering walls. Most everyone in the surrounding buildings had gone. Not everyone, but most. The stubborn, the helpless, and the stupid had stayed.

Like Daniel's friend, Tolley.

Tolley had stayed.

Stupid.

And now here they were in an empty building surrounded by empty buildings in an outrageous storm that had forced more than a million people out of the city, but Daniel kinda dug it. All this noise and all this emptiness, no one to hear Tolley scream.

Daniel turned from the window, arching his eyebrows.

"You smell that? That's what zombies smell like, brought up from the dead with an unnatural life. You get to see a zombie?"

Tolley was between answers right now, being tied to the bed with thirty feet of nylon cord. His head just kinda hung there, all swollen and broken, though he was still breathing. Every once in a while he would lurch and shiver. Daniel didn't let Tolley's lack of responsiveness stop him.

Daniel sauntered over to the bed. Cleo and Tobey shuffled out of the way, letting him pass.

Daniel had a syringe pack in his bag, along with some poppers, meth, and other choice pharmaceuticals. He took out the kit, shot up Tolley with some crystal, then waited for it to take effect. Outside, something exploded with a muffled *whump* that wasn't quite lost in the wind. Power transformer, probably, giving up the ghost, or maybe a wall falling over.

Tolley's eyes flickered amid a sudden fury of blinks, then dialed into focus. He tried to pull away when he saw Daniel, but, really, where could he go?

Daniel said, all serious, "I asked you, you seen a zombie? They got'm here in this place, I know for a fact."

Tolley shook his head, which kinda pissed Daniel off. On his way to New Orleans six days earlier, having been sent to find Tolley based upon an absolutely spot-on lead, Daniel decided this was his one pure and good chance to see a zombie. Daniel could not abide a zombie, and found their existence offensive. The dead should stay dead, and not rise to walk again, all shamblin' and vile and slack. He didn't care for vampires, either, but zombies just rubbed him the wrong way. Daniel had it on good authority that New Orleans held quite a few zombies, and maybe a vampire or two.

"Don't be like that, Tolliver. New Orleans is supposed to have zombies, don't it, what with all this hoodoo and shit you got here, them zombies from Haiti? You musta seen something?"

Tolley's eyes were bright with meth, the one eye, the left, a glossy red ball what with the burst veins.

Daniel wiped the rain from his face, and felt all tired.

"Where is she?"

"I swear I doan know."

"You kill her? That what you been tryin' to say?"

"No!"

"She tell you where they goin'?"

"I don't know nuthin' about—"

Daniel hammered his fist straight down on Tolley's chest, and scooped up the Asp. The Asp was a collapsible steel rod almost two feet long. Daniel brought it down hard, lashing Tolley's chest, belly, thighs, and shins with a furious beating. Tolley screamed and jerked at his binds, but no one was left to hear. Daniel let him have it for a long time, then tossed aside the Asp and returned to the window. Tobey and Cleo scrambled out of his way.

"I wanna see a goddamned zombie. A zombie, vampire, *something* to make this fuckin' trip worthwhile."

The rain blew in hard, hot and salty as blood. Daniel didn't care. Here he was, come all this way, and not a zombie to be found. Anything was good, Daniel missed out. A life of miserable disappointments.

He looked at Tobey and Cleo. They were difficult to see in the flickery light, all blurry and smudged, but he could make them out well enough.

"Bet I could kill me a zombie, one on one, straight up, and I'd like to try. You think I could kill me a zombie?"

Neither Tobey nor Cleo answered.

"I ain't shittin', I could take me a zombie. Take me a vampire, too, only here we are and I gotta waste my time with this lame shit. I'd rather be huntin' zombies."

He pointed at Tolley.

"Hey, boy."

Daniel returned to the bed and shook Tolley awake.

"You think I could take me a zombie, head up, one on one?"

The red eye rolled, and blood leaked from the shattered mouth. A mushy hiss escaped, so Daniel leaned closer. Sounded like the fucker was finally openin' up.

"Say what?"

Tolley's mouth worked as he tried to speak.

Daniel smiled encouragingly.

"You hear that wind? I was a bat, I'd spread my wings and ride that sumbitch for all she was worth. Where'd they go, boy? I know she tol' ya. You tell me where they went so I can get outta here. Just say it. You're almost there. Give me a hand, and I'm out your hair."

Tolley's lips worked, and Daniel knew he was about to give it, but then what little air he had left hissed out.

"You say west? They was headed west? Over to Texas?"

Tolley was dead.

Daniel stared at the body for a moment, then drew his gun and put five bullets into Tolliver James's chest. Nasty explosions that anyone staying behind would have heard even with the lion wind. Daniel didn't give a damn. If someone came running, Daniel figured to shoot them, too, but nobody came—no police, no neighbors, no nobody. Everyone with two squirts of brain juice was hunkered down tight, trying to survive.

Daniel reloaded, tucked away his gun, then took out the satellite phone. The cell stations were out all over the city, but the sat phone worked great. He checked the time, hit the speed dial, then waited for a link. It always took a few seconds.

In that time, he stood taller, straightened himself, and resumed his normal manner.

When the connection was made, Daniel reported.

"Tolliver James is dead. He didn't provide anything useful."

Daniel listened for a moment before responding.

"No, sir, they're gone. That much is confirmed. James was a good bet, but I don't believe she told him anything."

He listened again, this time for quite a while.

"No, sir, that is not altogether true. There are three or four people here I'd still like to talk to, but the storm has turned this place to shit. They've almost certainly evacuated. I just don't know. It will take me a while to locate them."

More chatter from the other side, but then they were finished.

"Yes, sir, I understand. You get yours, I get mine. I won't let you down."

A last word from the master.

"Yes, sir. Thank you. I'll keep you informed."

Daniel shut the phone and put it away.

"Asshole."

He returned to the window, and let the rain lash him. Everything was wet now: shirt, pants, shoes, hair, all the way down to his bones. He leaned out, better to see the Square. A fifty-five-gallon oil drum tumbled past the alley's mouth, end over end, followed by a bicycle, swept along on its side, and then a shattered sheet of plywood flipping and soaring like a playing card tossed out like trash.

Daniel shouted into the wind as loud as he could.

"C'mon and get me, you fuckin' zombies! Show your true and unnatural colors."

Daniel threw back his head and howled. He barked like a dog, then howled again before turning back to the room to pack up his gear. Tobey and Cleo were gone.

Tolliver had hidden eight thousand dollars under the mattress, still vacu-packed in plastic, which Daniel found when he first searched the room. Probably a gift from the girl. Daniel stashed the money in his bag, checked to make sure Tolliver had no pulse, then went to the little bathroom where he'd left Tolliver's lady friend after he strangled her, nice and neat in the tub. A little black stream of ants had already found her, not even a day.

Cleo said, "Gotta get going, Daniel. Stop fuckin' around."

Tobey said, "Go where, a storm like this? Makes sense to stay."

Daniel decided Tobey was right. Tobey was the smart one, and usually right, even if Daniel couldn't always see him.

"Okay, I guess I should wait till the worst is over."

Tobey said, "Wait."

Cleo said, "Wait, wait."

Like echoes fading away.

Daniel returned to the window. He leaned out into the rain again, watching the mouth of the alley in case a zombie rattled past.

"C'mon, goddamnit, lemme see one. One freaky-ass zombie is all I ask."

If a zombie appeared, Daniel planned to jump out

8

the window after it and rip its putrid, unnatural flesh to pieces with his teeth. He was, after all, a werewolf, which was why he was such a good hunter and killer. Werewolves feared nothing.

Daniel tipped back his head and howled to match the wind, then doused the candles and sat with the bodies, waiting for the storm to pass.

When it ended, Daniel would find their trail, and track them, and he would not quit until they were his. No matter how long it took or how far they ran. This was why the men down south used him for these jobs and paid him so well.

Werewolves caught their prey.

Los Angeles
Now

THE WIND DID NOT WAKE HIM. It was the dream. He heard the buffeting wind before he opened his eyes, but the dream was what woke him on that dark early morning. A cat was his witness. Hunkered at the end of the bed, ears down, a low growl in its chest, a ragged black cat was staring at him when Elvis Cole opened his eyes. Its warrior face was angry, and, in that moment, Cole knew they had shared the nightmare.

Cole woke on the bed in his loft bathed in soft moonlight, feeling his A-frame shudder as the wind tried to push it from its perch high in the Hollywood Hills. A freak weather system in the Midwest was pulling fifty- to seventy-knot winds from the sea that had hammered Los Angeles for days.

Cole sat up, awake now and wanting to shake off the dream—an ugly nightmare that left him feeling unsettled and depressed. The cat's ears stayed down. Cole held out his hand, but the cat poured off the bed like a pool of black ink.

Cole said, "Me, too."

He checked the time. Habit. Three-twelve in the A.M. He reached toward the nightstand to check his gun—habit—but stopped himself when he realized what he was doing.

"C'mon, what's the point?"

The gun was there because it was always there, sometimes needed but most times not. Living alone with only an angry cat for company, there seemed no reason to move it. Now, at three-twelve in the middle of a wind-torched night, it was a reminder of what he had lost.

Cole realized he was trembling, and pushed out of bed. The dream scared him. Muzzle flash so bright it sparkled his eyes; the charcoal smell of smokeless powder; a glittery red mist that dappled his skin; shattered sunglasses that arced through the air—images so vivid they shocked him awake.

Now he shook as his body burned off the fear.

The back of Cole's house was an A-shaped glass steeple, giving him a view of the canyon behind his house and a diamond-dust glimpse of the city beyond. Now, the canyon was blue with bright moonlight. The sleeping houses below were surrounded by blue-and-gray trees that shivered and danced in the St. Vitus wind. Cole wondered if someone down there had awakened like him. He wondered if they had suffered a similar nightmare—seeing their best friend shot to death in the dark.

Violence was part of him.

Elvis Cole did not want it, seek it, or enjoy it, but maybe these were only things he told himself in cold moments like now. The nature of his life had cost him the woman he loved and the little boy he had grown to love, and left him alone in this house with nothing but an angry cat for company and a pistol that did not need to be put away.

Now here was this dream that left his skin crawling—so real it felt like a premonition. He looked at the phone and told himself no—no, that's silly, it's stupid, it's three in the morning.

Cole made the call.

One ring, and his call was answered. At three in the morning.

"Pike."

"Hey, man."

Cole didn't know what to say after that, feeling so stupid.

"You good?"

Pike said, "Good. You?"

"Yeah. Sorry, man, it's late."

"You okay?"

"Yeah. Just a bad feeling is all."

They lapsed into a silence Cole found embarrassing, but it was Pike who spoke first.

"You need me, I'm there."

"It's the wind. This wind is crazy."

"Uh-huh."

"Watch yourself."

He told Pike he would call again soon, then put down the phone.

Cole felt no relief after the call. He told himself he should, but he didn't. The dream should have faded, but it did not. Talking to Pike now made it feel even more real.

You need me, I'm there.

How many times had Joe Pike placed himself in harm's way to save him?

They had fought the good fight together, and won, and sometimes lost. They had shot people who had harmed or were doing harm, and been shot, and Joe Pike had saved Cole's life more than a few times like an archangel from Heaven.

Yet here was the dream and the dream did not fade—

Muzzle flashes in a dingy room. A woman's shadow

13

cast on the wall. Dark glasses spinning into space. Joe Pike falling through a terrible red mist.

Cole crept downstairs through the dark house and stepped out onto his deck. Leaves and debris stung his face like sand on a windswept beach. Lights from the houses below glittered like fallen stars.

In low moments on nights like this when Elvis Cole thought of the woman and the boy, he told himself the violence in his life had cost him everything, but he knew that was not true. As lonely as he sometimes felt, he still had more to lose.

He could lose his best friend.

Or himself.